CW00860423

Rose

By
Lilly Adam

Also written by Lilly Adam:

May of Ashley Green
Stella
Poppy Woods
The Whipple Girl

This novel is a work of fiction. Apart from references to actual historical figures and places, all other names and characters are a product of the author's imagination and any resemblance to real persons, living or dead is purely coincidental.

CHAPTER ONE
1865

Rose Harper took one last look at Bushel Farm as she crept quietly away in the dead of night. With her young son of fourteen months cradled in her arms, his mop of soft golden curls barely visible beneath the thick woollen blanket, and with her second child growing in her belly, Rose knew that she had made the right decision to leave. She went for the final time to the graveside of her beloved Johnnie, taking with her the dried posy of flowers which she had saved and cherished since the best day of her life; the day they had married. The blackness of the night had never scared Rose, unlike many a young woman of twenty, and as she began her walk to freedom, guided only by the moon which tonight was shining brightly like a golden medallion, she prayed that she would have the strength to make it as far away as possible by sunrise. The events of the past few months had changed everything for Rose, leaving her once again, feeling alone and vulnerable in the world.

It had been a shocking day when Seb Harper had returned to the farm house with the devastating news on that first day in January of 1865, bringing an abrupt end to all the New Year's celebrations that Rose had planned for that evening.

"There must be something we can do......we can't just leave him out there, and presume the worst!" Rose cried out in desperation. She had never liked Sebastian Harper, and never trusted him. He was the complete opposite in every way to her darling Johnnie; half brothers with fifteen years between them. They shared the same father, who Seb now despised for not leaving Bushel Farm exclusively to him in his will. It was his opinion that he had far more rights on the property than Johnnie, who had been a mere boy whilst all the hard toiling was being done to make the farm what it was today.

"I'm telling you Rose, there was nothing I could do, that stupid husband of yours should 'ave bloody well listened to me, and he might then be standing here in the kitchen." Seb made a loud snorting sound and spat out a mouthful of phlegm into the sink, which dangled from the handle of a saucepan.

"So where's his body then!" screamed Rose, as she suddenly came over in a wave of nausea. "Why aren't you out looking for him instead of spitting in to my sink of dishes?"

Seb laughed, coldly, "I do love it when you gets so angry, little Rose, but like I said, I value my life, and if I'd have chased after his body in that freezing river, we'd both 'ave been goners; there's a right strong current pushing down river this morning, and it's near on freezing, then where would that leave you, sweet Rose?"

"Stay away from me!" screamed Rose, as Seb tried to take advantage of the situation and offer some comfort to her. She could already smell the rancid stench from his unwashed body, and clothes, which he refused to remove from his body all winter long.

"Ah little Rose, you'll soon come round when you see sense."

"Go and find my husband!" Rose demanded.

"What do you think your pa would think of you if he was alive?"

Releasing a loud chuckle, Seb picked up the last remaining half loaf of bread with his filthy hands, and began to chew on it, champing like a wild beast.

" Tomorrow, I'll go and look for his body; it's more likely to have been swept up onto the banks down river by then. Now, how about if I keep your bed warm for you this night, little Rose."

"*You*, Sebastian Harper, make me sick; now, get out of my way while I see to my crying baby."

Quickly leaving the kitchen in a flood of tears and racing upstairs, Rose made sure that her bedroom was bolted and a chair was jammed up against it as she sat down to nurse ten month old Alfie; the burning tears streaming down her face at the thought of becoming such a young widow, and poor little Alfie having to grow up without a Pa. Johnnie couldn't be dead, he just couldn't be, was all she kept telling herself as Alfie's wide eyes were securely fixed on his ma, as he filled his small belly. If Seb did find Johnnie's body in the morning, then Rose knew that her days living at Bushel Farm would be numbered. After settling Alfie back down to sleep, Rose returned back downstairs, where she found Seb devouring the special cake that she'd made for the New Year. His filthy boots were resting upon the table next to the cake, as he swung back and forth on the back legs of the tilted chair.

"This is a tasty cake Rose, my love...I always said you were wasted on that feeble half brother of mine, as was his share of this place too...our pa always favoured me you know, on account that my ma was his first and undying true love, and he only took in Johnnie's ma, so she could keep house for him. He never loved her, and never even married her if you must know, so what did that make your precious Johnnie, then? I'll tell you, it made him a bastard."

" I don't know why you're bothering to tell me this, Seb, because it doesn't make any difference to me, and I'd thank you to stop referring to Johnnie in the past tense, we don't know that he's dead, and if you had an ounce of decency in your lazy body, you would be out searching for him, not sat here filling your ugly face with cake."

Seb chuckled, coldly,

"Oh Rose, sweet Rose, you look so tempting when you're feisty, you're a temptress. You best make sure you bolt your bedroom door tonight, I might not be able to control my urge to visit you."

Rose stared in disgust at her foul brother in law as he crammed another huge chunk of cake into his mouth, choking on it and coughing out half the contents of his mouth back out onto the table. She would be taking the carving knife up to her room tonight, she thought, as she decided to try and ignore Seb with his teasing ways, hoping that he would then, perhaps, leave her alone.

The following day, Seb returned to the farm with Johnnie's cold dead body slung over his horse. Rose had spent most of the morning in the outhouse throwing up, realising that she was with child again; a bitter sweet discovery in these dire circumstances. Since Seb had told her that Johnnie's body was no longer recognizable, after being submerged in the river for twenty four hours, Rose could not bear to kiss him goodbye, and decided to keep the last memory of her beloved before he died in her heart. The New Year had begun beneath a gloomy shadow, and Rose couldn't believe she was a widow. The ice cold relentless winter weather showed no signs of easing up, and as Bushel Farm became buried in deep snow, cutting it off from the rest of the world, Johnnie was laid to rest alongside his parents and Seb's mother. Rose, who was determined to keep her newly discovered pregnancy a secret from Seb, took to wearing a loose black smock, telling Seb that she intended to remain in mourning until the summer sun could once again shine some warmth upon her hurting heart. Even though the new life inside of her was still too tiny to be noticed, Rose didn't want to take any chances and planned to be miles away from Bushel Farm by the time of her confinement.

Life for Rose was an endless chore just to keep Seb at arm's length from her. He was under the illusion that once Rose had ceased grieving the death of his half brother, she would consider becoming his wife, insisting on telling her how it would be the ideal solution to keeping everything on the farm ticking over nicely, and how he would provide for her every need.

Seb never failed to make Rose shudder with his inappropriate innuendos and his repulsive habits. As she waited patiently for the arrival of spring, she spent more and more time locked away with baby Alfie in their bedroom.

Seb was convinced that since Rose had nowhere to go and no living relatives, it was just a matter of time until she finished her ridiculous mourning and discarded the hideous dress which veiled her womanly figure, and gave in to becoming his wife. He longed for that day, and not wanting to jeopardize it or prolong its arrival, tried his hardest to behave in a gentlemanly way, and keep his hands to himself, until she was legally his possession. A day he dreamt about most nights.

It was one evening in mid April, when Rose had to face the truth that she couldn't stay much longer under the same roof as Seb. Feeling physically sick knowing that his eyes were constantly watching her, she didn't bear to think about what was going on in his head, and the only reason that she hadn't yet left Bushel Farm was due to Alfie having been unwell with a fever and a chest cold throughout March. The spring had been a long time arriving this year, and on this particular evening in April, Rose had finally settled Alfie for the night and returned downstairs to heat up a mug of hot milk. Earlier that day she had experienced the familiar fluttering sensations inside her belly, and knew that little Johnnie, as she had named her unborn child, was growing fast. Thinking that Seb had already retired for the night, it was a shock when he suddenly appeared in the kitchen wearing only his heavily soiled long johns and his filthy boots. He stood in the door way, a threatening blade in one hand, and a huge lump of cheese in the other, cutting away at it, as though he were whittling a piece of wood, and shoveling the cuttings into his over full mouth. Unable to speak, he merely grinned, allowing the chewed food to drop onto his bare stomach which hung grotesquely over his long johns. He sat down at the table, not taking his eyes from Rose for a single second.

"Can't you sleep Seb?" she asked, casually, trying not to let him see her awkwardness and fear.

"I was having the best dream, and then some bloody fox woke me up, trying to get into the chicken coup."

Rose hurriedly filled the small saucepan with milk, wanting to flee from the kitchen as soon as possible.

"Ain't you going to ask me about my dream?" Seb sniggered, "you were there, as large as life and looking right pretty, you know."

Rose felt her skin crawl, and wished with all her heart that her Johnnie hadn't been taken from her; she needed him more than ever, to be at her side, to protect her and their unborn child.

" Seb, I don't care to know about your sordid little dreams, or what goes on in that disgusting head of yours."

Seb just sat staring at her, his unblinking eyes fixed firmly.

" Rose! Are you fattening yourself up for our wedding night?" Seb teased, knowing full well that Rose was with child.

"How many times have I told you Seb, I will never wed you, so you might as well just put the idea out of your head before it does you some damage."

"You're definitely becoming more curvy, my delicious Rose. You were wasted on Johnnie; he

was nothing but a young inexperienced pup.
You need a real man Rose."

Thankfully the milk had come to a boil, and
Rose quickly left the kitchen.
"Goodnight Seb," she shouted annoyingly.
Behind her closed and locked door, Rose placed
a hand over her small protruding belly, knowing
that very soon it would be impossible to hide
baby Johnnie.

CHAPTER TWO

After barely an hour of walking, Rose was overtaken by sheer exhaustion, forcing her to take a break. Alfie had become heavier with every step, and the small of her back was throbbing with pain. As the sky had now clouded over, intermittently shielding the moon, Rose could only just make out the dirt track that was hopefully leading her far away from Bushel Farm, and from Sebastian Harper. With thick wooded forest on one side, and open farmland to the other, she took a slight detour from the pathway towards the farm land, and rested alongside the row of thick gorse bushes which stretched around the perimeter of each field. The spring air was becoming unbearably cold with a distinctive feel of a frost to it. Rose cuddled baby Alfie close to her body, feeling his warmth as she breathed in his delightful odour; she couldn't quite believe that they were huddled together in the middle of nowhere, in the small hours of the morning, and longed for the warmth and comfort of her bed. As much as she knew it was a sin to wish somebody's life away, over the past four months, she had lost count of how many times that she'd wished it had been Seb's life, lost in the ice cold river on that day, and questioned God as to why her darling Johnnie had been so cruelly snatched away from her.

Johnnie was worth a hundred of his disgusting half brother, and life could have been perfect, if only Seb did not exist. A small niggling thought crossed Rose's mind as she questioned whether this was her punishment for always wishing that Seb was not a part of their lives and that he didn't live under the same roof as her and Johnnie. Rose pulled out Johnnie's thick black overcoat from her bag, glad that she had grabbed it from off the hook on the back of the kitchen door as she'd left. It had been hanging there since Seb had removed it from Johnnie's body, and even though it had endured a thorough soaking after being submerged in the river, the familiar scent of Johnnie's skin still lingered, bringing about a feeling of safety and a stinging sentiment of longing for the love of her life. Rose traced her finger tips over the roughly sewn initials of 'JH' which Johnnie had stitched into the inner collar years ago when Seb had threatened to steal it from him. It was warm and twice as big as Rose, making an ideal blanket. Alfie began to stir, his chubby arms moving and stretching as his mouth imagined it was in possession of his biggest comfort in life. Rose quickly exposed her breast and within seconds Alfie was satisfying his hunger, without even opening his eyes. Resting on her side, with her and Alfie both wrapped in the warm overcoat, he continued to suckle contentedly. Rose caressed his golden curls, as she wondered if they would darken and become like Johnnie's brown hair as he grew older, or he had inherited her blonde hair.

Within minutes she had fallen into a fretful sleep, where grotesque images of Seb, chasing after her through the open countryside, soon woke her again, making her leap back up onto her feet. Shivering from the cold, exhausted, and hungry, Rose continued briskly along the gloomy track and for the first time for as long as she could remember, felt petrified of the dark shadows which engulfed her. Having no recollection of what time it was, or for how long she'd been asleep, and how many miles she'd covered, a feeling of anxiety suddenly overwhelmed her at the thought that perhaps Seb *was* trailing behind her; she wouldn't put anything past that unscrupulous savage. With these terrifying thoughts spinning around inside of her head, she quickened her pace, saying a prayer as she dragged her tired legs across the bumpy uneven surface of the country roads, every now and again becoming startled by the shining eyes of a fox, out hunting for the night.

When the usual yeasty aroma of freshly baked bread failed to stir Seb Harper, the following morning, he immediately had his suspicions that Rose had deserted him. The usual mouth watering smell never failed to lure him from his room and out of his strange bed, which adjoined the farmhouse kitchen. He'd constructed the peculiar wooden high bunk, which stood on tall stilts, nearly reaching the eaves of the roof, shortly after he and Johnnie had spent a week's hard labour adding on the additional room to the farm house, prior to Rose and Johnnie's wedding day. Claiming that sleeping at a height helped with his breathing and was much warmer, the real reason for the positioning of the monstrosity was to enable him to lay on his high bunk and peer through the purposely left gap, where the wall and ceiling met and where he had a bird's eye view to admire Rose as she moved about the kitchen like an elegant swan. Her soft hair was like a measure of golden silk, as it trailed down her slightly arched back. He had been infatuated by this beautiful fair haired girl from the very first day that Johnnie had introduced them, when he announced that Rose was soon to be his bride. A tidal wave of jealousy had washed over Seb that day; *he* was the oldest; he should be getting wed first, and he should get first pickings of the prettiest girls. As usual, he had done all the hard work, and his half brother had picked up the rewards. Seb truly believed that once Rose was living at the farm, she would soon realise that she'd made the biggest mistake of her life, by marrying the wrong brother, but for the time being the gap in the wall would give him his own special private time with her. Watching Rose as she glided her attractive curvy body around the room, often stripped of her top garment in the heat of the kitchen, would keep Seb enthralled, until Johnnie showed up. The newlyweds would often embrace in front of his eyes, causing a surge of jealousy to instantly turn Seb's mood, and within seconds he had left his bed like a shot and was in the kitchen, putting a stop to any possible encounters. Rose and Johnnie had never wondered why every time they had shared a kiss or an embrace in the kitchen, Seb was quickly in the same room with them.

As he stood in the desolate, cold kitchen, Seb could feel the anger raging up inside of him. His breathing became heavy, his mouth dry, and as he raced to the upstairs bedroom, he already knew that he was completely alone in Bushel Farm. Rose had taken her belongings and her baby, and deserted him. She *was* to be his wife, in fact , thought Seb, she practically *was* his wife since he was probably more familiar with her body than Johnnie had ever been; Johnnie didn't appreciate her beauty like he did, he had been an immature kid, and now he was gone, so that made Rose his. Slamming his hand down violently onto the dressing table in Rose's bedroom, Seb looked out through the tiny window, across the field; a hard frost had set over night, turning the landscape into a vast twinkling blanket beneath the early morning sky. She couldn't have got far by foot in this cold weather with the baby in her arms, thought Seb. He would go and search for her, bring her back to where she rightfully belonged and take good care of her and the child. He would even take care of the new baby that Rose thought she'd hidden from him; he had watched from his high bed, in amusement as she had looked lovingly down at her belly, rubbing it gently as she whispered words of endearment. The ripple of jealousy touched him again, as he wished that he'd been the one to plant that seed inside of her belly, but, he consoled himself that her third child would definitely be his very own flesh and blood.

Half an hour later, Seb had saddled up his horse and set out on the frosty track. Having no clue as to which direction Rose would be heading, he allowed the horse to choose. They headed south, through the quiet and deserted countryside, where it seemed the whole world was still in a deep slumber on this freezing morning.

By the time the first light of dawn was making its welcoming appearance, Rose had arrived at a tiny cottage which stood in solitude, surrounded by the never ending patchwork fields. Smoke was rising up from the chimney, making Rose yearn for the chance to warm her chilled body and rest in the safety of such a homely looking dwelling. As she knelt down by the white painted picket fence which enveloped a well cared for garden with its sharp cut borders, and

twisted path leading to the arched front door,
Rose imagined how beautiful it would look
during the months of summer, when the borders
would likely become alive with a rainbow of
vibrant colour and sweet intoxicating perfume. It
looked like the perfect little cottage in the ideal
location to raise her children, and far away from
Seb Harper, she thought, wishing that she could
have such a place of her own. She was suddenly
brought out of her reverie, as Alfie decided to
start bawling, his bottom lip had dropped, and
there seemed to be no consoling him. His little
body was wet and cold and Rose could not bring
herself to undress him out in the biting morning
air.

"There, there, my darling, Mamma will soon
make you better, hush now, hush, hush my
darling," she whispered, as she gently rubbed
Alfie's small damp back, trying to soothe him.
Evie Bancroft had been admiring the beauty of
the frosted fields from her window, when the
sound of a wailing baby suddenly diverted her
attention. Having raised eight children of her
own in the small cottage, she recognised the
distressing cry, as one which needed immediate
attention. She pulled back the door, poking her
head out into the piercing cold.

" Would you care to bring baby in to the warm,
and tend to his needs?" she called out across the
front garden.

Rose, who was still squatting down by the fence,

unsuccessfully trying to calm little Alfie,
immediately stood up and accepted this
elderly woman's kind offer. Lifting the latch off
the small gate, Rose hurried towards the smiling
face, and the comfort of a warm home.
"Thank you so much, he's cold, wet and as
always, hungry," replied Rose, a little nervously.
"And I dare say that you're not feeling too comfy
either, being out so early on such a cold
morning." Evie, had a full round face, which
matched her ample body perfectly and her
warming smile made Rose feel instantly
welcome.
"Thank you Mrs...."
"I'm Evie, Evie Bancroft."
"Rose Harper, and this is little Alfie."
Evie's smile faded away briefly, as her
eyes viewed Rose with a look of concern.
"And when's the new baby due?"
Rose was shocked that even though she was
wearing Johnnie's cumbersome coat, this woman
had spotted her unborn child.
Evie let out a chuckle,
"I can see it in your eyes, and in the fullness of
your lips!"
Rose swallowed hard, spontaneously placing her
hand on the small protrusion in her belly, before
replying,
"I think I must be about five months gone."
Evie, made no comment, but had turned her

back on Rose and was busily searching through the contents of drawer, which appeared to contain nothing other than babies and young children's clothing. Rose looked around the cosy, warm room, and Alfie, who was now wide awake, was also taking in his new and strange surroundings, and had thankfully stopped crying. There was a strong delicious aroma of chicken, which was causing Rose's stomach to rumble loudly and her mouth to water. It didn't take long for the blazing fire to warm them up, making Rose feel extremely sleepy.

"Here you are; this should fit the little man." Evie held out a thick knitted two piece set in dark blue, and a clean, off white napkin."

"You sort the little fellow out, while I fetch us a bowl of chicken broth, which never fails to aid a broken heart an' warm up a cold soul on such a chilly morn."

Rose was quite puzzled by Evie; in the few minutes that Rose had been inside her cottage, her observations had been very accurate, she seemed to be a woman of wisdom, but there was something odd about her too, which was keeping Rose on her guard. She slumped down wearily in the floral armchair, trying to change Alfie as quickly as possible before Evie returned. Alfie was being co-operative today, perhaps sensing his mother's nervousness. Rose planted a kiss upon his chubby cheek, making him smile. He kept his wide hazel eyes fixed like magnets on Rose the whole time, and was very shortly looking and feeling clean and fresh, and eager to climb down from his ma's lap to explore.

Evie returned to the room with a tray of steaming food and drinks. She sat on the small brown velvet sofa next to the large ball of bright red wool and pair of knitting needles, which had also attracted Alfie's attention.

She was soon up on her feet again, opening the door to a cupboard which was built into the recess next to the hearth. She pulled out a wooden box for Alfie to play with. Inside was an assortment of beautifully carved wooden farm animals, which, by the looks of them had once been painted. Alfie was delighted in the box of treasure, and Evie suggested he sat on the floor with them while Rose spoon fed him some of the chicken broth which she added, she'd let some soft bread soak into it, to fill Alfie's belly.

Rose was so grateful for Evie's kind and generous hospitality, and the break from trudging the harsh road, that it had given her.

"So who are you running from?" asked Evie, blatantly, as she slurped her broth, noisily.

"What makes you think that I'm running from somebody?" replied Rose, feeling a little annoyed by Evie's assumption, albeit correct.

Placing her spoon into the bowl, Evie pulled down her bottom lip with her aged dappled hand. Rose looked on, wondering what on earth this old woman was doing.

"You see this," she said, incomprehensibly, still holding on to her lip,
"I've got eight decades, and eight children behind me, I've buried more loved ones into the depth of the earth than you can count on your fingers and toes, and me bottom teeth left me mouth long before you even began to breath the Good Lord's air, so I'd thank you for some straight and honest answers, since I've been decent enough to invite you into me home. A young woman with her baby, don't find themselves wandering the wilderness so early on a freezing morn unless she's not quite all there in the head, or she's on the run from somebody, and my guess is, that it's your husband."

Evie picked up her spoon again and as her noisy slurping continued, an awkward atmosphere had filled the room, causing Rose to suddenly feel unwelcome, and a little wary of this strange old woman. How dare she be so presumptuous, thought Rose, as she tried to act normally, continuing to drink the broth, even though her throat felt suddenly constricted. Here she was escaping from that vile beast Seb Harper, wishing for nothing more in the world than to have her beloved Johnnie at her side, instead of in the Harper's family grave, and this woman, who was a complete stranger, was falsely accusing her.

"I'm not running from my husband, Mrs

Bancroft...because he is dead and buried. I am escaping from my brother in law. I believe he means me harm."

Evie stared, but for some reason, had her own version of the story in mind, and was beginning to see this flighty young girl as nothing but a heartbreaker. She was convinced that Rose was most likely pregnant with her brother in law's baby, and was merely trying to gain sympathy with her distressing tale.

"Where have you come from?" asked Evie, casually.

"Bushel Farm, in North Haddon. Are you familiar with it?"

Evie's mind had drifted off for a short period, as she tried to recollect such a place. She knew most local towns and villages, and most of the farms within ten miles of her home, but she had never heard of Bushel Farm, and even North Haddon sounded only vaguely familiar.

"So when did you set off on your journey?"

Having finished her broth in the time Evie had drifted off into her own little world, Rose was struggling to keep her heavy eyes open, and suppress her yawns. Sleeping in Evie's cottage had now lost its appeal, there was something unsettling about her, and Rose would rather find an old barn somewhere on her travels to nap in, and had already decided that she would soon be on her way.

"I left last night," Rose finally answered.

Evie just nodded.

" You must have covered a fair old distance then, reckon you're miles away from your home. Why, you're near enough in Oxfordshire."

Shocked by how far she'd managed to walk through the dark hours, Rose was relieved that there was now a good distance between her and Seb Harper, and she also decided that Oxford might be the ideal place for her to start her new life.

CHAPTER THREE

The bright April day promised to be a
welcoming, warm and sunny one. The early
morning frost was clearing quickly and the
white landscape was now lush green, with an
abundance of daffodils opening up to look like
groups of women, all wearing yellow bonnets as
they gently swayed in the breeze. Clumps of
perfectly formed snowdrops grew in scattered
clusters, adding splashes of white to the
beautiful picture. The signs that spring seemed
to have finally arrived, did not go unnoticed to
Rose, as she sat dreaming, gazing through the
small cottage window. Alfie had climbed back
onto her lap, and with his thumb in his mouth,
was once again, sound asleep.
Evie had swiftly cleared away the dishes, and
returned to her sofa, and now, all that could be
heard from her was the continuous clicking
sound of her wooden knitting needles which
were moving at such a speed, transforming the
thread into what looked like part of a small
jumper. Evie's concentration on her work was so
intense, that she failed to hear the clip
clopping sound of a horse, as it rode past the
tiny cottage, and then abruptly halted. Lifting
her heavy eye lids, which Rose no longer seemed
to have any control over, she stretched her neck
in order to see where the horse had gone,

freezing in horror as Seb Harper's unmistakable hefty body was dismounting from Blossom, one of Bushel Farm's mares who Rose had named herself.

"Oh, no!" she cried out, immediately causing Evie's knitting to stop, "it's him, he's followed me here!"

"Your husband?" questioned Evie, hoping to catch Rose out and hear the truth.

"Mrs Bancroft, I told you, my Johnnie is dead. That grotesque man outside, is his half brother, *and* his lifelong enemy. He means nothing but trouble. Please Mrs Bancroft, you must help me." Easing herself gradually up from her seat, moaning about her aching old bones, Evie hobbled to the window, rubbing her back as she took the few steps,

" He don't look so bad to me, in fact, he has a look of little Alfie about him."

"Please, Mrs Bancroft," begged Rose, in despair, don't give me away. I swear to you, he is *not* my husband."

Seb had now secured Blossom to the fence post and was marching down the narrow path, towards the front door.

" Go an' hide yourself and the little lad in the kitchen, and woe betide you if you're telling me a basket full of lies."

"Thank you Mrs Bancroft; trust me, I'm telling you only the truth."

Still unconvinced, Evie's face wore a frown while

she waited as Rose gingerly carried Alfie out to the kitchen, praying with all her heart that he wouldn't let out a sudden loud cry.

Evie opened the door slightly, peeping through the tiny opening at the heavily built stranger. Seb, in his normal uncouth manner stood breathing heavily, failing to remove his cap.

"Yes, can I help you young man?" asked Evie, abruptly.

Seb's eyes peered over Evie's head as he tried to glimpse the inside of the cottage.

" I'm looking for me wife and boy, Misses; she left in the night, and she's been a bit melancholy lately; I'm that worried that she might do something stupid."

"Well, I ain't seen nor heard a soul all winter long, young man. How old is your boy? Won't he see her safe?"

Solemnly shaking his head from side to side, Evie couldn't help thinking that this man was harmless and genuinely concerned for Rose and Alfie's welfare.

" Oh no, Misses, he's just a toddler, and we've got another one on the way too. I must find them, before it's too late."

Evie found herself in a quandary, she was usually able to see through a lie, but both Rose *and* this man, who was claiming to be her husband, both sounded so truthful and sincere in their claims. She didn't know what to do for the best. This man didn't appear at all threatening, maybe Rose *was* just suffering from a kind of melancholy; it wasn't unheard of when a young woman was burdened with the worry of childbirth and raising a young family, especially during difficult times.

"I'm sorry son; I do hope you find her soon. Tell you what, if you're coming back this way later and you haven't had any luck in finding her, knock on me door again, just in case she *does* come along this way. If she shows up, I'll be sure to keep her safe."

"That's right kind of you Misses, thank you kindly. I'll be sure to call back on me way home, if I ain't come upon them by then."

" God be with you young man," Evie called out as he hurried back to Blossom. Seb turned around, before she had a chance to close the door,

"Is there anything I can get for you on me travels, any provisions you need?" Once again, Evie was impressed by this man's thoughtfulness, making her doubt that Rose was being honest with her.

"I could do with a half sack of flour; my winter's stocks are just about depleted and perhaps a slab of cheese."

Seb raised his hand and waved, as he mounted the patient buckskin mare.

Having heard Evie's request for flour and cheese, Rose was feeling so angry that Mrs Bancroft should even contemplate allowing Seb

Harper to return to her cottage, and knew that she'd been lucky this time; thankfully, Alfie had not stirred from his deep slumber. She would have to leave quickly, she told herself, as she hurried to the window to see which direction Seb was heading in; it would be an absolute disaster to run into him on the road.

Rose returned from the kitchen, under the watchful eye of Evie, who seemed to be visually examining her.

"So that's your man is it? He don't appear to be the savage that you claim him to be. You got to let him take you back home Rose, he knows that you're ailing. He looks the sort to take care of his wife and family too."

Trying to hold her temper, which was now welling up inside of her, Rose couldn't fathom how Seb had somehow managed to sway this foolish old woman into believing his story.

" How many times must I tell you, Mrs Bancroft? That man is *not* my husband, I promise you. Why won't you believe me? If he *was* my husband, he would surely know that I am with child, but he is oblivious to that fact. *Now* do you believe me?"

Keeping her shock hidden from Rose, Evie had just heard all she needed to hear and was now convinced that Rose *was* telling her a pack of lies. She would keep quiet about the fact that Rose's husband had just declared how his wife was carrying his baby, and make sure that she remained in the cottage until he returned.

"Why don't you take little Alfie upstairs, you and him can have a nap on me bed; you look exhausted, and in your condition, you need to be taking care of yourself."

"Thank you, Mrs Bancroft, but I need to leave before Seb comes after me and the sooner the better, before the cold night returns."

Evie watched annoyingly, as Rose quickly bundled the large overcoat into her bag and wrapped a shawl around her shoulders. She finally tucked every strand of her rich golden hair beneath a drab brown bonnet, and wrapped a small square blanket around Alfie, who was still fast asleep.

"Which way are you heading then?" asked Evie, casually.

"I'm going to London. I'm sure there will be plenty of opportunities for me there, and Seb will have a difficult time in tracing me."

Within a couple of minutes, she was ready to leave, and bade her farewell to Evie Bancroft, thanking her for her kind hospitality. Rose had no intention of going to London, but knowing that Seb would be returning to Mrs Bancroft's cottage, she hoped to throw him off her trail, now convinced that Mrs Bancroft, for some bizarre reason trusted Seb, and would take pleasure in informing him as to where she'd gone.

The afternoon sun was still shining brightly,

feeling warm on Rose's back as she continued on her way. The countryside, with its new shoots flourishing beneath the nurturing sun was like an explosion of life and colour after the bleak harshness of the drawn out winter, and as Rose marveled at the bird song which filled the entire area, she was anxious and on her guard in the knowledge that Seb could suddenly appear at any moment. Hindered by her utter exhaustion too, she prayed that the coming night would be a milder one, and that she would manage to find somewhere safe to sleep.

CHAPTER FOUR

It had been a bitterly cold Sunday morning when the Baker girls were out playing in the snow. Being warned by their parents, not to go anywhere near the river which flowed past the end of their farmland, Beth had insisted that it was the only place where she would be able to find some exposed stones to use as the snowman's eyes. At twelve years old, she prided herself on being given the nick name of *the sensible one* by her ma, unlike ten year old Susie, who was renowned for often finding herself in trouble. On this occasion however, it was Susie who had foreseen how hazardous it would be on the slippery river bank. Beth, having a strong willed nature, refused to listen to her little sister's pleads to do as they had been told and to stay well clear of the river.

"Please don't go near the river, Beth, I'm sure we can just dig up some stones down by the footpath."

"Don't worry so much Susie; you're beginning to get on my nerves. Remember, I'm a whole two years older than you, so you *have* to do as I say."

Susie shrugged her shoulders, and kicked up the snow.

"Stop sulking Susie, and follow me. If we hold hands we will be fine, and no harm will come to us."

As they neared the river bank, Beth suddenly turned in alarm to her sister,

"Did you hear that?"

"What?" quizzed Susie, looking about her, slightly scared by her sister's terrified expression.

"I heard something; it sounded like a trapped animal; come on, let's go and have a look."

"I didn't hear a thing, and I'm freezing, and I can't feel my feet *or* my hands. Can we go back home now, Beth?" she pleaded, on the verge of bursting into tears.

"Oh, Susie, you're such a spoil sport. You've always got to ruin all the fun. We haven't even finished making our snowman yet."

"I don't care, I want to go home."

A sudden loud groan made both the girls cease their dispute and grab hold of each other's hands in trepidation. They stood motionless for a few seconds, not knowing whether to run back through the small thicket, and across the open field to their farmhouse, and the safety of their parents, or to go and investigate the source of the harrowing cry.

"I'm scared, Beth, let's go quickly. It might be a wild bear."

"Stop being so silly Susie, we don't have bears in England," assured Beth, trying to sound brave in front of her younger sibling.

As Johnnie Harper used every ounce of energy he could muster to crawl from the undergrowth, on hearing the sound of the girl's voices, Beth and Susie turned around and fled from where they'd been stood motionless since hearing the first of Johnnie's haunting screams.

Bursting into the warm kitchen of the Baker's farmhouse, Beth and Susie declared in unison what they had stumbled upon near the river bank. Lester and Nora Baker tried to calm their hysterical daughters, and comprehend what they were saying.

Grabbing his rifle off the high hooks on the kitchen wall, Lester was quick to go in search of the intruder who had induced such fear into his young daughters. Nora called out to him in vain, insisting that he should wear his coat on such a cold January day, but Lester's hot and angry temper was sufficient to keep out the cold.

"What happened out there girls? What did you see?"

Trying to calm her daughters, Nora wrapped her arms around them both. They were shaking from fear and cold, and Nora was suddenly overcome with worry, and the fact that her husband was now out in the open and in great danger from who or whatever it was that had filled her daughters with such dread.

"Beth, I want you to try and control yourself and explain to me exactly what you saw outside.

Remember, you're the oldest and you should be setting an example to your sister."

"It was a monster, covered with blood!" cried Susie, her bottom lip trembling.

"No it wasn't, *silly*," declared Beth, wiping away her tears, with the back of her hand. "It was just a scary man, maybe even a beggar."

"But he *was* covered with blood, *and* mud," insisted Susie.

Lester hurried back into the kitchen, visibly disturbed, and with an air of great urgency about him. Replacing his rifle back onto its safety hooks, he turned to his worried looking family, who were anxiously awaiting an explanation. Nora hadn't failed to notice the strained look shadowing her husband's face.

"Well, I won't need my rifle, but there's an extremely sick man down by the river. Nora, pass me a blanket, he's nearly frozen to his marrow...God knows how long he's been out there. I'm going to have to take the horse and cart to him; he's far too sick to walk, and I can't manage to carry him from such a distance."

"I'll make up a bed for him near the fire," said Nora, now concerned for her whole family, as she prayed that this sick man wasn't infected with a deathly disease, such as cholera.

Beth and Susie huddled together, still scared and now dreading the fact that their pa was going to bring the creepy looking man into their peaceful, clean home.

A straw filled mattress was placed near the kitchen hearth, and Beth and Susie were sent upstairs to their shared bedroom, and ordered to remain there until told otherwise.

Standing anxiously at the kitchen window, ten minutes had passed before Nora heard the familiar squeaking of the old cart wheels. It had begun to snow again, huge flakes, silently fluttering to the ground. The sky was nearly as white as the ground and Nora was overcome by a foreboding feeling, knowing that they would continue to be detached from the rest of the world until there was a change in the weather and now it looked as though they would be having a sick guest for the foreseeable future. Nervously wringing her hands, she was shocked when her eyes caught sight of the man who Beth and Susie had portrayed as some kind of terrible monster. He didn't look older than thirty at the most, just a young man, probably around the same age as her, even. He was obviously in a very bad way, the signs of chronic pain etched upon his blood stained face. Nora flung open the door, hurrying to assist her husband to carry this poor soul out of the cruel January elements. Unable to utter a word, Johnnie Harper was a stranger to every sight and sound. There was no feeling in his legs, and his eyes were devoid of all emotions and could only stare blankly, hardly blinking.

"Lay him down, Lester," ordered Nora, as they

struggled, literally having to drag him across the stone tiled floor to where the mattress awaited him. Both puffing, out of breath, as they stood in disbelief looking down on Johnnie, they both knew that a miracle was needed to restore any health to what they could only construe, was a victim of the harsh season. One of the worst winters in decades, the elder folk had announced, cutting farmers off from neighbouring hamlets, villages and towns as the relentless snow blizzards caused complete white outs, costing farmers the loss of many of their livestock as they became buried alive beneath huge snow drifts.

"Is there any chance that Doctor Tomlinson might come out to us and take a look at him?" questioned Nora. "He would stand a much better chance in the hospital."

After fifteen years of marriage, Lester knew exactly what Nora was thinking, and that her prime concern was the welfare of her family. He loved his wife dearly, and knew that her compassionate nature would soon overcome her fear, and she would do all she could to help this stranger.

"We might be able to persuade Doc Tomlinson to venture out here, love, but the roads to the hospital are completely cut off and impassable; it would be a miracle for a healthy man to get through. No, let's do all we can for him, and first thing in the morning, I'll try to get hold of the doctor. God willing, that the poor soul makes it through the night."

Nora, continued to study her patient, wondering where to start; he had such a vacant look about him, that Nora couldn't help thinking that it might have been better if the Good Lord had taken his soul and saved him from this torment. She would do all she possibly could for him. While Lester went to stable and feed the horse, Nora began the grueling task of cleaning Johnnie. Covered in dried blood and mud, it took a while to find the wounds which were thankfully all quite superficial. She cut away at his water logged clothing, leaving his long underpants for Lester to attend to when he returned. He had a handsome face, thought Nora, albeit in need of a shave, and his brown hair which was matted with clumps of dried blood, in need of attention. She wondered who he was and where he'd come from? He must have been out in the freezing cold for quite a while, she thought; was there a desperate family somewhere, worried sick about him; perhaps a distraught mother, out of her mind with worry? She gently bathed his face and hands, allowing some of the warm water to drip into his mouth. As his body began to warm slightly, his eye lids gently closed, his breathing was laboured, but Nora was convinced that he already appeared a little improved. Lester quickly returned, accompanied by a cold blast of the winter's air.

Covered in snow, he brushed his clothing and stamped his feet on the ground allowing the clumps of snow to fall away, onto the kitchen floor.

"How's he doing?" asked Lester, peering across the kitchen, as he hung up his wet coat on the peg.

"He's a little warmer, and seems to be more restful. Come and undress his bottom half Lester, while I go upstairs and find a pair of your long johns for him to wear."

When Nora returned with the under garment, and after being bombarded with a whole host of questions from Beth and Susie, who were eager to hear all about the ailing man, Lester had such a look of worry upon his face, that Nora instantly knew something was very wrong. She hurried to his side, and gasped in shock on seeing the blackness in Johnnie's lower legs. Lester was rubbing his face and slowly shaking his head from side to side.

" Poor lad," he uttered, solemnly.

"Is that what I think it is?" questioned Nora, her brow creased with concern.

"If I'm not mistaken, that looks very much like severe frostbite. I must go and fetch Doctor Tomlinson...he looks in a critical way, Nora."

"There's a blizzard out there, the conditions look merciless; Lester, please wait a while 'till it passes." begged Nora.

Still not having taken his eyes from Johnnie's

lower legs, Lester knew that if Johnnie was left much longer like this, he wouldn't last the night. He was a young man, with his life in front of him, and Lester knew that his conscience wouldn't allow him to stay in the warmth and safety of his home and witness the life leaving his fellow human being. He *had* to do something, even if it was only a feeble attempt.

"We don't have time on our side, Nora. There's no guarantee that this storm will surpass by nightfall. I have to reach the doctor by then; otherwise this poor young man won't stand a chance."

In the knowledge that nothing she could do or say would deter her husband from his urgent venture, Nora began to make a few preparations to help Lester on his arduous journey.

"Are you going on horseback?"

"By foot, across the farmland; it will be quicker. Don't worry my darling; I *know* these fields, every square inch of them."

Nora was already worrying, and praying hard for the safety of her brave and selfless husband.

CHAPTER FIVE

Beth and Susie had both hugged their pa goodbye, wishing him a safe journey.
With instructions to the three dearest females in his life, to take care of each other, he crossed over the threshold and out into the sub zero temperatures of the white wilderness. The sound of the howling wind seemed to laugh at him for leaving home in such hazardous conditions.
Nora kept up a continuous vigil of bathing Johnnie's lower legs in warm water hoping it might bring back a hint of normal flesh colour to them and save him from what she knew was likely to be the only treatment. It had been bad enough for all those unfortunate soldiers, who'd suffered so terribly on the battle fields during the Crimean War over ten years ago; to lose their limbs so brutally on the makeshift operating tables, miles away from home and from their loved ones. This young man had probably just slipped on the icy river bank and fallen into the river.
With the subdued atmosphere in the Butler's warm kitchen, all thoughts were now with Lester, as he made his dangerous journey to reach the doctor. Beth and Susie sat around the table, preparing vegetables for supper. Nora had decided to use their last rabbit to make a stew, hoping that perhaps, if her patient could manage

to get some warm food inside of him, it would aid his recovery; she doubted that he'd eaten in a while.

"It's all your fault, Beth!" whispered Susie, as she scraped away at the outer skin of the carrot in her hand.

"What do you mean? It's all *my* fault!"

"If you had listened to Ma and Pa, we would never have found him," she scolded, nodding her head in the direction of Johnnie. "They told us to stay away from the river bank; now it's your entire fault that Pa has had to go out in this dreadful snow storm."

"Oh, be quiet, Susie, you don't know what you're talking about; if it wasn't for me, that man would still be out on our field, maybe even *dead!*"

"*Girls!* That will do. This poor man needs peace and quiet; now hurry up with those vegetables and hold your tongues."

Johnnie half opened one eye, and for a brief second Nora thought he was about to speak, but then he sank back into a state of semi consciousness, leaving Nora with a dash of optimism that he might just pull through. If only she knew his name, she thought, as she continued to place warm soaked rags onto his blackened limbs, praying that her efforts would not be in vain.

It was no more than two hours later that the

backdoor to the Baker's kitchen was suddenly flung open, blowing in a whirlwind of dry snow and both Doctor Tomlinson and Lester, white clothed and red faced from the biting wind. Luck had been on Lester's side when he had miraculously met the doctor who'd been called out urgently to the neighbouring farm when the farmer's young son had been suffering from a high fever and chest pains.

The warming aroma of the appetizing rabbit stew which was simmering gently on the stove had to be temporarily ignored, while Doctor Tomlinson examined his newest patient. Johnnie was not a young man that he recognized from his local rounds, much to Nora's disappointment. She would have felt a lot safer knowing what sort of family the young man had come from.

Doctor Tomlinson's face expression spoke loudly and clearly of the severity of this young man's afflictions, he turned to Lester, ashen faced.

"It's not looking good, Lester... his condition is potentially life threatening."

He crouched down to examine Johnnie's lower legs again, taking the oil lamp from off the kitchen table. Lester and Nora stood in the background, solemnly, in dread as to what Doctor Tomlinson's prognosis would be, but both having an idea as to what would be the only treatment to save Johnnie's life. Doctor

Tomlinson who was in his early fifties, was an excellent and well experienced doctor, with a wealth of medical knowledge and modern ideas, after having travelled and practiced medicine throughout Europe. He had worked with some of the top surgeons, in the world, and was greatly inspired by the late Scottish, Doctor Robert Liston who was a remarkable surgeon and an expertise in the use of anesthetics and limb amputations. Having left his busy lifestyle behind him on returning home to Melksham in Wiltshire, to take over his father's practice, it had been years since he'd last had the misfortune of carrying out an amputation.

"You've done a good job in applying warm compresses to his legs, Mrs Baker," he announced, with the first sign of hope in his voice.

"I did my best for the poor man, doctor."

"You might just have saved him from losing one of his legs."

"Well, it was with the Blessing from The Good Lord, doctor; we have all been praying hard for the poor soul."

Doctor Tomlinson stood up again, his weary eyes surveying the kitchen before coming to a halt as he stared down onto the table. Lester already sensed what was coming next. Doctor Tomlinson's voice was low but serious,

"I'm going to need the use of this table to perform an amputation of this gentleman's right lower leg. Gangrene has already began to spread...so, the sooner the better." He paused for a couple of seconds as he watched the colour drain from Nora's cheeks,

"I'll need your assistance...are you up for that? I'm sorry, but it's the only option. The weather conditions make it impossible to transport him to hospital, but they could work in our favour in as much as I can use the snow to pack around his leg to stem the bleeding."

Nora let out a cry of despair, the thought of such a barbaric operation about to take place in her home, somewhat disturbing her.

"I'm sorry Mrs Baker; I didn't mean to alarm you."

"No Doctor, *I'm* sorry, we must *all* do whatever it takes to try and save his life," she declared, bravely looking down at Johnnie's limp body. "Now, Doctor Tomlinson, please inform us of exactly what you want us to do."

Lester took her hand, squeezing it gently, as he looked proudly at his brave wife.

Taking two bowls of the rabbit stew up to Beth and Susie, Nora was exceedingly stern in her instructions, for them to remain in their bedroom until further notice. Sensing their ma's strained voice, and the look of fear that she was trying so hard to hide from them, the hungry girls, took the food and promised to do as she had told them.

While Lester and Nora set about scrubbing the

already spotlessly clean kitchen table, Nora couldn't help thinking that meal times would never quite be the same again. The doctor prepared his patient, using a chloroform soaked sponge held over his airways, to insure that he would be completely oblivious to what was happening as he drifted into an anesthetized state. As Lester and the doctor carried his body to the improvised operating table, Nora caught sight of the gruesome saw, and swooned.

Half an hour had passed, until Doctor Tomlinson, had completed the operation, and Johnnie's leg had been successfully amputated just below the knee and the stump sealed. The next few days would prove to be traumatic for the young man, Doctor Tomlinson had declared. Nora had recovered from her episode of fainting, and was determined to nurse Johnnie back to health, no matter what it took, even if it meant forfeiting her sleep and the warmth of her bed for a few nights. Doctor's orders, were that the three of them all sampled a bowl full of Mrs Baker's delicious rabbit stew, to keep up their much needed stamina, essential for them to maintain the round the clock care that their sick patient needed. Nora insisted on keeping a little of the flavorsome stew aside, just in case her patient woke up feeling starving. The doctor, not completely convinced that Johnnie's left leg would escape being amputated too, realised that he'd have to keep a very close eye on him, but

for the time being Nora and the doctor
continued in their endeavor to bring the foot
back to life with warm water.

Over the next few days, a cloud of silent prayers
and held breath descended upon the
Baker's farmhouse. Even Beth and Susie seemed
to have taken a vow of silence, as they too spent
every day just waiting for a sign that the man
they had discovered would pull through his
horrendous ordeal. Doctor Tomlinson hadn't left
their home for days apart from the one journey
that he'd taken to collect medical supplies and to
inform his wife where he could be contacted in
case of any emergencies. For most of the time,
Johnnie was in a laudanum induced sleep,
waking sporadically in obvious pain, and
burning up with fever, where he would cry out,
'*Rose,*' and be given sips of water before
returning to his darkened world again.

Thankfully his left leg had greatly improved,
and was now a healthier looking colour,
reassuring Doctor Tomlinson that he would not
need to use his saw again.

On the fifth day, Johnnie's fever broke and he ate
his first meal. Lester and Nora were delighted
and with Doctor Tomlinson having returned
home on the previous day, they eagerly awaited
his next call, knowing how pleased he would be
to witness the improvement of their mysterious
patient.

Beth and Susie were now allowed to enter the

kitchen and looked in amazement at how different their mistaken beggar man now looked. Lester had given him a shave, and found and old truckle bed out in the barn which had been made up and positioned near the kitchen window, where Johnnie could view the tranquil farmland. Although still in a confused state, Johnnie had been able to remember his name, and when Nora mentioned to him how he'd been calling out for *Rose* during his delirium, she was warmed to catch the very first smile upon this man's face, as his mind wandered off for a brief moment before declaring that Rose was his beautiful young wife, and that he was also father to a baby boy.

CHAPTER SIX

"Here you are Mrs!" Seb declared, grinning widely as he delivered the sack of flour, cheese and a small poke of tea leaves to Evie Bancroft. "That's mighty thoughtful of you young man, do you want to come and share a pot of tea with me while your horse rests up?"

"Did my wife come this way?" Seb was impatient; exhausted and sore from being in the saddle all day, without any positive results. Not one single person who he'd come across on his long journey had passed by a fair haired woman with a baby in her arms, along the road. Seb could only draw to the conclusion that he had been heading in the wrong direction. Tomorrow he would travel north, he decided. She couldn't have vanished, and Rose belonged at his side where he could take good care of her.

"Are you coming in or not!" demanded Evie, ignoring Seb's question.

"So have you seen her then?" he persisted.

"Yes," Evie answered. Flatly, "*Now* I bet you'll step over my threshold, won't you?"

Seb let out a chuckle,

"You're a clever old bird, ain't you?"

"Enough of your cheek now, I dare say I'm old enough to be your grandmother, so just you remember that. Manners never cost a farthing."

Not having a clue as to where he'd found the

patience from, as he stood waiting while Evie bided her time brewing the tea, Seb suddenly caught sight of the half opened box of wooden animals by the side of the armchair. There was only one reason why an old woman would have these child's toys on hand, he thought annoyingly. Rose must have been here and that lonely old crow had probably invited her in to pass the time of day, just as she was doing with him. Seb's heavy breathing caught Evie's attention as she appeared from the kitchen, carrying two enamel mugs of tea. She placed the mugs down onto the antique sideboard, which had been in her possession for seventy years; a wedding gift from her pa when she was just a young bride of sixteen. She looked up at her house guest, thinking how she had not had any visitors in more than ten years and how this day was becoming more interesting with every hour that ticked by.

"What are you huffing and puffing about? Your nostrils look fit to emit red hot flames at any minute."

"Stop playing games with me Misses, an' tell me where me wife an' kid are. I know they've been here!" Seb's raised and angry voice did nothing to ruffle Evie, she remained calm.

"So what makes you so sure that I know where they are? I'm just a silly old woman, after all. Now drink your tea, and let's have a civilized conversation shall we?"

Evie pointed to the cup on the sideboard, as she kept her eyes firmly on Seb. She was feeling quite intimidated by his presence inside of her snug cottage. His bulky body was not without its unpleasant unwashed stench, and a little of her felt sorry for the sweet young girl who had stood in his footprints earlier. She would not allow an ounce of her fear to become apparent to him. If he was who Rose had claimed him to be, a heartless bully, who was her brother in law, she would have to tread carefully. She was now beginning to have her doubts that Rose hadn't been spinning a yarn.

"What makes you so certain that your wife and child have been here anyway?"

"Because you bloody well told me they had, less than ten minutes ago!" exclaimed Seb, now thinking that perhaps this senile old woman was just toying with him for her own amusement and enjoying every minute of it. "How often do you play with toy animals then? And don't tell me that you have family who visit, because if that was the truth, you wouldn't be in need of those victuals that I bought for you."

"Think you're a right clever young man don't you? Think that you can pull the wool over an old wise woman like me self, who's old enough and strong enough to give you a clip around the ear."

Seb let out a hearty laugh at Evie's words, which soon dramatically changed to anger, as the sudden thought of the empty cold farmhouse flickered through his thoughts, reminding him of what he would be returning to.

" I'd like to see you try, Mrs, but you're right of course; I do think I'm a clever young man, and if you want to see the sun come up in the morning, you had best use your wisdom, and tell me where Rose and the brat went," bellowed Seb angrily, banging his fist down hard onto the sideboard, as his face turned puce.

Shaken by the sudden change in this man's behaviour, Evie told herself to keep her fear concealed from this menace who now seemed to tower over her in a threatening manner. She was also convinced that Rose had been telling her the truth as her heart was thrown into sorrow that she'd been over hasty and misjudged the poor vulnerable young girl. A loving father would never refer to his missing baby as a brat. This man *did* possess a nasty mean streak, just as Rose had claimed. Now poor Rose was out on the lonely and dangerous road with that sweet baby; she should have offered her more help and showed her a bit of faith, she thought, angry at herself.

Evie laughed coldly, as she glanced at her treasured sideboard, more concerned for the piece of furniture than her own well-being.
"Didn't your ma teach you any manners?"
"Just cough out the truth if you know what's good for you, and let me be on my way. This is

your last chance," Seb growled, taking a step nearer to Evie, *"Where did she go?"*

Refusing to make it easy for this repugnant man, Evie decided to send him on a wild goose chase, it was after all, the only way that she could now help Rose, and she owed that much to her for being so disbelieving of her plight.

"Well, I ain't no coward, but the sooner you remove your stinking carcass from my home, the better, even me pretty daffodils have begun to wilt. They were here, earlier, if you insist on forcing the words from my mouth."

Seb's eyes sharpened as he fixed his stare on Evie's round face, unable to hide his excitement. "And where did they go, Misses?" Evie knew that Seb meant business, the malevolent look in his eyes cried out danger, causing every bone in her body to shake in trepidation.

"Now why would I divulge such information to you?" she foolishly teased.

"Maybe because you've got enough sense in that dried up old brain of yours to know what's good for you, Grandma!"

"Well, she headed off to Oxford. There, now take your foul-smelling body out from under me roof. I'd say that Rose had a lucky escape from you."

"Thanks, old woman, you've been very obliging." As Seb placed the empty mug back down onto the sideboard, he purposely knocked the vase of bright yellow daffodils over, bringing it crashing to the floor; shattering it into tiny splinters.

"Oh dear, how clumsy of me!" he declared, smugly, as he sauntered out of the cottage. Glad to see the back of him, and thankful that it was only a vase that he'd damaged, Evie was elated that she'd sent him to Oxford, remembering how Rose had told her that it was London where she intended to head for.

Rose had covered very few miles since leaving Evie Bancroft's cottage; every step she took was a huge drain on the little energy that she had left. With her carpet bag on one arm and Alfie, who was now barely visible, wrapped in Johnnie's overcoat, in the other, Rose was eager to find a shelter of some kind before the sunset and before the gathering dark clouds, burst upon her. Now in complete open countryside, which stretched out before her, never ending and never changing, Rose's nerves were frayed, knowing that if Seb should all of a sudden appear from any direction, mounted upon Blossom, she would stand no chance at all of concealing herself from his view. The thought immediately spurred her on to an increased pace, as she now prayed for the darkness of night to hasten.

Only a couple of horse and carts had passed her, since she'd left Evie's cottage, which, she thought, probably meant that she was a long way from civilisation. Feeling every sharp flint, stab her foot as she trekked along the twisting dirt track, her feet felt raw and swollen and she was desperate for a long rest. As daylight was slowly being consumed by the curtains of nightfall along with the now charcoal clouds, amidst the vastness of the surrounding fields, Rose spotted a solitary Oak tree, standing grandly, like a beacon of hope. Its dark silhouette appeared gloomy and foreboding, but it would make for a decent shelter. Huge raindrops had already intermittently begun to drop from above, and Rose knew it was only a matter of minutes before the Heavens opened. Breaking into a gentle run and using every remaining ounce of her energy, Rose crossed the recently ploughed field with caution, taking care not to twist her ankle on the uneven furrows. As the pelting rain fell like stair rods from above, Rose had just managed to reach the shelter, dropping her exhausted body down next to the massive trunk.

Alfie was now wide awake and had broken into a repetitive chant of 'mamma, mamma, mamma.' His adorable antics brought a smile to Rose's strained face. She had saved a few pieces of potato and some slices of carrot from Mrs Bancroft's chicken stew; thankfully they'd remained intact. She pulled the cold delights from her pocket, breaking them in half and filling Alfie's mouth with them. It wasn't enough, and when the last piece had been swallowed, he broke into an angry cry, as he rubbed his tender heels back and forth on the rough ground in frustration. Digging deep into her bag, Rose soon pulled out a crust of bread for him to chew on and peace once again ascended beneath the leafy tree. She pulled out the square wooden jewellery box, which Johnnie had given to her on their last Christmas together; a sharp stab of sorrow pierced through her heart, as she remembered that joyful day, bringing such a feeling of desperation about her. She missed Johnnie so much, and knew in her heart, that nobody would ever be able to take his place. She had fallen in love with him on their very first meeting, when he had offered her a lift home, on his horse cart, one sweltering summer's day. She had never known her parents, who'd both been tragically taken by a cholera outbreak which had swept through Northamptonshire when she was just a baby. The two rooms above the forge, on the outskirts of the town had been her home. Her grandfather was a skilled and hard working farrier, who doted on his young granddaughter, and her grandmother who was full of kindness and love, worked hard, weaving, straw hats and selling them at the local market; a skill which she had taught Rose when she was just a young girl of six. By the time Rose had reached the age of ten, her beautifully crafted straw boaters and bags were as good as her grandmother's and increased the family's income. Sadly, though, both her grandparents had left the world within ten months of each other, shortly after Rose and Johnnie had married.

Emptying its meagre contents into her bag, she took the box and its upturned lid to beyond the shelter of the Oak, allowing them to fill up with the rain fall; a drink for when morning arrived. Making a bed from the clothes in her bag and Johnnie's warm overcoat, Rose nestled down with Alfie, to suckle him, praying that The Good Lord would protect them both throughout the night. As Rose lay listening to Alfie's contented sighs as he lazily filled his belly and to the rain as it gently dripped from the lofty leaves, Rose felt the tiny baby wriggle inside her belly, reminding her of the heavy responsibility that she had; to take care of her poor fatherless infants.

CHAPTER SEVEN

Bushel Farm was cold, dim and lonely, on Seb's return from his unsuccessful day's journey. The kitchen was already in a desperate need of a woman's touch, but he was not about to attempt to wash any of the dirty dishes that were beginning to accumulate. There was no freshly baked bread, and no delicious stew simmering on the stove. Seb sat in the semi darkness sulking. He'd only lit one of the oil lamps, not wanting to view his desolate home in Rose's absence. Exhausted from his long day's travels and with the thought of another one when first light appeared, Seb was reluctant to turn in and get some sleep; he was a troubled man, and his mind was unable to unwind as he chewed over everything that had happened of late, especially back on that New Years day, when the events caused everything on the farm to change. Nobody really knew why or how he had been given such a name as 'Mad Master Monty,' Johnnie had always insisted that he had probably come from a wealthy and well to do family and that Master Monty was the last way that he could remember being addressed, before he lost his wits. Nobody knew how that had happened either, but this cumbersome crazed looking man, was totally harmless. Monty was probably in his early fifties, although looked a lot older due to his rough and unkempt appearance, and from years of sleeping out in all weather. Although mature in years, his mind wavered from being that of an excited five year old to an interested and curious sixteen year old. He had managed to escape being institutionalised and appeared to relish in the outdoor life, surviving by continuously moving from one place to another.

He would turn up at Bushel Farm without fail, every Christmas and sleep out in the barn for a while before moving on, working his way through the hospitality of the farmers who had come to know him over the years, and allowed him on their land. Even when Seb and Johnnie's pa was still alive, Master Monty would always be greeted kindly and offered any food that the family could spare. Like his pa, Johnnie had always possessed a far more charitable side to his nature than Seb, who had no patience or tolerance for the simpleton and in his youth had gained great pleasure from taunting him, much to the disgrace and condemnation of his pa. Seb would never have noticed how much Monty had been shivering from the freezing temperatures, like Johnnie had done on that morning, and Seb would never have even dreamt of lending him the use of his warm overcoat; that was by far too huge a sacrifice to make on such a harsh winter's day.

Seb's rumbling stomach forced him to leave his

chair and search the pantry, where he found some eggs and cheese; cheese which was still covered with his grubby finger prints. In his slovenly state, he cracked the eggs upon the table, and poured them one at a time down his throat, leaving a trail of the glutinous egg white dangling in slimy threads from his already filthy beard. Rubbing the back of his neck, Seb's mind wandered back to that day when he and Johnnie had been out on the land, to retrieve any rabbits caught up in the snares that they'd set up on the previous day. Monty stood waving like a small child as he waited next to one of the snares, ever eager to help. His wide grin displayed a mouthful of broken and rotting teeth as he jumped for joy, clearly euphoric at the arrival of Seb and Johnnie.

"Got yer self a fat an' tasty rabbit, Johnnie. Pretty Rose can make a juicy pie."

"Move out my way, you bloody idiot!" shouted Seb, angrily as he elbowed Monty, making him trip over his own awkward feet.

"Leave him alone," cautioned Johnnie, "can't you see how excited he is, poor bugger."

"I don't want his filthy hands touching my dinner," growled Seb, retrieving the stiff rabbit from the snare.

" There's more over the hill, Johnnie, one as big as a sheepdog." Monty held his hands apart, to emphasize its size, as he skipped along beside them, like an excited five year old. Dressed in a

pair of baggy trousers held up by a length of
rope, and a striped cotton shirt, Monty's thick
coat that he was normally turned out in had
been replaced by a thin summer jacket.
"Where's your warm coat, Monty?" asked
Johnnie, noticing how much Monty was
shivering.
"Did the deal with the nice man," he replied,
smiling joyfully.
"What nice man?" enquired Johnnie,
suspiciously.
"The nice man who gave me this." He tugged at
the thin worn out jacket, proudly.
"He said I'd get a wife wearing a smart jacket;
someone like Rose who can make pies and stuff."
"Monty, you *are* an idiot," announced Seb,
laughing out loud.
"Don't yer think the gals will like it then, Seb?"
Monty now had the look of a sad dejected child
about him, which didn't go unnoticed by
Johnnie.
"Come the summer, Monty, you'll be the
smartest man in the county; you'll even look
smarter than my loathsome brother, here, and
the women will be queuing up to kiss you."
The smile returned to his face, as Johnnie
removed his heavy black overcoat.
"Here, you go Monty, you can wear this for a bit,
an' I'll see if there's an old coat in the house for
you later. You can save your new jacket to show
off in the summer."

" You're as bloody mad as him!" declared Seb, "Now let's fetch those damn rabbits and get back home, it's bloody well freezing out here."

"You can come back to the house, Monty and have a bowl of Rose's stew, and I'll dig out that old coat for you too."

Seb looked annoyed, and issued a mean sideways glance at Johnnie. Just because Johnnie had the wife and kid didn't give him the authority to dish out the invitations to bloody empty headed tramps like Monty, he thought angrily. What gave *him* the right to take over; he was his junior, and Seb could still remember the days before he was even born, when it was just him and his pa working on the farm, and *his* loving ma, who's cooking was by far the best he'd ever tasted.

The amplified sound of the gushing river could be heard before they reached the small hill, the current was ferocious, taking with it hefty branches, that had been broken down during the earlier high winds. As all three stood watching, Johnnie explained to Monty that it was only the strength of the current that had prevented the river from freezing over.

Monty suddenly caught sight of a distressed duck, down by the river's edge, and before Johnnie had the chance to stop him, he'd scrambled down the slippery bank. The scared bird began flapping crazily as it turned in circles, pivoting on one wing, struggling to escape from the anticipated human intervention. There was a loud splash. Johnnie and Seb watched in disbelief as Monty's body was swiftly swept away, his arms desperately trying to grab hold of the overhanging branches.

"Seb!" yelled, Johnnie, "quickly, get a branch out to him, before he's swept completely out of reach."

Seb didn't move.

"Ahh, let him go, you'll be doing the poor bugger a favour."

Johnnie couldn't believe what he was hearing, and spontaneously leapt down the icy bank without a second's thought to the consequences as he slipped straight into the hostile gushing water.

Seb remained motionless, watching as his half brother disappeared from his sight. He wasn't going to risk his own precious life for those two and doubted that neither one of them would survive. The sudden realisation that everything he had been forced to share with Johnnie over the years would now belong to him alone, made it difficult for him to contain his triumphant smile.

The oil lamp began to flicker, leaving Seb sat in the darkness with his thoughts. He had never expected Rose to behave as she had, convinced that she would be grateful for a home to still call her own for her and the kid, Seb had presumed

that it would merely be a matter of time before
she saw sense and came around to his way of
thinking. *She* was a silly little fool too, no better
than her stupid husband, but that didn't stop the
ache that he felt every time he thought of her,
and pictured her teasing image in his mind. He
wouldn't be happy until she was back where she
belonged, and cradled in his arms; she was, after
all, a Harper just like him, and that surely made
her his very own possession now that Johnnie
was gone. As anger and frustration
overwhelmed him, Seb violently stabbed his
knife into the table, creating yet another
indentation. His violent temper was gradually
wrecking the kitchen table. Picking up a chair,
he hurled it across the room, causing its already
wobbly leg to fall off. He hadn't planned on
tricking Rose into thinking that it was Johnnie's
body he'd brought back to the farm for burial,
but when he'd witnessed the colour slip from her
beautiful face, and the sparkle disappear from
her sapphire eyes, he'd decided that it was the
kindest favour he could do for her; after all,
there would have been no way in which Johnnie
would have survived the ruthless cruelty of the
ice cold river. It would prevent Rose from
having to go through the trauma of knowing
that her Johnnie was lying at the bottom of the
river somewhere without any hope of a proper
burial. Consoling his conscience that he had
done the right thing, he dragged his weary body

out of the kitchen and instead of retiring to his own room he climbed the stairs, and took his rest in what had always been the Bushel Farm marital bedroom. The smell of Rose's perfumed skin upon the soft cotton sheets allowed him to drift off into a blissful sleep as he imagined that she was there, next to him. He could even hear her whispering sweet words of endearment in his ear putting a permanent grin on his unwashed face.

CHAPTER EIGHT

Awakening with the first light of dawn, Rose's entire body ached; she missed the comfort of her soft mattress and finding herself starving hungry, cold and damp beneath an oak tree was not the ideal start to the day. Alfie had begun to stir, his eye lids momentarily twitching; a sure sign that very soon he would be wide awake and hollering for food. The wooden Jewellery box had over filled with rain water, along with bits of tree debris during the night. Rose drank thirstily from the box as she stretched her stiff and aching limbs. The cool water was refreshing, but a hot cup of tea would have been far more pleasing. In a hurry to return to the road, and reach the nearest town, the reminder that Seb was still at large and knowing how stubborn he was, spurred Rose to quickly pack up her bag again. She was under no misconception that he would give up easily, especially as he was claiming that she was his wife; knowing Seb, he had probably already convinced himself that they had stood together in the church and taken their vows. He was such a great oaf of a man, with the most vulgar personality, not a bit like her dear Johnnie had been.

Alfie had the last piece of bread, which although, now quite stale, kept him contented and his little mouth busy. Rose had buried his soiled napkin beneath a pile of last year's dead leaves and twigs; she didn't want to leave any signs to assist Seb in his search for her. Hoping that the meagre crust of bread would keep Alfie satisfied until they reached a town or store where she could purchase food and drink, Rose was sure that she had no milk left to offer her poor son, the usual fullness in her breasts was missing, and her stomach ached with hunger. She prayed that her poor unborn child was not suffering too. The early morning bird song was a welcoming tonic, sounding more cheerful than she'd ever heard it before, as though a thousand birds were all chirping energetically to encourage her on her way. The sun was gently burning its way through the early morning mist, turning the hazy sky into a glorious stretch of rich unblemished blue. Alfie continued sucking happily on his crust, every so often shoving the soggy bread onto Rose's lips,

"Thank you Alfie, you're such a sweetie to take such care of your mamma."

Alfie smiled excitedly, wriggling in Rose's arms, making it difficult for her to hold him securely. The sound of horse's hooves nearing her brought an instant feeling of worry to Rose; scared to turn around, and knowing it would be pointless to try and run, she could only pray quietly under her breath that it wasn't Seb approaching. As the rattle of the wooden wheels upon the dirt track increased, Rose stopped in

her tracks to swap Alfie into her other arm.
"Wow, wow, ease up boy, wow," shouted the
driver, as the horse and cart pulled up just past
Rose, throwing up a cloud of dust behind it.
"Good morning, ma'am, I'm heading in the
direction of Oxford, if I could drop you off
somewhere along the way?"
Rose hurried the few steps to bring her
alongside the horse cart, a young cheerful
looking man, probably not much older than
herself was smiling down at her.
"You look like you're in need of a lift," he
declared, sympathetically.
The offer was far too tempting to decline,
"I would be grateful of a ride Sir, thank you."
"It's Dan, my name's Dan," declared Dan,
unfamiliar to any one addressing him as sir.
"I'm, Rose, and this is little Alfie," stated Rose,
smiling in sheer happiness at the thought of
resting her blistered feet.
"Here, let me take little Alfie, while you climb
aboard."
Rose did as Dan had suggested, although Alfie
wasn't as willing, and immediately burst in to a
fit of protesting screams, as he held his little
body rigid, making holding him extremely
difficult for Dan.
"I don't think he likes me," called out Dan, above
the racket coming from Alfie, as he held tight to
the wriggling infant, relieved when Rose had
clambered up beside him and once again had

hold of her baby. Alfie instantly became quiet, as he wrapped both arms tightly around his ma's neck, nearly choking her as he refused to look at the strange man.

Rose was blushing as she explained to Dan how Alfie always behaved in such a way around strangers and he would soon become friendlier towards him.

"Where would you like me to drop you off then, Rose?" inquired Dan, expecting Rose to ask for a lift to one of the approaching crossroads.

"Would it be asking too much if I travelled the whole journey with you?"

Flicking the reins as he commanded the horse to 'walk on' Dan turned to Rose, a little shocked by her request. He had a pleasant well shaven face, noticed Rose, with a neat brown moustache; his eyes looked kindly at her, showing definite signs of genuine concern.

"Don't tell me you were about to walk *all* the way to Oxford?"

"That *was* my intention, though maybe not in one day. How far away from there are we anyway. I was walking most of yesterday, so I'm not quite sure where I am anymore."

"Well, Rose, you are just outside of Helmdon, not that far away from Banbury. I'm planning to stop for an hour or so in Banbury, got to buy some plough parts and my ma and sisters have given me a whole list of peculiarities that they want me to purchase from Banbury market, it's like a complete new language to me...laces and gingham, tacking thread, bobbins… the list is endless."

Rose couldn't help giggling at the odd expression on Dan's face.

"It's no laughing matter, Rose; they put me through this embarrassment every time I go to Banbury. It's quite painful you know."

"Well, maybe I could help you, with your ma and sister's shopping, it does sound like a more feminine order."

"Rose, you have indeed, saved the day, and if you can stop me cheeks from turning bright red in front of those two old biddies down at Banbury market, then you have definitely got yourself a lift all the way to Oxford *and* back again if you so wish."

"Then we have a deal," declared Rose, happily, as they proceeded along the bumpy road.

"Please don't take this the wrong way, Rose, I mean no harm, but is that your stomach I can hear rumbling?"

"Oh dear, can you hear it too?"

Stretching his arm to reach down behind him into the cart, Dan pulled up a wicker basket, its contents covered with a piece of muslin.

"Here, take a look in this," he said, placing the basket down on the seat in between them. "My ma usually packs enough food to keep a whole regiment fed for a week!"

Rose removed the cloth, shyly, her mouth

already watering at the thought of something to eat.

"There's probably some chicken legs, there usually is; please help yourself, and let little Alfie get stuck in too, he might grow to like me then!"

The journey seemed to take on a complete new feel about it, the warm sun was shining, Rose and Alfie were enjoying Dan's generosity and Rose now felt safely assured that Seb wouldn't catch up with her. Every time she thanked Dan for the food he insisted that she should consume as much as she needed, telling her that unknown to his ma, he enjoyed eating in a restaurant whenever he journeyed to Banbury or Oxford, but didn't like to hurt his ma's feelings by rejecting the food hamper which she devoutly prepared for him every time.

Alfie had soon filled up on strawberry jam sandwiches, covering him in a sticky mess. The gentle motion of the trotting horse soon sent him back into a blissful slumber. Dan was desperate to question his stunning passenger, about the reasons behind her obvious escape from home, but didn't want to appear too inquisitive or risk upsetting this gentle female; he knew how fickle women folk could be, he had two sisters after all, and they gave him a difficult enough time with their moods and jealousy over the most trivial and ridiculous matters.

"So, Rose, do you live in Oxford?" he casually

inquired.

Although Rose had no doubts that she could trust Dan, she felt a little nervous about telling him her business, just in case, like Evie had, he would presume that she was lying, and by chance, Seb should later meet Dan on the road and asked after his so called wife.

"It's alright, you don't have to tell me a thing, there's no pressure, as long as you haven't just robbed a bank and are on the run," Dan joked.

"Do I look like a bank robber, with little Alfie here as my accomplice, of course!"

"Well, you can never tell these days, Rose." Dan turned to look at Rose, sensing that her casual banter was merely a cover for a very troubled young woman.

"I've got two younger sisters, you know, Rose, and I doubt that you are much older than them, and if I ,for one minute thought that either one of them was forced to be out on the road with a young baby, I'd move mountains to see them safe. I won't pass judgment, Rose, and if you decide to confide in me, well, I can promise you that I'm an excellent keeper of secrets. You never know, I might even be able to help. So what do you say?"

"Well, for someone who claims there's no pressure, you certainly don't make it easy for a woman to keep her private business to herself!" replied Rose, light heartedly, releasing a giggle. "And anyway, why are you trying to sound like some worldly, wise old man, I doubt that you're much older than me!"

"I'm twenty five, but me ma is always telling me how I have the wisdom and maturity of a forty year old."

"Ahh, but that's your ma! Maybe it's just her way of encouraging you to behave in a mature way, just as I tell young Alfie what a good boy he is, even if he's bawling down the house at four O' clock in the morning!"

Dan flung back his head in laughter.

"I certainly came upon a remarkable woman today."

Dan steered the horse and cart towards a nearby tree, off the track.

" Poor old Pepper is in need of a rest and some sustenance before we continue to Banbury."

Jumping down from the cart, Dan quickly pulled out a large flagon from the cart and proceeded to pour some water into a large metal pail, placing it near the grey speckled horse. He filled two tin cups for himself and Rose, passing hers up to her as she remained in the seat.

"Shall I help you down, Rose?" he suggested, holding out his hand to her, "we'll just let Pepper rest for ten minutes, before continuing."

Rose took hold of his hand as he politely helped her and Alfie down from the high seat of the cart. Feeling Dan's eyes glancing at the few strands of her golden hair which had escaped from beneath her bonnet, Rose felt strangely shy, and awkward, as she quickly tried to tuck them out of sight as soon as he'd let go of her hand again. She imagined that after so many hours spent on the road, with insufficient sleep, and grooming, she must look a sight, and attempted to make a few adjustments to her crumpled dress and obscure bonnet, while Dan was busy sorting out the back of his cart, dragging sacks of seed grain about from one side to the other, before jumping down triumphantly, announcing to Rose how he'd made a special secure section where Alfie could lay and sleep on the thick plaid blanket in safety, allowing Rose a respite from carrying him.

"That's wonderful," proclaimed Rose as she peered over the side of the wooden cart to view the snug and secure sleeping area, just behind her side of the seat. "Alfie will sleep like a little angel, thank you Dan; you have been so kind to me."

The strain of the past days and the lack of sleep had made Rose become quite emotional, and the thoughtfulness of this kind young stranger had somehow seemed to tip her emotions, making her break down into tears.

"Hey, steady on, Rose, it's only a blanket in the back of me cart!" exclaimed Dan, not sure whether he should follow his overwhelming instincts and take her in his arms to comfort her.

"I'm sorry Dan, what must you think of me?" Rose sniffed, wiping away her tears, "I've just had an emotional time of late."

Seeming like the most natural action to take, Dan took Rose in his arms and held her close, as once again she allowed her tears to fall freely. Up until this moment, it had not crossed Dan's thoughts that Rose might be with child; he still couldn't be sure though, but had his suspicions, which instantly made him conclude that she must be fleeing from an unhappy marriage. His heart went out to this beautiful, gentle soul, who didn't look as though she could have a mean bone in her body.

CHAPTER NINE

It was mid day when Seb eventually stirred from his heavy sleep. Looking around Rose's prettily decorated bedroom, he scolded himself for oversleeping, but couldn't find the energy to rouse himself from bed. As he lay day dreaming about Rose, wishing that she was under the same roof as him, and next to him in his arms, he came to the decision to wait for a week or two before continuing his search. By then, he thought, she might be a familiar sight around the streets of Oxford, making his task easier and would probably have realised, that it was no easy life for a young pregnant mother on the road. The farm was falling behind; he had neglected his work lately, especially after the extremely freezing and prolonged winter that the country had endured and now, without Johnnie around, everything on the farm was down to him; a huge and daunting mission for just one man. The acres of fields were still too tough for the plough to cut through them with ease, but Seb knew that if he wanted to produce any crops by late summer, there was no time to waste in sowing this year's seeds. The flock of ewes was about to start lambing too. In the past, Rose had always assisted with this task, priding herself on never yet losing a lamb.

Seb's thoughts transferred to his late pa, he

would be turning in his grave if he could see the state that Seb had allowed his farm to fall into since the beginning of the year, but even that didn't give him the incentive to rise from the bed and crack on, instead, he just pulled the blankets over his head, disappearing back into his imaginary world, telling himself that work would commence by mid afternoon.

"Johnnie, you're working far too hard, you know. As much as we appreciate all your help, we couldn't bear to see you back on your sick bed again." Nora pleaded with Johnnie, who she had grown very fond of over the few months that he'd been on the Baker's farm; he was such a considerate young man, always pushing himself to the limits to help around the place, even though Nora knew by his often creased brow that he continued to suffer unbearable pain. He seldom complained, and was so appreciative of everything that the Baker's had done for him, wanting to return the favours by helping out as much as he could.
"Oh, Mrs Baker, compared to what you and your family have done for me, if I worked till the end of my days, it wouldn't be enough to repay you."
"Johnnie, we only did what any other God fearing folk would have done, how many times must I keep telling you that; I consider that *we* are the fortunate ones to have been blessed with such a kind young man like yourself to help out

around the farm, especially with the harsh winter having left the land so crippled!" Immediately noticing his sad downcast look, Nora realised how unthoughtfully she'd phrased her sentence.

"Harsh winters have a habit of leaving a whole barrel full of cripples behind them, but I guess that's just one of life's trials," Johnnie replied, glumly.

"I'm sorry Johnnie; that was very insensitive of me."

"Please don't be sorry, Mrs Baker, you spoke only the truth. I don't want people having to be careful of their words when I'm around. I'm fortunate to be alive, and to have been rescued by such a lovely family."

"The good fortune rests entirely on us, now where are those girls, they will be late for school again, and I'll have grumpy old Madam Walters knocking on my front door come the end of the day. Thank Heavens it's Beth's last few months at school, though I don't think she'll be content staying home on the farm all day every day, she's got far too much energy, and you know what they say about idle hands."

Johnnie took hold of the crutches that Lester had expertly made for him, making his way towards the back door,

"Lester's been out there working from the break of dawn, I caught a glimpse of him leaving, but must have fallen back to sleep again," he informed Nora.

"And that means the poor man is working on an empty stomach. If you'd like to find him, and call him in, Johnnie, I'll make a start on the breakfast. He's probably out in the barn checking on all the heavily loaded ewes; spring is such a lovely season."

Johnnie strode across the yard towards the barn; he was becoming quite proficient in the use of his crutches, moving at a swift pace. He had endured a rough and painful couple of months, at one point when his wound had become infected it was touch and go whether he would pull through, but having youth and a strong constitution on his side and an excellent nurse in Nora, he had survived his ordeal. Although eternally grateful for all what the Baker's had done for him and how they had continued to welcome him in their home, even though he knew it was not practical for him to carry on sleeping in their kitchen, Johnnie was desperate for his foggy head to clear to enable him to remember his past life. Feeling as though he was living in a state of limbo, not belonging anywhere, but unable to proceed to the future, until he found his past, Johnnie was continuously tormented by the bleakness of knowing that somewhere he had a family. The Baker's continued to help in every way they could, coming up with many different ways and ideas in the hope to break through his memory loss. From Johnnie's knowledge of farm work, Lester was convinced that Johnnie had once worked on the land, or maybe even farmed his own place, but where this farm was remained a mystery; it was certainly nowhere near their farm in Wiltshire. Johnnie's knowledge that he had a wife called Rose and a baby continued to tease him way in to the dark hours of every night. As hard as he tried to remember about them, his mind seemed to enter a gloomy tunnel, leaving his heart and mind aching and sore and his eyes filled with tears of frustration.

Doctor Tomlinson, however, had explained that it was not uncommon for the brain to temporarily block out huge chunks of memory after such a horrendous trauma had occurred, plus the fact that it was highly likely that Johnnie had received a few blows to his head while he was in the river. The doctor's assurance that eventually most of Johnnie's memory would be restored to him, kept him from completely submerging into a state of depression every day, leaving him with a glimmer of optimism.

Lester heard the now familiar sound of Johnnie's crutches as they landed heavily onto the hard ground, causing the chickens to disperse noisily into every direction. He quickly hid the chunk of wood that he was clandestinely carving and shaping, behind a bale of hay, out of Johnnie's sight. The barn was filled with the cacophony of bleating ewes and the smell of new born lambs.

"Good Morning, Johnnie, how are you today?" It was a question Lester never failed to ask, every time they met.

"I'm very well, thanks, how about you?"

Lester nodded, giving Johnnie a wide smile as he pointed to the sheep pen,

"Take a look at the two young lambs; born early this morning, they were."

Johnnie made his way to the far side of the barn, immediately spotted a ewe which was clearly in distress as she tenderly nudged and licked her new born lamb as it lay lifeless next to her. Within seconds, Johnnie had managed to swing his legs over the hay bale which was acting as a fence, and was crouched down next to the limp lamb. Grabbing a handful of loose straw which covered the ground, he began to vigorously massage the tiny lamb's body. Lester had, by now, noticed that something was amiss and stood watching as miraculously, the life was gradually returned to the young lamb. Lester quickly joined him, congratulating and thanking him for his quick actions which saved the lamb's life.

"Now I know that you *must* have worked with livestock before, Johnnie," he joyfully declared, patting Johnnie on his back as he marvelled at the amazing sight of the ewe with its resuscitated lamb.

Johnnie smiled proudly suddenly remembering Nora's message,

"By the way, Mrs Baker sent me out here to bring you back in for breakfast."

Lester turned his attention to Johnnie,

"You know, you can just call us by our first names, all this Mr and Mrs carry on makes me feel like your old uncle, and if truth be told, we must be around the same age, give or take a few years either way."

"Still can't remember how old I am," said Johnnie, annoyingly.

" I'm thirty four, and Nora is a few years younger, but it would be more than my life's worth to reveal her precise age; you know what these women are like!"

Before Johnnie had a chance to reply, Beth appeared running across the yard,

"Pa, Pa, the breakfast is ready, and Ma said you're to hurry up before it all goes cold,"

"Take a look at our newest baby lamb, Beth, which Mr Johnnie practically brought back to life with his expertise," insisted Lester, not paying any attention to Beth's message.

" Ahh, it's so tiny and adorable," she quietly cooed, as if the lambs were sleeping babies, not to be disturbed. "I can't wait to tell Susie...come on Pa, we don't want Ma getting all annoyed, you know how she hates to see good food wasted."

Lester rolled his eyes jokingly, "*Females!* They aren't happy unless they're nagging someone."

"Oh come on Pa," continued Beth, smiling as she

took hold of Lester's hand and began to pull him across the yard. Johnnie looked on, in admiration at the loving bond between father and daughter. A twinge of longing filled his heart with such a need to find his Rose that he felt a cold shiver dart through his body. It was becoming more and more like a dream with every passing day; as he stood wandering if his mind would ever clear of the dense fog that shrouded his memory and his identity. In his darker moments he sometimes questioned whether Rose would be better off without him, now that he was a cripple. Would she repulse at the sight of his deformity? And on occasion, it sometimes crossed Johnnie's mind that perhaps there was no Rose and child; maybe that too was a figment of his imagination that his confused mind had persuaded him to believe was reality.

"Johnnie!" called out Lester, as he and Beth reached the back door, "are you alright?"

Johnnie broke out of his reverie, putting on his smile as he hurried back to the farmhouse.

The delicious aroma of fried eggs and freshly baked bread filled the kitchen. Beth and Susie sat politely, but impatiently, waiting for their parents and Johnnie to be seated around the rectangular table, while Nora poured the steaming tea from the huge brown earthenware teapot.

The conversation was mostly centred on the way in which Johnnie had leapt to the rescue of the newly born lamb earlier that morning, with the whole family praising his quick thinking.

"Well, I think Johnnie is welcome to stay with us for as long as he likes!" announced Nora, as she buttered her bread.

"Me too!" exclaimed Beth and Susie in unison.

"Well, then that's settled, but there *is* a condition attached to this invite," stated Lester, looking very serious.

All eyes immediately focused on Lester, Nora trying hard to hide her anger as she wondered what on earth her husband was about to announce.

"From now on, you must call us Lester and Nora, we are your dear friends and like Nora said, you must consider this your home too, and let's just pray that before long, Johnnie will be united with his dear wife, Rose and his child.

With everyone jubilant at Lester's announcement, especially Nora, who was smiling lovingly at her husband, the kitchen was filled with everyone's overflowing excitement, only to be suddenly broken by Nora's loud exclamation,

" Goodness, look at the time girls, you're late again.....off you go now, quickly. Tell Mrs Walters that your ma made you help with the chores this morning, since we're all busy with the lambing."

Within minutes, Beth and Susie were wearing their coats and hurrying out the kitchen door, calling out their farewells as they ran across the yard and along the meadow lane.

CHAPTER TEN

With it being such a gloriously warm and sunny spring day, Banbury market was thriving; It was as though every inhabitant from miles around had ventured out to celebrate the long awaited arrival of the new season, relived that the harsh days of insufferable cold had finally turned their back on the country. Alfie awoke from his nap on hearing the noisy chanting of the costermongers, as they all competed to sell their goods, and immediately burst into tears feeling insecure at not being cradled in his mother's arms, and on viewing his strange surroundings in the rear of the horse cart. As Rose quickly rescued and comforted him, peace was once again restored.

"Have you ever been to Banbury before, Rose?" Dan asked.

"No, I haven't really travelled further than Northampton. There's so many people here, it's awfully busy," replied Rose, looking around in bewilderment.

"I don't know about you, but I'm starving. Come on let's go and have a feast before business." Dan secured Pepper, and attached a nose bag around his neck, before helping Rose down off the cart. She looked tired he thought, and wondered what would become of her after he'd returned back home. She had yet to open up and disclose exactly why and who she was running away from, and had cleverly diverted all conversations away from her personal life during the journey. Dan would not give up, he was quite sure that she *was* expecting another baby too, but just in case he was mistaken, didn't want to voice the subject, for fear that it would only end up embarrassing Rose, and himself if he was mistaken. If only she would confide in him about *something*, he thought.

Dan searched the market for a good quality food stall. Rose was right, it was exceptionally busy today, and there were a few dubious looking characters hanging around that Dan didn't like the look of.

"Rose, do you mind if we eat on the cart, only I've such a load in the back, and like you said, it is very crowded."

"Of course not, if you like I'll wait by the cart and keep guard of it."

Knowing that Rose's presence would do little to deter any would be thief and with his overwhelming desire to protect and keep her and Alfie safely by his side, Dan politely declined her offer,

"Thanks, Rose, but I reckon it will be safe for a few minutes."

Rose held Alfie securely in her arms as they mingled amongst the bustling market stalls and the abundant crowds; his enquiring eyes viewed the many varied colourful sights with great interest. There were so many stalls which Rose would have loved to buy from, but knew that Dan was nervous about leaving Pepper and his supplies on the roadside, but recalling the list of haberdashery items which she was going to buy later for Dan's ma, she decided it would also be the ideal time to do her own bit of shopping. Dan purchased two sizable steaming hot meat and gravy pies; their golden pastry appearing particularly appetising. Banbury cakes were a favourite of Dan's and he couldn't resist buying enough of them to last a week. They were soon all sat back on the horse cart, indulging in the delicious food, with Alfie sharing the gravy soaked pastry of Rose's pie. It was decided that while Dan travelled the short distance to the nearby forge where they specialized in making the plough parts which he needed to buy, Rose would remain in the market place and do some shopping, and also purchase the list of items which Dan's mother required.

For a brief while, the seriousness of her plight seemed forgotten to Rose, as she waltz around the market, with Alfie in her arms, surveying the copious stalls and buying the essentials to keep her and Alfie provided for during the coming days. The temptation to purchase a new bonnet was quickly dismissed when Rose remembered that she had to be extremely thrifty with her meagre amount of funds, until an opportunity to earn more came her way, so it was napkins and

essential victuals which filled Rose's bag. She
soon understood Dan's reluctance to buy from
the haberdashery stall. The two elderly women
were quite a cheery, joking pair who kept up a
continuous banter as they worked. As all their
customers appeared to be female, she could
appreciate how Dan would feel a little
uncomfortable too. The pair of hefty
looking woman who must have both been in
their mid fifties, stood behind one of the most
extensive stalls in the market, with a mountain
of bolts of every type of fabric in every shade
and pattern precariously balanced on one hand
cart, and another stocked with an abundance of
ribbons and handmade lace, and every size of
bobbins and needles. The two hand carts were
separated by a stack of opened wooden drawers
all filled with every hue of sewing and
embroidery threads, and an array of buttons.
"Look at that handsome little boy, Violet,"
announced one of the women as Rose
approached.
"Ahh, what a darling, hello, my sweet little lad,
what's your name then?" she continued, giving
Alfie a peculiar little wave.
"Don't be ridiculous, Annie, he's far too young to
be talking; why don't you ask his pretty ma what
his name be?"
Alfie buried his head in Rose's neck, not happy
at having the attention of these unfamiliar
women both gawping, and paying far too much

attention to him. Rose gently patted his back, sensing his unease.

"Good day Madam!" declared Violet, as she quickly studied Rose from head to toe, noticing immediately that she was showing signs of being with child, either that, or she had a tendency to over eat. "And isn't it a glorious day today...makes you glad to be alive, does it not?" Rose smiled and returned the greetings, wishing there were other customers at the stall so that all the attention wasn't on her.

"What can we do for you today, my lovely?" asked Violet, as she continued trying to attract Alfie's attention.

"I ain't seen your face in Banbury market before; are you new to the area?" pried Annie.

"Oh don't take no notice of my sister," declared Violet, "She's too nosey for her own good, but she does have a point, I don't recollect seeing such a pretty face in Banbury market in a long while; everyone who shops from us usually has a face like a dried up old turnip!"

"Hold your tongue Violet; you'll make us loose all our customers," Annie warned, giving her sister a prolonged serious stare.

Taken in by complete amusement by these eccentric sisters, there was little that Rose could do but stand patiently and wait for their verbal jousting match to come to an end.

"So what brings you to Banbury market today? I hope you didn't have to travel too far to reach us?"

"Actually, I came especially to buy all of these items," declared Rose, waving the list which Dan had left with her under their noses. "I was told that you are the best stocked haberdashery stall in the whole of Oxfordshire!"

Annie and Violet looked astounded at each other; Rose's announcement had left them speechless as they stood open mouthed.

" The best in Oxfordshire, eh?" repeated Violet, smugly.

"I always told you that we were a darn sight better than those costermongers in Oxford, didn't I?"

"That you did little sister, that you did," confirmed Annie, nodding her head.

Violet took the list from Rose's hand with a renewed air of importance about her.

"Oh yes, we have all of these items in stock, *and,* I hasten to add, at a price you'll not find lower anywhere else."

"Oh Goodness gracious me!" exclaimed Annie, shaking her head from side to side, "now she's going to be full of herself for the rest of the day! Would your little boy like a gingerbread man? I baked them earlier today, they're not too spicy."

Alfie stared for a few seconds at the odd shaped biscuit, which Annie was holding out, before stretching his arm and clumsily grabbing it from her hand, immediately ramming into his mouth and letting out a chuckle of satisfaction. Rose

smiled proudly at her son, thanking Annie.
While Violet was busy assembling the order,
Rose thought it might be useful to inquire
whether these two women had knowledge of
any local work available, thinking that perhaps
she would remain in Banbury.

"You're quite correct you know. I am new to this
area."

Thrilled that *she* had found out some
information about Rose, before her sister had,
Annie stood beaming.

"I don't suppose that you know of any local
work that would be suitable for a woman with a
young child?" Rose asked, in a matter of fact
way.

"Can't say that I do," announced Annie, looking
quite vacant as her mind wandered off in
thought.

"What's up with you?" Violet asked, abruptly,
having collected everything from Rose's order,
"you look like you've seen a three legged horse!"

"I was thinking."

"Well, don't. The customers will think you're not
quite all there. What is it that's putting such a
drain on your poor little brain, anyway?"

Annie's face had turned a bright shade of
cherry,

"This nice young lady, was just enquiring if I
knew of any local work that would suit her."

"Oh was she indeed?" replied Violet, as she
stared at Rose, annoyingly.

"And what sort of work can you do with a
toddler in tow, and another on the way?"
Now it was Rose's turn to blush, wishing that
she'd never asked such a question, and wanting
to get as far away as possible from this rude
woman.
"How much do I owe you?" Rose ordered,
crossly.
Annie felt ashamed by the way in which her
younger sister had spoken to this woman, after
all she *was* a customer, who was purchasing a
large order too. She took Rose's money, as
Violet passed the sack full of goods to her, before
hurrying off to another waiting customer.
"Why don't you ask Mr and Mrs De Santis, over
there," Annie suggested, pointing to the couple
who were selling hot beverages. "They turn up
at nearly every market in Oxfordshire...*they*
might be able to help you."
"Thank you so much."
"I'm sorry about me sister, she can become a bit
standoffish sometimes; she means no harm
though."
Rose was grateful for Annie's kind words and
advice, but even they had failed in uplifting her
spirits after Violet's earlier harsh words. The
previous draining two days were now taking
their toll on Rose, she felt utterly exhausted and
it took nothing more than a kind or unkind word
to cause her tears to flow. Dan soon joined her
back at the market, noticing immediately how

fragile and emotional Rose was feeling. He insisted that she took a rest in the back of the horse cart, while he went to buy her a mug of hot sweet tea, from Mrs De Santis.

"You've been extremely kind to me Dan," she murmured, trying to keep her tears at bay, " I expect you're wishing that you'd just rode past me earlier; I know that I'm giving you a lot of trouble."

"Ahh, don't be silly now Rose, why, you saved me from those two at the sewing stall and that's worth *all* the trouble that you're giving me." Dan couldn't help laughing, seeing the indignation on Rose's weary but still incredibly beautiful face. He already knew that she had taken a firm hold on his heart; he wanted nothing more than to shield her and keep her safe; she looked so alone and vulnerable, but until he knew a little more about her circumstances, Dan warned himself to tread slowly and carefully.

After a refreshing mug of tea and a fifteen minute nap in the horse cart, while Dan took care of Alfie, Rose awoke feeling recharged and ready for the journey to Oxford, which she had now decided to be the best option for her. Alfie was now quite content to be in Dan's care and had quickly become accustomed to him, provided that he still had sight of his ma.

"You didn't tell me who it was that you're going to stay with in Oxford, did you Rose?"

mentioned Dan, casually, as the sights and sounds of Banbury were gradually left behind them, and once again they became surrounded by the peaceful lush green landscape, and shaded copses, where carpets of dazzling bluebells covered the land.

"Oh, Dan, I really *would* like to tell you everything, but please believe me when I say that I have good reason for keeping my private business to myself."

Pepper's gentle trot turned into a canter as Dan flicked the reins and passed a sideways glance to his enchanting companion. They exchanged a smile, both inwardly knowing that their arrival in Oxford would mean the parting of their ways.

CHAPTER ELEVEN

As the journey into Oxford continued, Dan found himself deep in thought, rattling his brains for a way in which he could perhaps remain in contact with Rose after they had reached their destination. He knew that he was being stupid, and behaving like a fool, but the thought of never seeing Rose again left a terrible desolate feeling within him. She probably had relatives in Oxford, parents in fact, he told himself. Maybe she wasn't running away at all, and maybe her husband was away on business, or even a soldier, stationed in foreign parts. She didn't owe him an explanation, he was merely some farmer who had offered her a lift, and had gone and fallen in love with her. Dan imagined the look on his ma's face, not to mention the string of cruel cutting remarks that his sisters would rain down upon him if he should disclose the fact that he'd fallen for such a woman, but even that didn't deter him; he was determined to be persistent until Rose gave him some kind of elucidation.

With a full belly again, Alfie had fallen into a blissful sleep, and was cocooned in the snug sleeping place which Dan had made for him. Rose was struggling to keep her eyes open, and to suppress her continuous yawns. She remained quiet, as she pondered on what would become of her and Alfie, and how she would survive. She had little money left, and no idea of who would offer work to a pregnant woman with a young child, but at least she could still just manage to hide her unborn child and even if someone employed her for a few weeks, it would be a start. Dan was suddenly bought out if his thoughts as Rose suddenly spoke,

"What sort of place would offer me work, Dan? Do you have any ideas?" It was said in a casual manner, but Dan could sense the underlying urgency in Rose's slightly cracked voice.

"Hmmm, that's quite a tough one. If Alfie was older it might be easier, but I can't really think of any job where you could keep Alfie at your side all day, and he certainly won't be content to be away from his ma."

"I know, you have voiced my very own thoughts."

"Why do you need a job Rose, aren't you going to visit relatives in Oxford?" ask Dan, slyly.

"Did I tell you that?"

"I don't quite recall, I just presumed."

"Well, you presumed wrongly, I'm a widow you know, not some silly girl taking a leisurely journey from town to town just for the sheer fun if it." In her tired and troubled state, Rose had suddenly lost her cool composure and could no longer pretend to be a woman in control of her life.

Dan pulled hard on the reins, bringing Pepper to

an abrupt halt at the side of the road.

"Come on," he said, turning to look at her with such concern etched upon his face, "Pepper could do with a drink and another rest."

Dan jumped down and fetched the water from the back of the cart, before steering pepper on to the grass verge where he immediately began to graze on the fresh new spring shoots.

The dry stone wall made a good back rest as they leaned against it in the warmth of the mid afternoon, sipping water. Dan produced the bag of Banbury cakes, that he'd bought earlier, but neither of them had any appetite.

"You know Rose, you *can* trust me. I care for you Rose, and I wouldn't do anything to harm you or put you in any danger."

Rose already had an inclination that Dan was harbouring feelings for her, it had not been the first time that a complete stranger had fallen for her; she seemed to have that effect on men. Her grandmother had always said that the beauty and fairness she had been blessed with would become a burden and a disadvantage to her, and she had been right. Rose had always imagined though, that after being married and having a child, men would see her in a different way, but she was sadly mistaken. Women tended to view her as a flighty heart breaker, and men became infatuated by her. No matter how she felt about Dan and she *had* taken to his kind and gentle ways, and he *was* a gentleman, quite dashing in his appearance too, she knew that any relationship between them would only cause him trouble. Dan had spoken so lovingly about his family, they could only want the best for him, and would not welcome another man's widow and children into their hearts easily. Rose couldn't even think to place Dan into such a position where he would become cast out from them, he had been an absolute saviour on this day, and Rose would never forget him, but that was as far as it could possibly go.

"Rose, are you hearing what I'm saying?" prompted Dan, noticing that Rose was sat with her eyes closed.

"Oh, sorry, Dan, I was just relishing in this glorious sunshine, it's been so long since we've seen such weather."

Dan, once again, realised that Rose wished to avoid his interrogation, it saddened him, but there was little he could do, other than try to gently coax the truth from her before they reached Oxford.

"When did you lose your husband Rose?" Dan persisted.

"On New Year's day, there was an accident; he drowned in the freezing river."

Dan was left speechless; he could feel the pain in every word that had come from Rose's sweet mouth, making him realise how devoted she was to her late husband, and how she loved him more than he could ever wish for her to love him. He now knew why it had been so difficult for her to explain her circumstances.

"That's terrible; I'm so sorry, Rose."

They sat in their own thoughts for a while, the sound of joyous spring birds breaking the silence with their continuous elation that spring had finally arrived, and the creation of new life was imminent.

"But, I don't understand, Rose, what made you leave your home?"

"It wasn't my home anymore, not after my husband had gone. You see, the farm was owned by him and my brother in law. It became awkward after....you know… just me and him alone there day after day." Rose surreptitiously wiped away a falling tear.

Dan understood too clearly what sort of man Rose's brother in law was, already feeling every muscle in his body tense up in anger.

"Don't worry Rose; I will be your chaperone until you find somewhere safe to stay, and a suitable job, in fact, I might just have the ideal temporary solution to your problem," declared Dan, with a glint in his eye.

Rose hoped that she wasn't being too forward and giving off the wrong messages as she took Dan's hand in hers,

"Thank you Dan, you have become a dear and trusting friend to me on this day. It's been a long time since anyone has shown me any genuine kindness; I value your friendship immensely."

Alfie's sleepy head with his tangle of flaxen curls
poking up over the side of the horse cart as he
sang out loudly,
"Mamma, Mamma," his appearance brought
about a smile on both Rose and Dan's faces,
instantly reducing the tension.
Alfie buried his head into Rose's chest as
Dan held out a Banbury cake for him, leaving
him feeling slightly embarrassed when Rose
explained that it was *mother's milk* which Alfie
was hankering after.
Half an hour later the trio was back on the road
again, a little refreshed and with Dan now
having a better understanding of Rose's
circumstances.

After stopping off to deliver the sacks of seed
grain to a farm near Bicester, by the time they
reached Oxford, a chill in the air and the setting
of the sun was bringing about an end to the
day's first real glimpse of spring. A fine drizzle
had began to descend, slowly soaking Dan and
Rose as they sat in, a now, subdued mood upon
the cart. Alfie was sound asleep, snuggled in his
designated place, which was now sheltered by
the large oil cloth which Dan had secured over
the back of the horse cart to keep everything dry.
Dan lit two lanterns, hanging one on each side of
the cart. The rapidly fading light was made
worse by the ominous dark clouds which
shadowed across the moon, causing an eerie

sight, and even though Dan had assured Rose that he would see her safe, she had a fearful foreboding feeling deep in her gut. They hadn't yet reached Oxford's city when Dan encouraged Pepper to slow up as he pulled in off the main road, taking the cart down a narrow road and coming to a halt.

"Why have you stopped here?" questioned Rose, her tone confused.

"Two reasons really." Dan twisted in his seat, gazing into Rose's eyes, his face dripping with rain water which had now saturated his moustache. "I have to deliver a fruit cake which me ma baked. You see this shop here?"

"Shop?" Rose viewed the small end terrace house on the corner where Dan had pointed to. The peeling brown paint from the grubby windows framed even grimier lace curtains that perhaps in another lifetime were once white. There was no sign above the shop, nor anything visible for sale displayed in the window.

"It doesn't look anything like a shop. What does it sell?"

Dan laughed at the confused look on Rose's face, " I quite agree, but when you see the owner, you'll understand why. She does sell the essential commodities; tea, sugar, flour, you know. Primrose Atkins used to be a neighbour to my late grandmother, and was always extremely kind to her, apparently. Over the years, my family has kept in touch with her and now whenever I take a trip to Oxford, I am put in charge of the famous fruit cake delivery."

"That sounds intriguing. How old *is she?* Does she live all by herself?"

" Yes she does, sadly, and I'd say she must be getting on for two hundred....I've never seen such a wrinkled creature in my life, but she is as sweet as a shriveled up prune," joked Dan. "How would you feel about staying with her for a while, just until you find something more suitable?"

Rose's confusion turned to shock, as she stared into Dan's face.

"You're not even joking are you?"

"Don't be alarmed, Rose, at this time of day, you won't find anyone willing to take on staff; these things take time. I got to thinking about old Mrs Atkins, and I reckon it to be the ideal short term solution. She won't be able to pay you, but she will surely give you a room in return for some home help and at least you and Alfie will be safe there; you'd both be doing each other a favour. Don't worry Rose, she's a game old bird, and she still has all her wits about her."

Rose took a peak beneath the tarpaulin at Alfie who was still in a deep sleep. She knew what Dan was saying was true, she would never find anywhere to stay for the night, unless she spent every last penny she had on a room in an inn somewhere, leaving her in exactly the same predicament tomorrow. It wasn't fair on poor little Alfie to drag him around the streets, if anything happened to him, she would never see a day's happiness again.

Rose turned to Dan, she *did* trust him, even though they had only been acquainted for a short period, and she knew that what Dan was saying made complete sense.

"Maybe she won't want me in her home; these old ladies can be rather set in their ways you know."

"Let's go and have a word with her then. I'm sure she will welcome some company and some help."

Dan jumped down from his seat; he hung a bag of oats over Pepper's head and tossed a blanket over his back.

"There you go, boy," he said, patting the loyal animal on his side, before gently lifting Alfie from the cart and passing the sleeping infant into Rose's outstretched arms.

The shop door was still unlocked, and as Dan and Rose crossed over the threshold the jingle of the door bell, was quickly followed by Mrs Atkins frail voice calling out,

"I'll be with you in a jiffy."

Dan smiled at Rose, briefly, as they stood in silence listening to the sound of Mrs Atkins shuffling her feet along the linoleum.

Rose glanced around at the sparingly filled shelves, which displayed more dust than stock.

The glass counter was dull and stain covered and in its recess were piles of old boxes and newspapers. There was very little about this grubby space that resembled a shop, and Rose found herself itching to restore some freshness to the place as she wondered if the rest of the house was in the same sorry state.

CHAPTER TWELVE

"Dan! Is that you? Young Dan?" exclaimed Mrs
Atkins, her squinting eyes fixed firmly on him.
"Mrs Atkins! Yes, it *is* me, how are you?"
She broke into a broad smile as she recognised
his voice, revealing only gums which reminded
Rose of little Alfie's smile. He stirred in her arms,
opening one eye to view his ma before returning
to sleep.
"How wonderful to see you Dan, and is this your
little family? How lovely, and such a pretty
young wife too."
"No, Mrs Atkins, I'm yet to marry. This is the
wife of a good friend of mine, who sadly lost his
life recently and now she finds herself in a bit of
a predicament."
"Come on through to the back, and we'll have a
brew. Dan, put the lock on the door will you, it's
far too late for customers and it looks to be a
wild and windy night as well. I've got a good
strong fire ablaze in the back."
Exchanging a quick glance and a smile to each
other, Rose and Dan followed behind at a slow
pace as Mrs Atkins shuffled her way back to her
parlour. The heat of the room and the pungent
tang immediately hit them. If Rose had to give a
name to this room, it would definitely be *'the
brown room.'* Everything was in the same dull
shade, brought about by the buildup of dust and

grime over the years; even Mrs Atkins was an image of brownness, her head was covered with an aged and snagged knitted bonnet in sepia, it's ties undone and hanging loosely. Rose wasn't sure if her dress was once another shade or like everything else within eyesight, had succumbed to a decade or more of filthy living conditions. Inwardly shuddering at the thought of sleeping under this roof, Rose knew that her options would most likely be far worse. She *did* feel sorry for such an old and wizened woman left to struggle and fend for herself though, and if she was offered the opportunity to stay with her, she would definitely endeavour to make a difference to the living conditions of the house and the life of Mrs Atkins.

"Ooh, you have a baby too!" declared Mrs Atkins, suddenly catching sight of Alfie.

"Yes, Mrs Atkins, this is Alfie," informed Rose, smiling kindly at the old woman.

"Dan, go and wet the tea leaves, that's a good lad, kettle's just boiled a minute ago; get me best cups and saucers out, we can't have this young lass drinking out of chipped mugs, now, can we?"

"You see, Rose, Mrs Atkins might look a touch feeble, but she can be an incredibly bossy old dear!"

Rose looked in shock on hearing the way in which Dan spoke in front of Mrs Atkins, but he obviously knew her well, and they appeared to have a reciprocated understanding for each other.

"Don't think I'm too thin and feeble to give you a wallop, young Dan, I remember when you was as tiny as this here baby," she joked, nodding towards Alfie.

"Sit down my dear, sit down," she ordered Rose. The small room was cluttered with piles of what Rose could only describe as junk. Mrs Atkins was a hoarder, like so many elderly people, and was surrounded by a lifetime's memorabilia. There were piles of letters, newspapers and magazines in rows, leaning against every spare bit of wall. Rose thought of how Alfie would relish in being allowed to play in this room and would soon have these paper mountains tumbling down around him. There were also small heaps of clothes scattered over the floor, pushed to the sides to leave a clear pathway so that Mrs Atkins could make her way safely from the kitchen, through to the shop. A small threadbare sofa and two similar shoddy armchairs were placed around the blazing fireplace, with a rickety looking, table in the middle. Rose noticed the tall glass cabinet in the far corner, which displayed an abundance of crockery, ornaments, books, and a variety of strange and random objects, including bouquets of dried up and disintegrating flowers.

"What's your name, lass?" asked Mrs Atkins, who was seated in the chair opposite Rose, and studying her curiously.

"Rose."

"I had a feeling that it would be a name from the garden, on account that you be as pretty as a flower in bloom, and *a rose*... well, that is surely the queen of all flowers. I was named after a flower too, you know. My dear ma, God rest her soul, gave me the name Primrose, but folk used to call me Rose...all except me ma; with her it was *always* Primrose."

Rose smiled, and wished that Dan would make haste with the tea.

"You have a lovely home, Mrs Atkins." It felt like a ridiculous statement to come out with, but was the first thing that sprung into Rose's head.

"Well, it used to be dearie, it's a bit like me now....old, tired, and run down. This house used to look like a little palace, there weren't a speck of dust to be seen; me lace curtains were sparkling white and I even had all the neighbours asking how I got them so clean, you know. Don't think that I've lived like an old vagabond all me life, Rose; old age is a mean old bugger, that creeps up on you slowly, and starts to remove your very self, bit by bit."

"Would you like a slice of Ma's fruit cake, Mrs Atkins?" asked Dan, in a loud voice, as he came in carrying two steaming cups and saucers in his hands.

"I *do* have a tray, out there you know, and I'm proud to boast that I haven't lost me hearing yet...it's about the only function that *hasn't* got up and ran off, so there's no call to shout, young Dan boy."

Rose sat in amusement as Dan received a scolding from this scrawny old woman, who wasn't hesitant to say exactly what she was thinking. Now shackled by her aging years, Rose couldn't help thinking that she must have been an exceptionally forceful woman in her youth.

"And yes please, Dan, cut me a healthy wedge of cake, 'cos it will be the first morsel that has past me lips since yesterday."

Rose's desire to help this poor old woman was growing with every passing second; she found herself remembering her own grandparents, and recalling how many chores she used to do for them about the home; it was no wonder poor Primrose Atkins was living in such squalor, she was far older than her own grandma, and so very lonely.

"Are your family well, Dan?"

"They are, thank you, Mrs Atkins, and they send their warmest regards to you."

She pursed her lips and nodded her head, as her mind wandered back down the years for a brief moment.

"So tell me, Dan, what's to become of Rose and her child?"

The untimely question had sprung from Mrs Atkins' mouth just as Dan had hungrily sunk his teeth into his slice of fruit cake. Primrose Atkins

turned her attention to Rose,
"You could always stay with me for a while, 'till you sort yourself out...I could do with a bit of company, and a hand around the place. What do you say?"

Dan raised his eyebrows, as Rose glanced his way.

" Well, if you're sure that would be alright, and you don't mind a noisy baby disturbing you, I would love to accept your kind offer, Mrs Atkins." Rose could feel her tears welling up, the enormous feeling of relief, that she now had a safe place to stay overwhelming her.

"Then that's settled," declared Mrs Atkins, before slurping down her tea and, looking as though she hadn't drank in a long while neither.

"There is one thing I think that you should both know," announced Rose, suddenly, her face flushed and looking nervous.

Dan and Mrs Atkins ceased consuming their cake and tea, now with all their focus on Rose. A sudden silence seemed to fall upon the overcrowded room with only the gentle crackling of the fire now audible.

"I'm going to have another baby in a few months!"

"Well, that's marvelous news!" exclaimed Mrs Atkins, "I presume that it *is* your late husband's child?"

"Of course it is Mrs Atkins, what do you take me for?"

Dan's lingering question had finally been answered and he knew that it hadn't made the slightest bit of difference as to how he felt about Rose.

Dan continued on his way feeling happy in the knowledge that Rose was safe and today would no longer be the parting of their ways. The simple fact that he now knew the truth about her condition was a relief to him and only made him more determined to protect her. Rose had protested strongly when Dan insisted that she took two pounds from him, to tie her over until she found a means of making an income. In the end she took it as a loan, assuring him that she would definitely pay him back one day, although Dan failed to see how she would manage such a task, with a young family to support. With all of the day's delays, it was now far too late for Dan to visit Garsington Farm to purchase his supplies, but another journey back to Oxford in a few days time no longer seemed such a burden, and Dan's new aim in life was to help beautiful Rose in every way possible. He prayed that she might, one day, fall in love with him. He also intended to mention his encounter with Rose to his ma, in a very casual way, just to test the water and see her reaction, but would have to be careful not to let his feelings show, not yet anyway. Dan's mind was overflowing with thoughts and images of Rose as he journeyed home, making the time pass quickly.

He *was* however, keeping an eye open for a glimpse of Master Monty on the road, his ma and pa were only saying this week that he hadn't shown up on their land as was his custom every spring time. His strong, extra pair of hands was always welcome at this busy time of year.

CHAPTER THIRTEEN

It was the following week when Lester had completed what he considered to be one of his finer, and by far the most useful pieces of carpentry. He nervously watched the changing expression on Johnnie's face when he presented him with the finely carved wooden leg, complete with as near to a foot shape on the end as he could create. Most wooden legs were merely shaped like a straight peg, but Lester wanted to design something that would not be obvious to the rest of the world, especially once Johnnie had mastered the skill of walking on it, and added a matching boot to it as well. It was in the privacy of the barn, after another busy few hours of attending the lambing ewes, where Lester presented the gift to Johnnie. Hours would pass without a single birth and then as one ewe went into labour, it seemed to trigger another half a dozen off, keeping Lester and Johnnie fully occupied. Johnnie had no inclination that Lester had been busy, in his spare time, for the past few weeks, carving and sanding the block of wood to perfection and was quite stunned when his eyes caught sight of the wooden limb. He had never envisaged a day when he'd receive such a gift. "Lester, you are the most thoughtful of friends that any man could wish for!" declared Johnnie, slightly choked at the sheer oddness of the gift.

"It almost looks like my real leg! It must have taken you hours."

"Ahh, didn't take too long, Johnnie, I just hope it fits good enough." Lester continued to focus on Johnnie's face, still not sure if he was truly pleased, as he held the leg in his hands feeling its smoothness, come about from the hours of sanding which Lester had devoted himself to.

"How about trying it on for size?"

"Yes, yes, that's a good idea," replied Johnnie, still a little stunned with the unexpected gift. He sat down slowly on a hay bale, and Lester decided to leave him to himself for a while.

"Just gonna clean out a few pens, take your time Johnnie, and give me a shout if you need any help."

The leg was a perfect fit, and the correct length; Johnnie imagined that Lester might have clandestinely been measuring him while he slept at night. He stood up, feeling quite strange to be standing on two legs again, but it felt good, so good in fact that he had difficulty in keeping a straight face, and beamed like a child who'd been given a new toy. Taking it slowly to begin with, and still holding on to the crutches, Johnnie walked the width of the barn. He felt proud and tall again, like a man, not a cripple. Backwards and forwards he walked, becoming accustomed to his new leg. Discarding one of his crutches, his sheer determination spurred him on to continue pacing back and forth, lost in his deep concentration as he insisted on conquering this new skill. Lester's loud applauding suddenly caught his attention; Johnnie walked towards him grinning joyfully.

"Lester, how can I ever thank you? You have given me the most wonderful of gifts, and made me feel human again."

Lester laughed out loud,

"My dear friend, I don't think that there has ever been a time when you weren't human! But I'm so glad it fits and you appear to be mastering its use."

Allowing his second crutch to fall to the ground, Johnnie shook Lester's hand and embraced his kind friend, finding the new experience too emotional to prevent his eyes from becoming watery.

"Come on, let's go and show Nora and the girls, they'll be amazed to see you walking with only one crutch."

"What are you talking about *one crutch?* I'm going to make my entrance with no crutches at all!" announced Johnnie, courageously.

"Steady on now, we don't want to rush into this now... Nora will blame me if you end up falling on your face! You know how she nurses you!"

"Don't worry so, I can do it, just be at my side in case *I do* wobble and lose my balance!"

Nora's screams of delight could be heard across the whole farm, as she jumped up and down in jubilation.

"Beth! Susie!" she yelled from the foot of the stairs, "quickly, come and see Mr Johnnie."

"If anything warrants a celebration, then this is it," declared Lester.

"Yes," agreed Nora, cheerfully, "no better time to bring out the strawberry sponge cake, even if we haven't yet had supper."

The small party went on until bed time, the entire Baker family proud of Lester for his skill in making the celebration possible, and optimistically happy that perhaps Johnnie would be less likely to fall into his dark moods now that he was near enough able to walk properly again.

"Give him another few days, and I reckon Johnnie will be running!" delighted Nora.

As spring transformed into summer, Johnnie had settled into a life of living and working on the Baker's farm, but still constantly troubled that little of his memory had returned to him. He made routine monthly visits to Doctor Tomlinson, who was now pursuing his fellow colleagues who specialised in such afflictions. There had been a few times when certain incidents seemed to jog Johnnie's memory, like the time when he had sat listening to Lester and Nora discussing the price of a bushel of grain. The word, 'bushel', seemed oddly familiar to him, but when he mentioned it to Lester, he was assured that this wasn't an uncommon word amongst farmers, even though Johnnie was convinced that it meant more than that.

Beth and Susie had now finished school for the summer; Beth would not be returning, and was constantly nagging her parents to allow her to go into service. They were reluctant to let her go, even though they knew what a sensible girl she was, they felt that she was too young to leave home and weren't ready to lose their daughter yet, especially since there were no suitable positions available locally, and it would mean her having to travel and live as far away as Bath. Beth yearned to leave the countryside and reside in a busy city, dreaming of one day meeting her future husband, and determined not to marry a farmer and spend her days toiling like she had witnessed her ma doing over the years as a farmer's wife. She had her sights set on a doctor, or a lawyer, or perhaps even a successful business man who would be dressed smartly every day, and not have permanently soiled clothes and hands. Keeping these dreams to herself, for fear of offending her parents, Beth spent every spare minute she had when she'd completed her chores, engrossed in reading the books which Mrs Walters had lent her, allowing herself to be swallowed up in the romance and heroes between the pages, and ignoring Susie's pleas to play games and take adventures out on the land.

"Look what happened the last time we went on an adventure!" Beth would protest, " we ended up finding Mr Johnnie, and now it looks as though he's going to be stuck with us forever, just giving Ma more work to do, as if she doesn't have enough already!"

" At least he helps Pa quite a lot around the place. Don't you like Mr Johnnie then?" Susie would question, alarmingly.

"Of course I like him, but sometimes I think he's just fibbing about having a wife called Rose, and a baby. Maybe he hasn't lost him memory at all, but just wants to live with us. There was a man in one of the books I read, and *he* pretended to lose his memory just because he'd fallen in love with the wife of the man who'd rescued him."

Susie took a sharp intake of breath, her eyes widening in alarm,

"You don't think that Johnnie has fallen in love with Ma, do you, Beth?"

"Well he does look at her with his smouldering eyes sometimes."

"What are smouldering eyes?" quizzed Susie, looking even more confused.

"Oh, you're far too young to understand."

This was a sentence which without fail would send Susie off in an angry mood. She hated the way in which Beth would try to appear so mature and knowledgeable, as though there was a generation between them, and not just two years.

She didn't believe a word of what Beth was saying; Mr Johnnie was a kind man, and he didn't look the sort to make trouble. Beth had just been reading too many books.

After months of neglect, Bushel Farm was now in a dilapidated state, no longer resembling a working farm. Seb had failed to sow a single seed yet alone plough his acres of land. His livestock had wandered off into the neighbouring farms through the broken fences which Seb had not repaired, and he had not bothered to make any effort in retrieving them. His weekly journey to Oxford had so far been unsuccessful and he had yet to have a single sighting of Rose, or talk to anyone who had seen her. He would vent his increased anger after each return journey on the nearest object to hand, slowly demolishing the inside of the farm house, as one by one each piece of furniture or item of crockery found itself flying through the air and smashing against the wall. The sweet perfume of Rose's bedroom no longer filled his nostrils every night and was replaced by his repulsive unwashed stench and heavily soiled from the filth which adhered to his boots. None of the few local women wished to have anything to do with Sebastian Harper; he was viewed like a leper, and given a wide berth on his few journeys to the village store and market place. He had even failed in employing someone to come and clean his home; no father or brother would risk allowing their women folk to venture anywhere near Seb Harper's land. He had, over the years gained a reputation of being something of a *wild boy*, with everyone always favouring Johnnie and his beautiful young wife, feeling sorry for them having to share Bushel Farm with Seb. Local gossip as to why Rose and her young baby had seldom been seen, after the tragic death of Johnnie took on many different tales, which was another reason why folk stayed far away from his land, no matter how much they empathised with poor Rose Harper.

CHAPTER FOURTEEN

"Please Mr Rutherford; let me have the stock in advance of payment. I promise you will get every single penny back by next week, and hopefully I will be in a position to purchase more from you. Please, just give me the chance to get this shop up and running again, that's all I'm asking of you, Sir."

Mr Rutherford twisted his sideburns between his finger and thumb, finding himself torn between wanting to help this attractive young woman and worried about what his superiors would have to say if he were to commit to such a risk, especially if it didn't pay off. He was impressed, however, at the transformation of Mrs Atkins' shop, and it *was* in an ideal position, he assured himself, near the railway station, surrounded by overcrowded terraces, *and* the only grocery shop within a mile. Just the sight of this striking woman would surely entice customers to keep returning to make their purchases, her pleasing nature, and natural beauty were indeed a tonic for the soul, thought Mr Rutherford. He prided himself on never yet having made a bad business deal and even though, this was not a normal way of handling his sale of stock, he had a strong inclination that he was making the right decision, though he'd decided that he would only allow her to have half of the stock which she'd requested.

"You place me in a very difficult predicament, Mrs Harper, but on this occasion I think I will allow you to have half of the stock which you requested, and I expect fifty percent of the payment by next week. Is that understood?"

Rose was delighted and could feel her insides dancing for joy, though she kept calm and business like, not wanting Mr Rutherford to witness her sheer jubilation.

"Thank you so much, Mr Rutherford, you won't regret it, and I will not let you down, you just wait and see."

Mr Rutherford replaced his bowler onto his balding head, as he glanced around the shop once more,

"How is Mrs Atkins, today?" he enquired, suddenly remembering that in his delight in chatting to her new assistant, it had completely slipped his mind to ask about her.

"She is very well thank you, Mr Rutherford, and taking a well deserved rest."

"Will she be serving in the shop anymore, now that you are here?" Mr Rutherford asked in a laid-back manner.

Surprised by this odd question, Rose decided to give him the answer she knew he wanted, for the sake of business only,

"Oh no, I will be a permanent fixture behind the counter!"

Mr Rutherford looked relieved, and smiled

broadly at Rose.

"Expect your delivery first thing in the morning, Mrs Harper, and I wish you all the best in your business."

"Thank you again Mr Rutherford."

Bowing his head to prevent it crashing against the door frame as he stepped back out into the summer sunshine, he took a last look back at Rose,

" Until next week then, Mrs Harper."

"Goodbye Sir."

Rose was so full of excitement that she was unable to stop herself dancing into the parlour to announce her good news to Mrs Atkins. Alfie immediately responded to his ma's look of joy and left his toy train, running to snuggle up to Rose's knees, which was as far as his height reached.

"Mr Rutherford is letting us have the provisions that I asked for, well, half of it at least, and he said we only have to pay him *half* the amount by next week!"

"Oh my dear Rose, you *have* turned my life around; God blessed the day when you stepped over my threshold and into my life."

Rose noticed the tears in Mrs Atkins faded eyes and hurried to give her a hug. She now smelt of sweet lavender, and wore a freshly laundered, pretty blue floral print dress.

In the two months that Rose had been staying

with Primrose Atkins, she had, as Primrose would often say, 'worked a miracle' on the place. She had toiled hard all day and every day, putting her heart and soul into restoring Mrs Atkins' shop and home. Her dedicated commitment had at least taken her mind away from her troubles, and now with Mrs Atkins insisting that she should consider this as her home; Rose had a renewed sense of belonging, blotting out all her fears of losing her children to the workhouse, or living on the streets. That one night sleeping under the oak tree in the middle of nowhere was more than enough to determine Rose to avoid such a situation again, at all costs. She had made sorting out and cleaning the living quarters a priority over the shop, finding many beautiful items of clothing in amongst Mrs Atkins' scattered heaps, most of which she had now washed and ironed and hung up in Mrs Atkins' wardrobe. Although she slept downstairs, finding the stairs too difficult to climb with her painful and inflexible hips and knees, Rose was now in the habit of bringing her down a clean dress to wear at least once a week. Rose had got Dan to bring the truckle bed down from upstairs, which was now neatly placed against the wall where her piles of cloths had once been. The glass fronted cabinet had been sorted out, cleaned and now displayed the elegant china which had previously been haphazardly shoved in the cupboard above the stove just waiting to tumble out and break, and a small chest of drawers which Rose had found in the back yard now housed her abundance of letters, books and keepsakes which she had collected over the decades. Mrs Atkins had given Rose full use of the two bedrooms upstairs, thankfully they were a lot cleaner and less cluttered than the downstairs rooms, and according to Mrs Atkins, had not been in use for the past ten years, when she had become an octogenarian. Most importantly Rose was intent on transforming the shop into a functioning money making business again, and had Mrs Atkins' full support and encouragement, as she witnessed Rose's youthful and energetic enthusiasm. The shop seldom sold more than a poke of tea and a bag of flour each week, with many passersby not even noticing that it was in fact still open. The grubby looking lace curtain was discarded, and Rose had persuaded Dan to scrape off the peeling paintwork and repaint the outside window and door frames. He needed little persuasion and was amazed to see how enthusiastic Rose was about running Mrs Atkins' practically redundant business. The old ripped and greasy linoleum was pulled up, and to Rose's delight, revealed beautiful quarry tiles which cleaned up a treat, and gave the shop a smart new look. The glass counter was scrubbed laboriously, and cleaned with vinegar until it sparkled, and Dan had also given the shelves a fresh coat of paint.

Rose had asked Dan if he could spare a bale of straw from his farm, to which he obliged, though a little confused as to what she needed it for. Every evening when Alfie had gone to sleep for the night, Rose would sit listening to the copious stories which Mrs Atkins enjoyed recalling, while her fingers were busy plaiting and weaving the straw to produce, beautiful straw bonnets and boaters, which not only looked attractive threaded up in the window on display, but were selling quicker than Rose could put them together. Mrs Atkins was frustrated that her gnarled fingers wouldn't allow her to assist in their production. The smaller sized girl's straw hats were particularly popular, especially now that summer was casting her sizzling sun so generously every day. Rose decorated them with colourful ribbons, silk flowers and dyed feathers. Mrs Atkins declared one night,

" Rose, these hats that you make seem a darn sight more popular than general groceries; maybe we should just sell these and nothing else."

"Ah but come the cooler months, when nobody wants to don a flimsy straw hat, we will be out of business." Rose reminded her.

"You young people these days, it seems you've all got a sharp eye for business."

"But didn't you tell me that the shop used to be

thriving back when you first opened up? I expect that your eyes were just as focused back then Mrs Atkins."

It didn't take much to send Mrs Atkins back down memory lane; she would often drift off in her day dreams, with a twinkle in her eye, and a slight smile upon her thin lips.

"Now Rose," Mrs Atkins suddenly burst out, "It looks to me as though we are going to be living under the same roof for some while, so you're going to have to stop calling me Mrs Atkins all the time, it's just too formal, and did I tell you that little Alfie is already calling me *Nanna,* the word just rolled off his tongue as naturally as breathing air."

"That's, fascinating, he's such a clever little boy," said Rose, proudly. "I hope he won't feel too put out when this new baby arrives." Rose gently rubbed her ever growing belly, a painful lump sticking in her throat as she remembered Johnnie.

"Do you have any suggestions as to what I should call you, Mrs Atkins?"

"You could call me Aunty or Ma....it's up to you of course, whichever one you're more comfortable with."

"Well, which one are *you* more comfortable with, that's the important question?" teased Rose.

"Oh, just call me Ma, even though it's a physical impossibility, but at least if makes me feel young, and I know that your birth mother passed on when you were a nipper, so I'm not treading on anyone's toes, so to speak. Are you happy with that, young Rose?"

"Yes I am Ma, very happy indeed, now, would you like some cocoa or some warm milk before bed? We have a busy day tomorrow; the stock will be arriving in the morning, and hopefully it won't take too long for me to stack the shelves, and then just pray that we have a stream of wealthy customers paying us a visit."

Primrose Atkins laughed gently to herself, it had been a long time since she'd been so happy, and it was lovely to feel like part of a family after so many years of loneliness. She had only been able to mother one child and he had passed away fifteen years ago, causing a huge gap in her life.

"Well, I guess I'll be playing trains and building bricks again tomorrow!" laughed Mrs Atkins.

"Alfie has taken such a shine to you, Mrs.....whoops I mean Ma; you give him enough attention for both of us when I'm busy," called out Rose from the kitchen as she put the saucepan of milk on the stove.

"That reminds me, Rose, the next time Dan pays us a visit, we must ask him to climb up into the attic, there's a box of toys, amongst other things stored away up there; Little Alfie will love them. I'm sure it won't be more than a few days 'till that lad shows his face again. I've seen more of Dan Heyford in these last two months than I've seen of him in the past five years. If ever there was a young man completely smitten, well then, *he's* the man."

Rose pretended not to hear the last part of Mrs Atkins conversation; it was nothing that she didn't already know. It was far from being the appropriate time in Rose's life for romance, her heart continued to ache for her darling Johnnie, and with her confinement rapidly approaching, she was more than happy to keep Dan as a good friend for now. He was the best friend that anyone could wish for, but Rose *was* aware of his feelings for her, and wished not to take advantage of them, or break his heart in any way. A slow and gentle pace to their relationship was probably the best solution for all.

Eight O'clock saw the cart load of groceries delivered to the new spruced up shop. Rose artistically displayed a sample of the stock in the window, which was framed by the selection of golden straw head wear. She had neatly painted in bold lettering, the words **'OPEN FOR BUSINESS'** on to a plank of wood which took centre place in the window, hopefully catching everyone's eye as they walked past. By nine O'clock Rose had taken the lock off the door and declared the shop open, praying that it wouldn't just be her straw hats to be the only items in demand; she had to prove to Mr Rutherford that she could turn this old abandoned corner shop into a thriving business again.

CHAPTER FIFTEEN

The balmy summer heat and long days on the Baker's farm, would forever remind Johnnie of the laborious days he spent learning how to walk again, not that it had taken more than a few hours for him to master the skill of walking with a wooden leg; he was aiming for perfection and to be able to walk without the slightest detection of a limp. Refusing to saddle up a horse to ride out across the acres of farm land, Johnnie insisted on walking everywhere. It was the first week in July when Johnnie was striding out across the field, on his way to open the gate to allow the flock of sheep to move on to higher, richer grazing land, when it suddenly sprung to his mind that it had now been six months since Lester had rescued him, six months and he was still no closer to discovering where he'd come from, and more importantly, what had become of his wife and son. Putting more thrust into his long confident strides he broke into a chant as he walked, he called out loudly with every step, *"Johnnie and Rose, Johnnie and Rose, Johnnie and Rose....."* he carried on, determined to move the dense fog which lay dormant inside of his head. If anyone had witnessed his bizarre behaviour, they would surely imagine him to have taken leave of his senses, but in his trance like state he was oblivious to his surroundings.

"*Johnnie and Rose,*" he repeated for the hundredth time.

"Johnnie and Rose Harper, Harper. *Yes,* Harper!" he hollered as loudly as was physically possible.

"My name *is* Johnnie Harper *and* Rose Harper is my wife."

He had made a miraculous breakthrough, and knew that Harper *was* his family name, and not just a name that he'd dreamt up in a state of desperation. Something was happening inside of his head, as though a strong gale had entered and was forcing the heavy and stubborn clouds of confusion to crack open, allowing tiny glimpses of his previous life to flash across his vision. Feeling giddy, Johnnie squatted down in the middle of the field. A few of the sheep made bleating sounds, as though objecting to his presence, but soon continued with their grazing, ignoring the strange human who had come to join them in their field. Johnnie could clearly see a man in the river; he was being swept away by the raging torrent. Johnnie stared at the panic on this man's face. There was another face, a laughing, mocking face. Johnnie felt an icy cold shiver rush through his body. He remembered feeling so bitterly cold. The man in the river was wearing his coat, while the other man stood smiling wickedly, telling Johnnie to leave the drowning man to his fate. Johnnie was all of a sudden hit by the sheer coldness of the icy water as he plunged in; in a desperate bid to save the

man who wore his coat, he called out,
"Seb, Seb!" and watched in horror as Seb turned
his back, making his way up the river bank, as
though nothing was happening. Johnnie hugged
his knees, his whole body shook, and the biting
cold had penetrated deep into his bones.
Suddenly distracted by the sound of horse
hooves, and a voice calling out to him, Johnnie's
disturbed mind had made him completely
disoriented for a few moments,
"I brought your water flask, Johnnie. You left it
behind. I thought you could do with a drink on
such a sweltering day!"
Lester's initial thoughts were that Johnnie had
taken a tumble and maybe injured his good leg,
but as he jumped down from the saddle, he
noticed how Johnnie's teeth were chattering
feverishly, as though it were the middle of a
bitter winter's day. Johnnie's whole body was
shaking; his taught face was as white as one of
the nearby sheep, and the oddest expression
upon it.

Back in the farmhouse, Nora fussed around like
a mother hen, wrapping a thick blanket around
Johnnie's shoulders, and holding the beaker of
hot tea, laced with sugar to his lips,
" Looks as though he's in shock, Lester," she
announced, a worried look causing her brow to
crease.
"Are you sure you didn't see anyone else up on

135

the field, Lester?" she demanded, abruptly.
Susie sat observing, whilst at the kitchen table
painting pictures of flowers. She remembered
Beth's words, and studied her ma with a
renewed intrigue, wondering if there was some
truth in what Beth had told her.
"I'm sure Nora, like I said, he was just sat in the
middle of the field; he was supposed to be
letting the sheep into the top field. There was
nobody within miles; I would have spotted them
if there were." Lester *was* becoming a little tired
of his wife treating him like a foolish child as she
made him explain to her what had occurred for
the second time. He cut himself a wedge of
apple pie, not in the neat way in which Nora
always insisted upon,
"I've got work to do. I'll be back for lunch."
Lester went out through the open door, annoyed
that his wife hadn't taken any notice of him, and
jumped back into the saddle. Cramming the pie
into his mouth, he forced the horse into a speedy
gallop. Johnnie viewed him through the open
window, watching as clumps of earth flew up
behind him and knowing that Lester was upset
about something.
"Are you feeling better, Johnnie?" enquired
Nora, softly.
"Thank you, Nora, I'm sorry for the trouble I've
caused for you and Lester, I don't know what
came over me, but I did remember my name, I
now know that it's Harper, I'm Johnnie Harper."

"Well, they do say that every cloud has a silver lining! That's marvellous news, now perhaps it will be a bit easier to trace your dear wife. I'm going outside to ring the emergency bell, to call Lester back in, he'll be over the moon to hear your breakthrough. No wonder you took a funny turn out there; did you remember anything else?"

"No, just my name, but that's good enough for now," replied Johnnie, not wishing to disclose any more, especially seeing Nora's ecstatic mood.

"Please, don't bother poor Lester again. I've caused enough trouble this morning and anyway I'll see him back on the field shortly, I feel fully recovered now, and, like Lester said, there's work to be done."

"Oh very well then, if you're sure, but you take it easy, mind, the work will still be there tomorrow. Now, if you're positive that you are fully recovered, I must go and collect the eggs."

"Do you want me to fetch them, Ma?"

"It's alright darling; you carry on with your beautiful painting, I'm in need of a bit of fresh air, it looks like being another roaster; I pray that's there's a bit of a breeze in the air today."

"Do you love my ma?" Susie suddenly blurted out after Nora had left the house, taking Johnnie by complete shock. "My sister thinks that you've fallen in love with her. Is it true?"

He noticed the look of anguish on her young

freckled face, a look which reminded him of how he was perhaps trespassing on this loving family, and then, from out of the blue, he had a startling flashback of that same man who had stood laughing on the river bank, the same man who had walked away when he was struggling to survive the freezing strong current of the river. He knew now who it was; Seb Harper, the man who had trespassed on *his* family, just as he was doing to this family. He knew exactly how Susie felt. He had turned into one of those overbearing visitors who moved into a family, and proceeded to out stay their welcome, the sort of guest who everyone ended up detesting, and he knew it was time to move on.

"Susie, your parents have been so kind and hospitable to me, in fact your whole family have treated me like I belong here, and I love you all as anyone would love such a lovely family; your ma is like a dear caring sister, and your pa like the best brother that any man could wish for."

Susie smiled, and turned her concentration back to her painting. Johnnie could not help but notice her look of relief.

"Where's Beth this morning?" Johnnie asked, wanting to return the conversation back to normality.

"Oh she's reading, as usual," Susie replied, along with a heavy sigh.

"It must be a good book then, to keep her inside on such a fine summer's day."

"She's got her head stuck in Pride and Prejudice, *again*. She must have read it at least ten times! She's no fun anymore; I hope she *does* go into service, as she keeps saying she will, because she's the most boring sister ever."

"Don't you like to read Susie?"

"No," she quickly answered, "I have enough of that when I'm at school."

Thankfully Nora returned to the kitchen, armed with a basket of eggs and putting an end to the strained atmosphere.

Johnnie was quick to get back onto his feet and leave the farm house, with a jumble of thoughts spinning around inside of his head. He would confide in Lester, and tell him that it was time for him to be on his way. It would be for the best anyway, he told himself, especially since it looked as though his memory was slowly returning. He *had* to go in search of his roots, and make every effort to be united with his darling wife and son; there would be no peace of mind until they were able to reunite, and he would not be complete until that day. Lester and Nora had been like true saints, but today had suddenly made him realise how Beth and Susie saw him as a threat to the stability of their family, and he wanted no part in bringing unhappiness to a family that had treated him so compassionately.

It was three days later when Johnnie said his

farewells to the Baker family, promising to keep in touch and write; keeping them up to date with his progress. They were all sad to see him leave, but had always known that this day would eventually arrive.

"You just make sure to take good care of your health, Johnnie," came Nora's stern instructions, "and as soon as you find that wife of yours, you be sure to bring her here to meet us."

Johnnie was finding conversation difficult; he was on the verge of breaking down, which was the last thing he wanted to do in front of this adoring family, who now felt like his kin; he kept telling himself to be brave.

"That's right Johnnie, you're welcome to come back here whenever you want, consider it your home; you definitely feel like my own brother." The crack in Lester's voice didn't go undetected, and within seconds he and Johnnie were locked in an emotional embrace, as they said their goodbyes. As the whole family stood waving until Johnnie was completely out of sight, Susie wondered if perhaps it was partly her fault that he was leaving so soon, after she'd questioned him about his feeling for her ma.

CHAPTER SIXTEEN

"Are you sure you don't want me to mind the shop for a while, Rose? I don't like the look of your swollen ankles, and you're looking extremely flushed," Mrs Atkins asked for the third time in an hour.

"I'm really feeling fine, Ma, and *I am* sitting down now, at least."

"Mmm, you need to be lying down, with your feet up."

"I promise, as soon as closing time arrives, I will do just that. Is Alfie behaving himself?"

"Alfie always behaves himself for his nanna; it's his ma who won't listen to reason."

Rose sat smiling as she listened to the familiar shuffling as Mrs Atkins returned annoyingly to her parlour, she could vaguely hear her continuous chatter to little Alfie, and imagined her to be complaining about her to him. They had grown so attached to each other over the past three months, with Mrs Atkins now having a new and refreshed look on life, even her aching bones seemed to have improved and she was able to move around with greater ease these days. She didn't think twice when hurrying to restrain Alfie when he was getting up to mischief. Primrose Atkins spoke frequently of an evening how she had considered her life to be over before Rose and Alfie had turned up on her doorstep.

"I was just biding my time, and waiting for The Good Lord to call for me," she would say, with unshed tears in her eyes.

Rose would always voice her gratitude and tell Mrs Atkins of how her great kindness of taking them in had been an absolute life saver and had given *her* a new and secure way of life too.

They had become a devoted extended family, with Primrose eagerly awaiting the birth of what she considered to be her second grandchild.

The shop had now become a thriving business and was generating a reasonable income after the initial sticky patch at the beginning of its transformation. Local residents had been so accustomed to the small grocery shop never having any essential stock that it took a while to be noticed, even though Rose had made the display in the window as alluring as possible. Rose didn't have all of the fifty percent repayment for Mr Rutherford after the first week of business, and not wanting to lean on Dan for any more funds, she was forced to sell Johnnie's woollen overcoat, and a couple of small silver spoons which Mrs Atkins had overlooked when she had sold every item of any worth over a decade ago. The mean pawn broker paid only a pittance to Rose, just enough to cover her outstanding debt, probably taking one look at her bulging belly, and sensing her desperation.

But thankfully, word soon travelled that the corner shop was now a grocery store where you could find almost everything needed, and if not, the charming new shop keeper would order it in promptly.

Rose prayed hard that her forthcoming confinement would be relatively easy and that she would only have to close the shop for a couple of days; she wouldn't even contemplate allowing Mrs Atkins to serve in the shop *and* take care of Alfie.

Having already warned all of her regular customers, most of them had decided to purchase extra stock prior to the month when Rose anticipated the birth of her baby, but as everyone knew, babies were more in the habit of arriving when it suited them, and not their mothers. She had also received offers of help in abundance, to which she was most grateful to, and if her hopes for a speedy recovery didn't materialize, she would certainly accept the kindness of her new friends and neighbours.

The sweat dripped profusely from Seb Harper, as he callously dug his heels into Blossom, forcing her to gallop fast and hard across the baked terrain in the sweltering heat of mid day. He had woken up with a throbbing headache and a hangover. After surveying the slum which had once been a spotless home, filled with the feminine touches of Rose's sweet hands, the permanent odour of her flowery perfume, the smell of fresh bread straight from the oven and simmering appetising stews, he had sworn an oath to himself that he wouldn't return to Bushel Farm until he had found his Rose and brought her home with him, no matter how long it took. His days of lazing around and being full of self pity were over, he told himself, he would bring Rose home and together they would turn Bushel Farm around after its months of neglect and soon have it back to how it used to be, resuming a new life there in true bliss, like a happy family.

By the time He had reached the outskirts of Banbury, Blossom had refused to gallop, no matter how hard Seb slapped her rump, or kicked her sides. The exhausted mare neighed angrily as she shook her mane in protest.

"You lazy bloody mare!" Seb yelled, in frustration, attracting the attention of the Banbury folk who were out enjoying the pleasing summer weather.

"Your days with Seb Harper are numbered, it's high bloody time I got shot of you and found me self a fearless young stallion."

Seb was oblivious to the crowds, as he continued to shout and have a one-sided argument with the horse; they were now finding his crazed looking antics amusing. Children giggled, and their parents smiled under their breath, passing comment to each other purely by movement of the eye. It wasn't until Seb had reached the heart of Banbury, and the busy market place that he suddenly took notice of how the tranquil countryside was far behind him, and that he had now arrived in the bustling town. He ceased shouting and cussing at Blossom and alighted from the poor horse, securing her next to a trio of horses, who were drinking from the town's long wooden water butt. Seb splashed his face with the same water and drank from his heavily soiled cupped hands. Passers-by continued to stare at him, now feeling uncomfortable at having such a rough and unsavoury looking character amongst them. He looked about him, before heading towards the hub of costermongers as he followed the smell of food like a starving hound. Not having eaten all day, it suddenly became apparent to him as to how empty his stomach was. Detecting the wafts of steam from the hot meat pies, a trail of saliva trickled from Seb's open mouth, as he pushed his way through the family groups and couples, not giving a care as he elbowed and shoved them from his pathway.

"I'll take three of them pies, Mister," he ordered the costermongers, who had watched Seb arrive and taken an instant dislike to him.

" That'll be one and six, *Sir*," he said, overcharging him, as he handed him the bag of piping hot pies, not giving him the usual warning of how dangerously hot they were.

"Bloody expensive in Banbury, ain't it?" declared

Seb as he parted with his money and rudely snatched the bag out of the man's hands.

"You're paying for excellent quality meat Sir; you'll find no gristle in these pies, top quality is that."

Seb grunted like a wild animal, and sauntered away.

Two seconds later every single person in the market place could hear the string of abusive words which flew out of Seb's mouth, after he'd taken a massive bite into the baking hot pie. He spat it out, his eyes watering from the pain, "What are you bloody gawping at?" he yelled to the shocked onlookers, who were quick to disperse, feeling slightly intimidated by this uncouth stranger who'd arrived on their patch. Seb's watery eyes suddenly caught sight of the back of a young woman; he stood in disbelief; he'd found her a last, and it turned out to be a lot easier than anticipated. He just wanted to hurry across the thoroughfare and grab her, but warned himself not to make any rash moves. Slowly edging his way towards the haberdashery stall where a length of powder blue fabric was being measured out, Seb could almost see Rose dancing in his arms in the finished dress. The sweet smell of Rose's perfume formulated in his nostrils, and within seconds he was stood behind her, so tempted to take her in his arms. Annie and Violet looked dubiously at this great oaf of a man. They had witnessed his earlier despicable behaviour and were feeling quite vulnerable and nervous, by his presence, both with the same thoughts that he had arrived to rob them. They were easy victims after all. Seb eyed the strands of golden hair which were visible below the pretty duck egg bonnet which adorned Rose's head; his mind drifted back to all those times that he'd watched her through the hole in the wall, and had yearned to feel it's soft silkiness between his fingers. He quickly wiped away his dribble with the back of his hand. The young woman had become aware of someone close behind her, feeling Seb's heavy hot breath on the back of her neck; she also noticed the sudden change in the casual conversation she'd been having with the women serving her.

"I always knew this day would come, sweet Rose!"

The woman turned around, viewing Seb with instant repulsion.

His jaw dropped, leaving him with an ignorant vacant look upon his heavily whiskered face.

"Sorry ma'am, I thought you was me wife."

"Did you lose your wife in Banbury market?" quizzed Violet mockingly, where upon she received a surreptitious kick from Annie, beneath the wooden hand cart.

The young woman quickly paid for her goods and hurried off, relieved to be free from the sickening stench emitting from Seb Harper.

"I lost me wife near on three months ago, when she took me only son and disappeared."

"We *might* have seen her," spoke up Violet.

"No, we've never seen such a woman," declared Annie, giving Violet a severe warning glare.

"Anyway, what woman in her right mind would run away from such a handsome husband like you?" teased Violet.

Seb felt awkward as Violet and Annie continued to mock and laugh at him, but he had a strong inclination that they were hiding something and knew more than they were letting on.

"You *would* tell me if my Rose came this way, wouldn't you, only I'd hate to see either one of you sweet old ladies coming to any harm...do you know what I mean?"

They certainly *did* know what he meant, and hadn't liked the look of him from the moment he'd turned up in the market place.

Annie nudged Violet with her elbow, hoping that she would understand that as a sign to keep silent, but Violet wasn't about to take any chances, and concluded that whatever she told this man, if that *was* his wife and son who they'd seen all those weeks ago, they could be anywhere by now.

"Yes, there was a pretty young woman with a baby here a couple of months back, but I haven't a clue as to where she went. She was travelling with a smart young farmer; they left together in his horse cart."

Seb had heard enough, instantly feeling his blood boiling and with a chunk of pie stuck at the back of his throat, he looked in horror at the two women.

"She wasn't on her own?" he yelled, angrily.

"Like I just told you, young man, she was travelling with a young farmer. Now I've told you all I know, and would be obliged if you would leave us to our business." Violet spoke directly and bravely, not wanting Seb to detect her hidden fear.

He violently threw down the remains of the half eaten pie which splattered across the floor, spraying gravy up onto the bolts of fabric.

"You're bleeding pies stink, and so does this bloody market."

Kicking the wooden hand cart, Violet and Annie both leapt to try and catch the mountain of fabric rolls as one by one they toppled on to the ground. Witnessing the commotion, a couple of heavily built costermongers had left their stalls and arrived to send Seb on his way.

"*That will do,*" one of them commanded, "you're not welcome 'ere, now on yer way, and don't come back, otherwise we'll 'ave you arrested."

Taking hold of his arms they began marching him from the market place. Seb wasn't going to leave peacefully and yanked his arms free from their hold.

"Take your filthy bloody hands off me; don't worry, I ain't staying in this stinking pit for a

second longer; now let me go and fetch me
'orse!"
The locals breathed a sigh of relief as they
watched the troublemaker gallop off like a man
possessed, in the direction of Oxford.

CHAPTER SEVENTEEN

'Travelling with a smart young farmer,' Seb couldn't dislodge these words from his head; they were stinging his heart and increasing his angry rage.

"I'll smash your bloody smart farmer's head to bits if you've laid one bloody finger on my Rose!" he shouted to the wind, as he raced like a mad man along the road towards Oxford. He could feel the bile rising in his throat, his stomach was churning over, and he regretted consuming any of the meat pies.

It took little time to reach Oxford, where he headed straight for the city's centre. Looking distinctly out of place, he dismounted from Blossom and sauntered through the High Street, his eyes scrutinizing every person in sight. He peered through each shop window in the hope that by some miracle he might suddenly stumble upon Rose. His exhausted mare hung her head as Seb led her through the old city; she had been greatly ill-treated and under nourished on this day, but stood loyal to her unkind master. Seb regretted not setting out from Bushel Farm earlier, it would soon be dark, and there would probably be very little chance of finding Rose. Feeling out of place as he continued through Cornmarket and into Broad Street, Seb couldn't spot one man who wasn't attired in a tailored suit or a black gown. These inhabitants all looked toffee-nosed and well-to-do, thought Seb, and he was beginning to feel as though he'd arrived in a foreign land; these weren't his kind of people and he found it difficult to imagine Rose settling in these parts; she was a country girl, she had all the skills of a country lass too, he'd never seen anyone more at home in the dairy or the lambing shed, he thought to himself as his attention was drawn to how fancy the women of Oxford looked as they glided through the streets in their fancy apparel, all perfectly colour coordinated. Rose could turn her hand to anything, and she'd always make a brilliant job of it, she could even make baskets and hats from straw, which he doubted any of these buttoned up women could turn their hands to. It was at that moment when the words of the market woman in Banbury sifted through his mind again, giving him the devastating notion that Rose's smart young farmer was the new love in her life, and she was miles away with *him* on his farm. Could it be possible? He asked himself, would another man want to be saddled with a pregnant woman who already had a kid? It took less than a second for him to answer his own question. Rose was a beauty through and through, there wasn't one aspect of her to dislike, she was a temptress; alluring, and any man would be blind if he couldn't see that. Seb had once again managed to work himself up into a frenzy, and what made it worse was that Blossom had come to an abrupt standstill and no matter how hard Seb tugged on her reins, she was adamant that until she was fed, she wouldn't move an inch. Realising that he had neglected feeding the mare, Seb just managed to catch the last nearby grocery store that hadn't yet closed. The shopkeeper was having difficulty in returning the heavy display boxes from the shop's frontage; he tried dragging them across the pavement, in-between rubbing his back and swearing under his breath,

"D'yer want a hand?" Seb asked.

"That damn lad ran off early 'cos his ma got sick, left me to bring these in knowing darn well that me lumbago's been playing me up all week. You couldn't have come at a better time; I'd be most grateful of some help."

Seb had no intention of helping unless it was to his advantage; he was already worn out, hungry and in need of a tankard of ale.

"You got anything for me poor horse? She's refusing to move on account of her being starving."

The shopkeeper looked around at his stock,

"I don't have any proper horse feed, but I can give you a pound bag of oats, and a couple of pounds worth of apples and carrots; that should put her out of her misery. There'll be no charge if you carry these boxes in for me," he declared, feeling intimidated by Seb's rough and uncouth

look and quite nauseous from his rancid odour.
"That's a deal then," agreed Seb, offering his
grimy hand to shake on the deal. The shopkeeper instantly let out a loud groan, as he
placed both hands on his lower back, and in a
strained voice said,
"Yes, Sir we'll call it a deal."
After all four crates had been returned to the
shop and Seb was in possession of his payment,
he asked casually before leaving,
"I don't suppose you've seen a beautiful young
woman with a toddler around these parts?"
The shopkeeper looked at him curiously,
convinced that this stranger was slightly loopy.
"*Sir*, I'm a shopkeeper, I see young women with
babies and toddlers every day of my life."
"But this one would be new to the area."
"No, sorry, can't say that I've noticed any
newcomer recently. Now if I could trouble you
to vacate my premises, it's been a long day, and
my wife is going to be none too pleased that my
supper is going cold," he replied, slowly losing
patience with this obnoxious man, and wishing
him gone from his sight.
Seb still didn't budge.
"You don't happen to know of a cheap place
where I could hang me boots up for the night?"
The shopkeeper rubbed his back again, now
nervous that he was about to be robbed of his
days takings and deciding that they would be
safer left locked in the money drawer for the

night rather than allowing this unsavoury stranger to set his eyes upon them. He picked up the bunch of keys from under the counter, and gently escorted Seb towards the front door and out onto the street.

"You could try over west Oxford way, beyond the railway station; there are quite a few families who take in lodgers in that area, *and* they're affordable. Now I bid you goodnight my friend, and thank you once again for your assistance."

Seb grunted, and watched as the shopkeeper locked up his shop and marched down the road, before striding over to where Blossom was stood; allowing her to feed, as darkness rapidly descended around him. Leaving her securely tied up with the apples in easy reach, Seb took himself to the nearby *Red Lion*, ale house; he had lost his appetite for food, now only craving a tankard of ale to wet his dry throat, and in need of a place to sleep for the night.

"Now you listen to me, young Rose, and rest yourself on that couch for the remainder of the evening," Mrs Atkins ordered, "little Alfie went to sleep quickly tonight *and* without any fuss, didn't he? You were only upstairs with him for a short while. Bless him, he must sense that his mamma needs to rest."

"Oh Ma, I hope we will all manage when the new baby is born," sighed Rose, feeling completely exhausted and now finding her heavy load draining her out by the time afternoons arrived.

"You're just tired and worn out, and what woman isn't when her time approaches. Now you drink this brew and eat these cheese and pickle sandwiches that I made for us."

Rose was becoming impatient and finding everyday an exhausting challenge; her nights were disturbed by the growing baby causing her discomfort every time he moved in the tight confinement of his space and during the day her legs, together with her ever swelling ankles, felt as though they could barely carry her weight; she just longed to deliver the baby and return back to normal once again. Dan's visits had been less frequent of late, convincing Rose that he was repulsed by her heavily pregnant appearance; she always looked forward to his visits; with Alfie so young and Mrs Atkins in her twilight years, Rose found Dan's company fun and their conversations meaningful, she also realised how attached she had become to him over the months, but knew it would be too much to hope for, to expect Dan to want to settle down with a woman who had so much baggage.

"We haven't seen Dan for a while have we?" she announced, as Mrs Atkins slyly lifted Rose's hem to check on the state of her ankles.

"Well, he *is* a farmer, and I dare say it's a busy time for farmers in the summer," assured Primrose Atkins, not quite convinced with her theory but not wanting to give Rose any more problems to worry about.

"You're forgetting Ma, that I'm a country girl and know for a fact, that the busiest time for farmers is during the harvest and lambing season."

"Ahh, them farmers is always busy doing something or other, now have one of these ginger biscuits, they taste a treat dipped in tea."

"Ma! Have you been pilfering the stock again!" laughed Rose, "We'll never become wealthy at this rate!"

"Don't blame me, it's your son who has a liking for these, his little face lights up like a lit candle when he catches sight of the packet."

Rose remembered the haberdashery stall in Banbury market,

"I blame those costermongers in Banbury, they were the ones who introduced Alfie to gingerbread....They *were* an odd pair."

"Well I expect folk around here say that about us!" She declared, as she sunk the gingerbread biscuit into her hot tea.

Seb had stayed in the *Red Lion* longer than he'd intended, finding the chair too comfortable to leave once he'd sat down, and not looking forward to searching for a cheap bed for the night. The summer air was still balmy when he finally left, and Blossom was stood in the same place, and had now devoured the small pile of food that had been left for her. Seb swayed towards the horse, as he struggled to get his bearings. With blurred vision he only just noticed the large sign, indicating the railway station and remembering what the shopkeeper had told him, he mounted Blossom in a somewhat clumsy and undignified manner and guided her in the right direction. Past the railway station and under the bridge the main road opened out into a broad highway where affluent detached houses stood boasting well manicured and flourishing gardens. Leading off from this road there were an abundance of narrow cobbled roads, all tightly packed with modest terrace homes. Seb could only imagine that it was in these side roads where the lodgings were to be found and his assumptions soon proved correct when he began seeing the occasional signs in windows reading, *'LODGINGS FOR RESPECTABLE GENTLEMEN ONLY.'*

It was half an hour later and after knocking on half a dozen front doors, where the only response he'd received was the twitching of the curtains, when Seb concluded that he wasn't viewed as a respectable gentleman. He left a trail of phlegm on the shiny doorsteps of each unopened door, sniggering as he imagined the owner's reaction in the morning. As he proceeded down the next narrow road, still, nobody opened their doors to him. He stood on the corner for a while next to a small grocery shop, straining his eyes in the darkness in search of a suitable place where he could bunk down for the night. He heard a young child crying out, 'Mamma, Mamma, Mamma.' Silence ascended once again, as Seb stared into the shop window. The display of straw boaters immediately brought him to his senses. He stared hard at them, and had the strangest feeling that they had been made by Rose's fair hands. They were identical to the ones she used to make and wear on her pretty head in the summer months; he could picture her in his mind. She would make them for her friends and the women folk who came to Bushel Farm of a harvest time to help out. He was, at last, a step closer to finding his Rose, and felt triumphant that he'd soon have her by his side. He would wait until the grocery store opened in the morning, and enquire after the supplier of the straw hats; maybe even making out that he too was interested in placing an order for his farm workers. With a renewed buzz of excitement, his tiredness seemed to have suddenly disappeared. A nearby bridge which passed above a small stream was to be Seb's resting place for the night. A wrought iron bench made for an adequate bed, and Blossom seemed content with the small patch of nearby grass. As Seb gazed at the bright stars that seemed to be sharing his excitement, he closed his eyes with the image of Rose at the forefront of his mind.

CHAPTER EIGHTEEN

It was the combination of a flutter of eagerly chirping thrushes that were perched in a row along the rooftop, and the uncomfortable cramping in Rose's back which woke her early the following morning. Daylight was only just showing her clear complexion which looked to be another cloudless sunny day. Alfie was peacefully sleeping in his cot on the opposite side of the bedroom, his head of cascading golden curls fanned out around his head on the pillow forming an angel like halo. Rose was tempted to leave her bed and kiss his firm chubby cheeks, which reminded her of two perfectly formed hills either side of his tiny button nose and pretty pink lips, but instead, decided that a longer period of peace and quiet would be more beneficial; once Alfie was awake, there was barely a quiet moment or a chance to relax, until he took his next nap. He was becoming a handful of mischief these days. Rose often wondered how Mrs Atkins managed to take care of him and remain so calm and relaxed at her age, whilst she was busy serving in the shop; she *was* an amazing old lady, who Rose had become extremely fond of over the months. Primrose Atkins had become her new and only family now, and Rose knew that she couldn't have managed on her own, without her or Dan's unconditional support. Her days at Bushel Farm with Johnnie seemed so long ago now, it had been seven months since she had lost her first love, and her darling husband, and even though she had recently vowed that a future marriage was now out of the question, she *had* really missed Dan's visits over the last few weeks, and prayed that he was well; she *had* fallen in love with him, but not wanting to cause any trouble, she had convinced herself that his family would be against any possible union between them and kept her feelings to herself.

Unable to get comfortable in bed, Rose decided to go downstairs and prepare some breakfast for her and Mrs Atkins, hoping that perhaps they could enjoy a calm and peaceful breakfast today whilst Alfie slept. It would make a change to be able to have an uninterrupted conversation over breakfast, and to spoil Mrs Atkins a little.
By the time the tea had brewed and the bread had been toasted, Mrs Atkins was sat up in her bed, delighted by the mouth watering smell which teased her taste buds,
"You should have let me do that!" She exclaimed, with a wide gummy smile upon her face as she viewed the neatly laid table.
"Are we supposed to be eating that marmalade Rose? I thought you told me it was unpaid stock." Mrs Atkins was, as ever, conscious of everything that went on in the shop, often

amazing Rose, with her sharp memory for someone of her age.

"Yes, I did tell you that, but I *have* paid for it, and besides, we both deserve a little treat."

Mrs Atkins wrapped her shawl loosely around her boney shoulders, and took her seat at the small table, still with the same fixed smile upon her deeply lined face.

" Looks like we're in for another lovely day," she exclaimed, peering up at the sky through the tiny window.

The sound of Alfie shaking his cot noisily and calling out to be freed from its confines made Rose and Mrs Atkins both laugh out loud,

"So much for our peaceful breakfast! I knew it was too good to be true!" laughed Rose, slowly lifting her heavy body to climb the stairs.

"Ahh bless him," cooed Mrs Atkins, "bring the little angel down; I expect he's hungry and has probably smelt the toast!"

Rose quickly dressed while she was upstairs, it would save her the effort of climbing the narrow staircase again later, and now, only having one dress which actually stretched around her swollen belly, there were no choice decisions to be made; she couldn't wait to be able to fit into her clothes again.

"Mamma!" exclaimed Alfie, with his arms stretched out in readiness, hoping to be picked up, his broad smile displaying four milk white teeth, "Alfie, toast!" he stated clearly, "Alfie, toast."

"So, my handsome boy, Nanna was right, you *did* smell the toast, you little scallywag!" Rose planted a kiss on his cheek, leaving him disappointed that she still hadn't lifted him from the cot.

"Let Mamma get dressed quickly, then Alfie can eat toast."

"Toast!" he repeated, shaking the cot and grinding his teeth on its bars as he waited patiently.

With Alfie sat down filling his mouth with toast and crabapple jelly, and Mrs Atkins fussing over him as usual, Rose remembered that she had promised to deliver three straw boaters to old Mrs Greenbank who lived a few doors away. She was leaving to Hastings to stay with her son and his family for the summer months, and had ordered three identical hats, for her young granddaughters, each with a pink ribbon and silk daisy trim.

"I'm just going to quickly pop to Mrs Greenbank's, to deliver those hats that she ordered. I'll only be a couple of minutes,"

"No you won't my dear, not if old Mrs Greenbank decides to tell you one of her long winded stories." Mrs Atkins tutted loudly, "that old woman don't know how to stop once she's started!"

"Well hopefully, she'll have a train to catch

today, and won't have time for any stories; besides, I can always pretend that the baby is on its way if I need to make a quick escape from her." Rose couldn't help laughing at how Mrs Atkins referred to her neighbour as an old woman, when, at sixty eight, she was young enough to be her daughter.

"I'll be back in a couple of minutes, Ma."

"Alfie pop out!" came a little voice, muffled from his full mouth.

"No, my darling, Alfie be a good boy for Nanna."

Seb had woken, feeling numb from the uncomfortable sleep on the firm metal bench. Blossom, now with her front hooves in the stream, was bent over drinking the gently rippling water.

Joining her to splash some water on his face, Seb's filthy and dishevelled appearance was already attracting some hard stares from the early morning business men who were heading towards Oxford Railway station for their commute into London. Their spotless smart apparel a complete contrast to that of Seb Harper's. On this morning, though, Seb had other things on his mind rather than fighting with the stuck up locals. He had drifted off to sleep with Rose on his mind; dreamt of her in the short period that he'd slept and now couldn't wait to return to the nearby grocery shop to enquire about the straw hats that just *had* to be the handiwork of his darling angel.

Mrs Atkins heard the knocking on the front door of the shop, as she sipped her third cup of tea, "Come on little Alfie, let's go and open the door for your Ma, sounds like she's forgotten the key, and locked herself out."

"Mamma," repeated Alfie, as he climbed down from the chair, his face and dimpled hands covered with sticky jam.

The moment her weak fingers had lifted the latch, Mrs Atkins was nearly bowled over as Seb came stampeding into the shop, filling its space with his overbearing body. His dim eyes immediately caught sight of Alfie who was cautiously poking his head out from behind Mrs Atkins, shocked that it had not been his Mamma stepping over the threshold, and unsure of the strange and unfriendly looking man.

"What do you want?" Mrs Atkins sensed that this uncouth man was not a customer, merely arriving early at the shop. Her heart was racing. "Alfie, go and finish your toast my darling," she encouraged, wanting him out of the way, just in case this rogue became violent.

"ALFIE!" yelled Seb, only recognizing the toddler by his head of distinctive curls and his name; he had never given much attention to Johnnie's child when he was living at Bushel Farm, he was just a screaming baby to him, and once again, Johnnie had beaten him in achieving

another one of life's milestones, making him even more jealous of his lucky half brother. Alfie stared up at Seb, cowering slightly, but inquisitive to find out more about the stranger who'd bellowed his name out so loudly.

There were very few things in life which managed to scare Primrose Atkins these days, but this beastly looking scoundrel had made her quake; his very presence seemed to fill the entire space with evilness, and she had a strong feeling that no good was going to come of his visit. She was lost for words; even when she *had* managed to speak; her tiny voice was insignificant and meaningless. The lingering odour of toast had reminded Seb that his stomach was empty, he grabbed a packet of biscuits from the shelf, and shoved them into his pocket, under the watchful eye of Mrs Atkins who was powerless to stop him or take any action.

"Where's Rose?" he suddenly demanded, pushing his way past Mrs Atkins and Alfie as he hurried into the private quarters.

"Get out of my home!" Mrs Atkins continued to repeat in vain. Seb took no notice, but proceeded to search every room.

"Where is she, old woman? I know she's 'ere." Seb had cornered Mrs Atkins, breathing his nauseating breath heavily upon her. She feared for Rose's safety more than her own, and prayed that old Mrs Greenbank *had* kept her chatting.

"She's not here; she's gone to London on the train

and won't be back 'till late." It was the first and only answer that entered her head; she hoped it would be enough to send Seb away, if only temporarily, until they would have a chance to find a safe place to escape to, and inform the local peelers of this menacing intruder.

"I don't believe you, old woman, you're bloody hiding her from her husband, and that's a bleeding crime you know!" Seb's face was barely an inch away from an extremely shaken Mrs Atkins, but she kept up her brave stance. His cold eyes focussed on Alfie, who was now clinging to Mrs Atkins and sobbing uncontrollably as he cried out for his mamma. "Right then, have it your way!" Seb suddenly declared, as he leapt forward, roughly yanking Alfie up and holding him in the crook of his arm, like a sack of flour. Alfie hollered and Mrs Atkins screamed hysterically, pleading with Seb to put the infant down.

" *She'll* know where to find him, and tell her to come alone. I don't wanna see no fancy young farmer lad on me land. You got that old woman?"

Mrs Atkins fell to the ground, weakened by the trauma, as she watched her darling little Alfie disappear through the shop door and from her sight, her tears streaming down her face in shear despair.

"Safe journey, God willing, Mrs Greenbank; I

pray you'll have a pleasant stay with your family." Waving as she left Mrs Greenbank on the doorstep, Rose was about to make her way back to open up the shop, when she was suddenly alerted by Alfie's distinctive and far from happy voice. Then her eyes saw a harrowing sight. She froze on the spot as the unmistakable shape of Seb Harper with a screaming Alfie hooked under his arm, sped along the main road and across the top of the narrow side street.

"ALFIE!" she yelled out in disbelief at what she was witnessing. A searing pain shot through her body as her belly contracted, becoming as hard as stone. She doubled up in pain on the dusty road. What was Seb Harper playing at, by running off with her son, she asked herself. As the pain slowly faded away, she hurried in a frenzied state to the corner of the street, only to watch him gallop past on Blossom and out of her sight, with Alfie screaming and kicking as Seb held him tightly.

"Oh Dear God! My poor little Alfie!" she cried out, as a morbid thought, that Seb had harmed Mrs Atkins, suddenly struck her.

She found Mrs Atkins in an inconsolable state, as between sobs she struggled to explain how she'd opened the door to such a savage beast. Rose tried as best she could to console her, telling her that it wasn't her fault and that even if she hadn't opened the door, Seb would still have found his way in, because, he was pure evil.

Rose felt utterly helpless; the shock of the terrible morning's events had induced her labour, making it impossible to follow after Seb. Her fear for Alfie's safety brought her to despair; she knew how careless Seb would be of her son, and prayed that Alfie would come to no harm. As her sudden pains intensified, Mrs Atkins managed to find some inner strength, knowing that Rose now needed all the support she could muster. Thankfully, Mrs Greenbank had arrived at the shop after viewing Rose fall to her knees at the end of the street; she hadn't witnessed the kidnap of Alfie though, so Mrs Atkins quickly filled her in before she went off to fetch a doctor and a police constable.

CHAPTER NINETEEN

"Pull up, Wilkins, pull up, man!" instructed Sir
Hugh Whitehead, knocking the embossed silver
handle of his walking stick against the roof of his
carriage, as he caught sight of the sickly looking
man slouched down on the grass verge.
Wilkins rolled his eyes; he had hoped that his
master would have dozed off to sleep by now,
during the long journey from Bath to Bicester,
but it appeared that it was impossible for Sir
Hugh to ever over look a potential charity case.
This would no doubt end up as another talking
point at one of Sir Hugh's many diner parties.
Since becoming a widower five years ago, when
poor Lady Whitehead had been killed outright
in a tragic riding accident, Sir Hugh seemed to
have undergone a complete personality
transformation, which had changed him from
the quiet reserved man, who was always content
to spend his leisure time reading and taking
country strolls, to a man who was in his element
when socialising with a house full of over
indulgent and rowdy guests. Rumour had it that
Sir Hugh had suffered some kind of mental
breakdown, after his wife's death, though many
people were convinced that this was the *real* Sir
Hugh Whitehead, who had been restrained by
his wife throughout their thirty years of
marriage and was now making up for lost time,

behaving like some caged animal who had
finally been set free. Wilkins however knew the
true reason behind Sir Hugh's eccentric
behaviour.

On hearing the carriage pull up, Johnnie's tired
eyes partially opened.

"I say; are you quite the ticket?" enquired Sir
Hugh, as he alighted from the pristine bottle
green and gold carriage, marching briskly
towards his next project. Wilkins sat rigidly in
his driving seat, refusing to even glance at his
master. He missed the days when Lady
Whitehead had full control of the running of
Westmead Abbey, *and* control of Sir Hugh as
well; he missed Lady Whitehead, she was
special.

"Thank you Sir, you're very kind, but the only
problem I have, is tiredness and I was just taking
a nap."

Viewing the unshaven and dishevelled state of
Johnnie, Sir Hugh felt obliged to persist in
offering his help in some way.

"Where have you travelled from, young man?
And more to the point, where are you heading?"
Johnnie got to his feet, feeling embarrassed at
the state of his crumpled and soiled clothing and
scruffy appearance. He'd been sleeping rough on
the land since leaving the Baker's farm, taking
advantage of the fine weather and saving the
little money which he had. It was hard to believe
that it was only three weeks since he'd waved

goodbye to Lester and Nora, and hadn't so far had any fortune in finding any where that reminded him of home. It was as though his roots had been severed, never to be connected to him again.

"It's quite a long story, Sir, but I'd be grateful if you could tell me exactly where I am."

"Good God, man!" spluttered Sir Hugh, "you mean to tell me you are traveling blindly?" He looked curiously up at this strange lost man who towered above his short stature. There was an honest air about him that Sir Hugh was drawn to and he took an instant liking to him.

"As I said, it's a long story, Sir, and I can see that you are on your way somewhere, and I don't wish to hold you up."

Sir Hugh was even more intrigued and eager to find out more about this young man.

"Poppycock, young man, I won't hear another word. You look as though you could do with a decent meal and a bath, so I'm inviting you to Westmead Abbey and I won't take no for an answer." He tapped his stick onto the ground a couple of times as he watched anxiously for some kind of reaction.

"That's very generous of you, Sir, but I really must continue with my search."

"Search?" Sir Hugh bellowed out, his voice seeming too loud for his small and feeble build. "What are you searching for? Because I dare say I might be able to assist, my family has lived in

Oxfordshire for generations. What's your name, man, or is that what you're searching for?"
Sir Hugh flung his head back as he chuckled at his witty remark, but stopped abruptly as he noticed the solemn look upon Johnnie's face.
Wilkins peered down from his high position, his face expressionless,
"Would Sir care for any assistance?"
"No, Wilkins, stop mothering me, if I want your assistance, I'll bally well ask for it."
A red faced and infuriated Wilkins turned to look in the opposite direction, cursing Sir Hugh under his breath.
"I'm not searching for my name, Sir, I'm Johnnie Harper; it's my family who I'm in search of."
Sir Hugh held out his hand.
" I'm Sir Hugh Whitehead of Westmead Abbey."
As they shook hands, Sir Hugh insisted,
"Now how about you take me up on my offer, Harper, I have an excellent listening ear, and I *might* be able to help you."
Enticed by the thought of a decent meal and an opportunity to bathe, Johnnie replied,
"Thank you Sir Hugh, you're most kind."
"Well, you'll be pleased to know, we're only about another five minutes ride away from Westmead Abbey, which is in Bicester."
Johnnie followed Sir Hugh as he marched towards the carriage, waving his stick in the air at Wilkins,
"Stop daydreaming Wilkins, and look sharp, Mr

Harper is joining us."

Wilkins looked exceedingly displeased.

The inside of Sir Hugh's luxurious carriage was like sitting inside of a perfectly moulded kid skin glove. The superior crafted tan leather seats were a complete contrast to the rough ground to which Johnnie had become accustomed to of late.

The Journey was, as Sir Hugh had correctly said, a five minute one, in which Sir Hugh spent most of the time complaining about the detestable attitude of Wilkins, stating how he had always shown far more respect and fondness to his late wife, and how he probably should have got shot of him a long time ago, accusing him of spreading malicious gossip amongst the staff.

Johnnie thought it a little odd that he was expressing himself so open heartedly to a complete stranger, but clearly he had lost all respect for his coachman.

Westmead Abbey was an impressive looking mansion, with a large and airy glass and wooden porch to the centre, and two adjoining identical buildings symmetrically placed on either side. The sandstone bricks and the clean white paintwork, together with the soft grey slated roof, gave it a light and inviting appearance. A perfect circle of grass surrounded by a gravel driveway made for a spacious and inviting entrance, and with the scattering of

mature conifers, oaks and beech trees, the
picturesque luscious green grounds were a
delight to the eye.

"Welcome to Westmead Abbey, Harper, I trust
that your stay here, however long or short it
turns out to be, will be one that you'll always
look back upon with fondest memories."

"I'm sure it will be, Sir," replied Johnnie, now
thinking that perhaps it hadn't been such a good
idea to have accepted this offer from a complete
stranger, and one of a completely different class
to himself.

Wilkins pulled the carriage to a standstill
directly outside the front porch,

"Will Sir be requiring the use of the carriage
again today?" He called out, with a touch of
sarcasm in his tone.

"Dash it Wilkins, I'm no clairvoyant!"

No sooner had they stepped over the threshold
into Westmead Abbey, when a young maid
appeared and was greeting her master and
relieving him of his top hat, and walking stick.
She held out a silver tray to him,

"This arrived earlier for you, Sir Hugh."

"Maisie," he declared, snapping up the small
cream envelope from the tray. "This is Mr
Harper; you are to show him to the blue guest
room and make sure he has everything he needs,
including a change of clothes, while his are
being laundered. Is that understood?"

"Yes, Sir," Maisie looked to Johnnie, would you

care to follow me Mr Harper?" Maisie asked in a soft voice.

"Join me down here for luncheon, Harper, when you've refreshed yourself; shall we call it an hour?" suggested Sir Hugh, flipping his gold pocket watch open. Johnnie viewed the bulky grandfather clock which stood in the hallway, wondering if it was showing the correct time, and if it was, why Sir Hugh hadn't noted the time of day from it.

" Very well Sir," answered Johnnie.

Sir Hugh swiftly disappeared through double oak doors, leaving Johnnie to follow Maisie up the wide staircase which split into two separate ones and into two opposite directions after the first flight. Maisie led him up the east side. Although Johnnie's limp was barely visible whilst walking, climbing the stairs was a different matter and took Johnnie far longer than an able bodied man; one step at a time putting his good leg forward first on every step. Maisie turned to see why he was lagging behind.

"Sir Hugh didn't mention that you had an injury; are you sure you can manage, Mr Harper?" Johnnie felt the colour rise in his cheeks, feeling embarrassed about his disability for the first time, as he quickly dismissed this pretty young girl's sympathy,

"I'm not injured, I have a permanent disability." Maisie said nothing, but slowed her pace until Johnnie had caught up with her. They soon arrived at the door to the so called *blue room*, which was strangely not as Johnnie had expected it to be. The only shade of blue came from a blue damask winged chair which was positioned next to the window looking out onto the grounds at the back of Westmead Abbey, a calming view of a modestly sized lake. The large guestroom was mostly decorated in sage green and cream, with matching soft furnishings, and a rich brown mahogany bedroom suite. A white bath looking slightly odd and out of place stood in the corner of the room. Johnnie eyed it enthusiastically, longing to take a soak. It was a far cry from any room or home that he'd ever stayed in, making him feel considerably out of place. Maisie had hurried from the room, muttering incoherent words under her breath, only to return five minutes later with a change of clothes for Johnnie; a change of clothes which were peculiarly almost identical to the ones he was already wearing.

"These look like they will fit you Mr Harper, just leave your clothes in here; Sir Hugh said they were to be laundered."

"There's no need, I might need them in a hurry if I suddenly decide to leave."

Maisie had a look of disbelief on her flawless face, as she shook her head from side to side, "Oh no, Mr Harper, Sir Hugh instructed me to have them laundered."

"But they're *my* clothes, and I'm happy with

them as they are, if that's alright?" Johnnie felt a surge of compassion for this timid girl, who was obviously intent on following everyone of her master's orders and maybe feared that she might lose her position if she didn't, "don't worry Maisie, I won't tell Sir Hugh." Looking shocked that Johnnie had taken note of her name, a sudden look of relief befell her as she performed a quick bob of a curtsy and fled from the blue room.

Feeling cleaner and more refreshed, Johnnie waited in the downstairs lobby where he had left Sir Hugh an hour ago. A gallery of portraits hung from the high walls, many of them portraits of the same austere looking woman, who Johnnie deduced to being Sir Hugh's late wife. There were no portraits of him, or of any males even slightly resembling a likeness to Sir Hugh.

"Ah, I see you're admiring the gallery!" Sir Hugh seemed to come from nowhere, very quietly, startling Johnnie. "Damned ugly looking bunch, apart from my dear Lady Ophelia, she was a *true* rose amongst the thorns."

Johnnie's mind switched to *his* darling Rose, a clear picture of her beauty flashing in front of his eyes.

"Now come along Harper, let's go through to the drawing room and partake in a spot of luncheon. I trust Maisie has taken good care of you; she tends to be a bit of a dreamer at times, but the poor girl does put up with an awful lot, working at Westmead Abbey."

"She took jolly good care of me," replied Johnnie as he followed Sir Hugh.

"Good show! Good show!" he declared.

Rays of light flooded through the floor to ceiling windows in the drawing room, which looked out on to the tranquil lake and assortment of mature trees, it was a picture far more delightful to the eye than any of the oil paintings hanging in the lobby. A marble topped table held silver trays piled high with petite salmon and cooked meat sandwiches and a selection of sweet pastries; a fine bone china set and a solid silver tea service completed the elegant layout.

A long honey coloured leather couch and two matching armchairs, bordered the low table, and made for the perfect position to enjoy the breathtaking landscape of the Westmead Abbey estate.

"Sit down Harper, sit down!"

Johnnie did as he was told, beginning to feel like a child again under Sir Hugh's constant orders, and still curious as to why Sir Hugh had invited him in to his home and was treating him as an equal.

"Sir Hugh, you do realise that I'm a humble farmer, and more to the point, a farmer who has actually *lost* his farm."

Sir Hugh's mind was focussed on food; he was starving, and paid little attention to Johnnie's declaration, and merely handed him a plate insisting that he should begin eating.

"Plenty of time for truth telling later, Harper; now I suggest we simply enjoy the delights of luncheon."

CHAPTER TWENTY

The following few hours at Westmead Abbey were spent relaxing in a shaded area of a well manicured lawn outside the grand French doors of the lounge. Sir Hugh kept his fingers busy by fiddling with his thinning grey beard as he began to tell Johnnie a little of his life's story, puzzling Johnnie, as he had been under the impression that it would be the other way around. Sir Hugh had obviously loved his wife deeply, and after five years, was still struggling to come to terms with his great loss. His eyes clouded over as he spoke so fondly of her to Johnnie, who was more than content to listen tentatively to his host's recollections.

"You see, Harper, my Lady Ophelia was the whole world to me, she guided me through life's ups and downs and was able to run the house and organise every single aspect of our lives with such ease and perfection. She was blessed with a remarkable way of being able to communicate with everybody and anybody, no matter what class they were from, and that is one of the reasons why I've slowly had to dismiss most of the staff since her death. You see, Harper, my good man, they just didn't take to me giving them orders after their Lady Ophelia had departed , and in a strange way they all collaborated to ruin my good name; to

make me look like a crazed fool, who had been afflicted by a mental breakdown.
I did a terrible and wicked thing after my Ophelia lost her life, and until today, there is only one person apart from myself, I hope, who has any awareness of it."
Johnnie, who had been in an almost sleepy state, as he relaxed in the warmth of the sultry summer's afternoon with a full stomach, listening to Sir Hugh's declaration of love and bereavement for his late wife, was suddenly drawn to attention. He wondered what huge hidden secret his ears were about to hear. Looking directly at Sir Hugh, he noticed the awkwardness in his demeanour as he proceeded to open his heart further to Johnnie.
"My Lady Ophelia was a superb and experienced rider, she was a natural in the saddle, and could soften and tame the most difficult of horses, solely, with her gentle voice. Horses were a large part of her life, and she always talked about increasing the stock and venturing into horse breeding, it was one of her dreams and ambitions, but she kept putting the venture off for one reason or another...."
Sir Hugh stopped to dig deep into his trouser pocket, pulling out a handkerchief. Johnnie took a sideways glance at him, noticing a falling tear. He thought of his Rose, and felt such a yearning for her, that his heart skipped a beat, making him question as to why he was sat wasting time

in the surroundings of a completely different world, when he should be using every morsel of energy to pursue his search for her and for his home, which still remained engulfed in a dense fog. He swallowed hard, fighting back his tears. Sir Hugh dabbed the beads of sweat from his brow along with a lone tear, took a deep breath and continued,

"On the day of my Lady Ophelia's disastrous accident, I completely lost control of my rational thinking. I behaved like a lunatic; grief took hold of me in such a way, it was as though the devil himself was prompting me to take such drastic and evil actions. We had to shoot the mare that my Lady was riding...broken leg. I was quite happy when Wilkins told me this news the following day, I thought to myself, why should that damned horse live, when my beloved had been so cruelly snatched away from me. I returned to the stable late that night, thinking that the staff had all retired."

Sir Hugh paused for a second to face Johnnie with a renewed seriousness in his voice,

"Now, Harper, I beg of you to try and understand how fragile my mental state was when I tell you what my next actions were; I took my pistol, and proceeded to shoot every one of my Lady Ophelia's poor horses."

Johnnie's jaw dropped; he couldn't believe his ears; Sir Hugh looked far too meek to even contemplate such a crime, let alone carry it out.

Sir Hugh's face was ashen; he shivered, even though the afternoon temperatures were soaring. Johnnie remembered the harrowing flashbacks that he'd experienced back on the farm, and felt immediate empathy for this fragile looking man, who was reliving one of the darkest moments in his life. He placed his hand on Sir Hugh's arm, and applied a gentle tap. "The moment that I stood in front of those six majestic animals as they lay before me, I was filled with an overwhelming flood of guilt and remorse. I could almost see and hear my Lady Ophelia condemning me. I asked myself, who *was* I to take away the life of these fine creatures....I had no right; it was a callous and evil inspired action, one which will haunt me until my dying day. I had, on the spur of the moment, decided to lie about these events, intending to report to the local constabulary that someone had broken into my stables during the night and committed an act of sabotage, a totally cowardly action I know, but I justified it by telling myself that my state of mind was temporarily on the brink of collapse. As I was about to leave the stables, a terrified looking Wilkins suddenly appeared from the tack room, he was brandishing a pitchfork and obviously feared for his own life, thinking that I had completely lost my wits. He had apparently noticed how unsettled the horses had become and taken the decision to sleep in the stables that night. Horses are such sensitive and intelligent creatures, and they were missing, if not actually mourning the loss of the horse which had to be destroyed. I must have appeared like the devil himself, arriving at the stables and shooting them all in cold blood.

I broke down into a pathetic excuse of a man, of my station, and for a while Wilkins gave me his support. But sadly that is where it ended, and he has spent the past five years blackmailing me with this secret, and threatening to report my actions and cause a terrible scandal. For the sake of my dear Lady Ophelia, I could not possibly allow her most respected family name to be tarnished."

Sir Hugh let out a cynical laugh,

"You know Harper, he carries a pistol on him at all times, probably even keeps one under his pillow at night. Stupid fool thinks I might kill him."

Johnnie sat up straight, intrigued and somewhat disturbed by Sir Hugh's confession. The sleepiness had left him.

"I don't quite understand, Sir Hugh, couldn't you have just paid him off and sent him on his way?"

Sir Hugh laughed out loudly, shaking his head, "Oh Harper my good man, if only it had been that simple. Don't you think I would have gladly parted with my money to be rid of that blood sucking swine? It turned out, that he had a soft spot for my Lady Ophelia. The stupid fool had convinced himself that she too harboured affections for him and was only restrained by their class difference, and by my very existence."

"But surely, now, after five years isn't it high time he got over the past?" Johnnie questioned, as the image of Sir Hugh's story cast a vivid picture in his mind.

"Where Wilkins is concerned, nothing is that logical, it's become a kind of obsession with him; I believe that he thinks he's punishing me on behalf of my dear Lady Ophelia. The man is beyond reasoning and believe me Harper, I've offered him a good many deals over the years but it seems that the more generous my offer becomes the more he digs his heels firmly in to the ground, refusing to even consider their benefits. He is enjoying ruining my life and having such a strong hold on me."

Sir Hugh picked up the brass bell from off the wrought iron table, shaking it vigorously until Maisie appeared from inside of the house.

"Yes, Sir Hugh?" She puffed, as she straightened her white apron.

" We are in need of some refreshments, Maisie."

"Yes Sir." Maisie performed a half curtsy as she awaited more instructions.

" Has your mother made any of her delicious lemonade, Maisie?"

"I think she has Sir."

"Splendid! Splendid!"

"Will there be anything else Sir?" Maisie was

very eager to please her master, thought Johnnie as he sat observing how the wealthy folk went about their life.

"That will be all for now Maisie."

"Thank you Sir." Maisie hurried back to the small entrance where she'd come from, leaving Sir Hugh to once again turn all his attention to Johnnie.

"She's still training, early days, early days, but if she turns out to be like her mother, well there'll be no regrets. Her mother is my cook, and an exceptional one at that. Yes, every member of staff has slowly left since my wife....." his voice trailed off sadly. "I'm not sure, if Wilkins is behind that...I sometimes get the feeling that he's hoping to take over Westmead Abbey. But I trust dear Harriet; she and her daughter have been in my employment for about ten months now, and I have warned them both to stay clear of Wilkins, and to have as little to do with him as possible. They are both aware of his devious ways."

Maisie soon arrived with a refreshing jug of cool lemonade, giving Johnnie a shy smile as she poured out two glasses.

"Thank you Maisie, we can manage now."

"Very good Sir."

Johnnie sat thinking of a way in which he might be able to do something to help Sir Hugh's predicament,

"Sir Hugh," he suddenly exclaimed, "Why don't

you just dismiss Wilkins, if he wants to make trouble for you, surely it's your word against his; it happened so long ago now and who would believe *his* word over yours?"

"Because my dear Harper, he claims to have evidence. You see, a few months after the incident, Wilkins left to Cornwall, his mother had passed away down there. While he was there I made the most foolish mistake of writing to him, offering him a large sum of money and an excellent reference on condition that he didn't return."

Sir Hugh looked downcast, combing through his beard with his finger tips, deep in thought.

" How exactly did you word the letter, Sir Hugh? Did you mention anything about the horses?" asked Johnnie eagerly.

"That's just it; my state of mind back then was such that I can't remember a blessed thing that I wrote, other than my offer."

Johnnie shook his head; he felt like a detective on a case,

"Sir Hugh, you're an intelligent man, and it's my guess that you wouldn't have put down in ink anything about the details of that incident. I think Wilkins is calling your bluff, and probably realises that you weren't quite yourself during that murky period in your life."

Gulping down the cold liquid, Sir Hugh reminded Johnnie of a guilty child, even though he must be in his sixties.

"But can I take that risk, Harper, that's the question that has haunted me for years; can I take that risk?"

"Maybe there *is* a way we can find out," Johnnie suggested, causing Sir Hugh to bolt upright in his seat.

"Dash it Harper, I was hoping you'd suggest that. I know a sincere face when I see one, and I have the feeling that you and I will be acquainted for many years to come."

A few minutes silence fell upon these two completely dissimilar men, broken only by the afternoon melody from the chirping of the abundant song birds that went unseen but managed to create an amplified tune from on high. They both had their problems, thought Johnnie; problems which were disrupting their lives and Johnnie wondered if it *was* possible for them to assist each other somehow. Since Sir Hugh had yet to ask about his own circumstances, Johnnie decided to take it upon himself to enlighten him.

CHAPTER TWENTY-ONE

Doctor Chapman stood in the small back parlour, as both Mrs Atkins and Mrs Greenbank threw a barrage of questions at him, in between insisting he drank tea and ate biscuits. He had been upstairs with Rose for more than ten hours, it had been a long and difficult birth, brought on by the shock of little Alfie's abduction. There had been complications and at one stage Doctor Chapman feared that he would lose both mother and baby, but by a blessed miracle they had pulled through, leaving Rose extremely weak and poorly. Her beautiful daughter, seemed to have come through the ordeal in a considerably healthier state than her poor mother, she had already taken her rest, and was now screaming out to be fed.

"Mrs Harper is going to need around the clock looking after until she regains her strength, ladies," he addressed the two elderly women, "and I am also entrusting the care of her daughter into your very capable hands."

"Don't worry doctor," assured Mrs Greenbank, who had taken charge since arriving at Mrs Atkins' home. "I'll send a telegram to Hastings and tell my family that I'll be delayed, I know how Mrs Atkins struggles with the stairs, and she's had a terrible shock today with that villain confronting her like that, and stealing that

Precious little boy. I'll make sure to take care of everyone under this roof, Doctor Chapman." Doctor Chapman's weary face showed a glimmer of satisfaction in the knowledge that poor old Mrs Atkins would not be left alone to cope.

"Perhaps, Mrs Greenbank, you could help Mrs Harper to feed her daughter, she is barely able to move, we need some peace and quiet and the infant is in need of nourishment. "

"I'll go right away doctor, perhaps Rose will be able to tell me where that scoundrel might have taken little Alfie."

"I would refrain from troubling her mind just yet, Mrs Greenbank; Mrs Harper has suffered a great trauma, and is very poorly indeed," he ordered, "I'm sure the police are doing their best to find the little lad." As Doctor Chapman prepared to leave, Primrose Atkins broke down into heart breaking sobs, again,

"Oh that poor little soul, I can't bear to think of him with that *beast* of a man, far away from his mamma and his nanna; he'll be distraught. He'll never settle…Oh my poor sweet Alfie."

Mrs Atkins buried her face into her palms as her shoulders shook with every sob. Doctor Chapman felt obliged to remain a little longer until Mrs Greenbank came back downstairs. There was at least no sound of the baby's cries, he noted, so hopefully Mrs Greenbank was doing a good job, and would soon rejoined them.

"Did you not say that this man is related to the child, Mrs Atkins?" he asked, trying to put a stop to her wailing.

" It won't make a farthing's worth of difference; he means nothing but harm to that sweet family. He's a brute, a savage, and my poor Alfie is at his mercy." Her sobs continued. Doctor Chapman was desperate to leave.

"It's been a long and harrowing day for all of us, Mrs Atkins, and we should all be grateful to The Almighty that upstairs little Alfie has a healthy little sister, and a Mother who has survived an extremely difficult birth. Count your blessings Mrs Atkins, today could have ended in a very tragic way, and I'm certain you will all soon be reunited with the little lad again." Doctor Chapman managed to conceal his underlying fears, not wanting to subject these women to any more worry than was necessary.

Primrose Atkins knew exactly what he was saying; he was right, she thought, the day *could* have been one of complete disaster. Pulling herself together, Mrs Atkins dried her tears and began to tidy the table, piling up the days crockery from her and Mrs Greenwood's copious cups of tea which had aided them through the traumatic day. Doctor Chapman took another check on Rose before leaving, promising to return in the morning before he opened his surgery. There was little change in her, but, she was young and strong, and in caring hands, and he had every confidence that she would pull through.

As daylight slowly hid behind the black silkiness of night, Seb had still not managed to bring any peace to Bushel farm. Having screamed himself to sleep a couple of times, Alfie was once again wide eyed and wailing. His continuous chanting of 'Mamma, Mamma, Mamma.' was driving Seb into a state of despair. With his dirt stained face now reddened from his unrelenting sobs, and his soiled napkin chaffing his tender skin, he hollered out rowdily every time Seb yelled at him to shut up. The farm house was now in a state of stinking filth, with black mould growing from every surface, and fungi sprouting from the cracks in the walls. Nothing had been cleaned, nor a single dish washed since Rose had left, and the vermin had moved in; their trail of droppings now covering every square inch of the house. The fact that there wasn't an edible morsel of food in the house only angered Seb more; starving, thirsty and exhausted from his two days in Oxford where he had gained little sleep, the thought of a night listening to the piercing screams coming from Alfie's mouth, had swayed him into taking some drastic actions. He remembered the large basket which Rose had made for the child and where he used to sleep before Rose had taken leave of her senses and ran off to Oxford. Taking the small crib out to the barn, he forcefully squeezed a much grown Alfie into its tight confines, leaving him cocooned in the crib with his little legs hanging over the edge. In his ignorance, he assumed that Alfie would soon fall fast asleep in his old familiar crib. The barn door was shut tight and Seb took himself off to the nearest ale house, a couple of miles away, and out of ear shot from the disturbing child, now convinced that since Rose hadn't yet shown up at Bushel Farm for some bizarre reason, it was guaranteed that tomorrow morning would see her pretty face upon his property once more.

Mrs Greenbank had taken control of the situation and persuaded a stubborn Mrs Atkins to turn in for the night, while she quickly tidied up the house, before turning all of her attention to seeing to the needs of Rose and her beautiful baby girl. Mrs Greenbank slept lightly in the adjoining room with one ear listening out all night long in case she was needed. It was at four in the morning along with the dawn chorus that the sound of the new born echoed through the rafters and alerted Mrs Greenbank. Rose was ashen faced and still looking extremely weak; she was asking for water.
Mrs Greenbank laid the small noisy bundle next to Rose allowing her to suckle while she hurried off downstairs to the scullery. Tiptoeing around

Primrose who was snoring soundly in her bed, Mrs Greenbank prepared a small feast of boiled eggs, bread rolls, jam and a pot of tea. Her second journey upstairs would be to carry the bowl of warm water so that she could give both mother and baby a wash. By the time the sun had risen, a little colour had returned to Rose's cheeks and she was sat up and becoming acquainted with her daughter. Mrs Greenbank had put fresh linen on the bed assisted a shy Rose with her ablutions, and washed the baby, and after consuming the breakfast and two cups of tea, Rose was looking much improved.

"Congratulations, Mrs Harper, You have a beautiful, healthy daughter," declared Mrs Greenbank, cheerfully, "she's going to grow up to be as pretty as her Ma."

Rose's stare was fixed on her daughter as she stroked her soft dark mop of hair.

" She certainly has my Johnnie's hair, Alfie was blond when he was born and he had such a tiny wisp of it upon his head. You are going to be just like your dear pa, my love," Rose sadly declared. She suddenly ceased talking, a look of desolation flooding her face,

" Oh my poor Alfie!" she cried out, "He should be here to meet his new sister, what's to become of him?" Rose suddenly swung her legs over the side of the bed, pulling back the patchwork coverlet.

"I know where Sebastian Harper has taken him; I

must go, he's not capable to have a toddler in his charge. Oh, my Alfie, he must be so upset..." Overwhelmed by pain and a weakness which didn't allow her to rise off the mattress, Rose sank back down in tears.

Mrs Greenbank was quick to rush to her side, "Rose, my dear, you have been through such a difficult birth, and you *must* remain in bed; that was Doctor Chapman's orders, and I dare say he'll be back soon to check on you. It's paramount that you rest, my dear."

Rose flopped back onto the pillow.

"Did I hear you say that you know where that awful rogue has taken little Alfie?" enquired Mrs Greenbank, softly, not wanting to subject Rose to any more stress. "The constable is going to call in this morning, we need to tell him anything that will help the peelers find Alfie and bring him home."

"Bushel Farm, in Northamptonshire," cried Rose, barely able to keep her heavy eyes open.

Mrs Greenbank repeated the address a few times under her breath, hoping that her memory wouldn't let her down on this occasion; she didn't wish to keep disturbing Rose, who needed all the rest she could get in order to recuperate.

" Now, I want you to have a good rest my dear, I will take baby down...."

"*Hope*," whispered Rose weakly, "her name is Hope."

Mrs Greenbank felt a tear roll down her face and

drop onto her ample bosom.

"What a delightfully, meaningful name," she said, choking on her words.

"Is it alright if I take little Hope downstairs for a while, Mrs Atkins is just longing to see her, and so annoyed that she can't climb the stairs. I will bring her back as soon as she's in need of a feed." Rose gave a slight nod of her head as she drifted back to sleep.

A sudden knocking on the front door interrupted the two elderly women as they sat cooing over baby Hope.

"That's sure to be either the constable or the doctor," deduced Mrs Greenbank, as she gently rocked the baby in her arms.

"I'll go then, since it looks as though you've managed to rock Hope to sleep." Primrose was still somewhat nervous after her last experience of opening the door, but knew she had to be brave and conquer her fears.

"I need to loosen up my stiff joints too. I'm so used to chasing after little Alfie all day, that my old bones are beginning to seize up with all this sitting around guzzling tea. Oh, I *do* miss that sweet little lad, I pray that he is safe," stated Primrose as she shuffled as fast as she could through to the shop, deciding that she would first take a look through the shop's front display window before turning the latch.

It was neither the constable nor the doctor, but Mrs Atkins had never been so pleased in her life to see the familiar figure waiting outside. She struggled in her excitement to get a grip of the latch with her gnarled fingers.

CHAPTER TWENTY-TWO

"Dan!" Mrs Atkins tearfully exclaimed, taking hold of his arm and almost dragging him over the threshold, as feeble as she was. "You *are* a welcome sight. Oh Dan, it's been such a carry on, these past few days, I'm out of me mind with worry. Something *dreadful* has happened."

"Are you alright Mrs Atkins?" Called Mrs Greenbank from the parlour, "Who is it, a bobbie or the good doctor?"

"What's been going on Mrs Atkins, and where is Rose?"

Little Hope began to cry,

"Rose has had her baby!" Dan blurted out, finding the whole atmosphere in Mrs Atkins' home tense and gloomy despite the obvious good news of the new born baby. It was a spontaneous second thought which struck Dan like a piercing arrow, instantly giving him the conclusion to the odd feelings he was experiencing. *"Oh no!"* his voice cracked with the strain, "please don't tell me that Rose didn't make it."

" What's keeping you, out there, for goodness sake?" called out Mrs Greenbank, "I'm taking little Hope back upstairs to Rose; she's hungry again, bless her little heart."

Dan was looking confused, but was at least now

happier in the knowledge that Rose was, by the sound of it, confined to her bed upstairs.

"Come on through lad, and put the kettle on to boil. I'll fill you in before the local peeler and the doctor arrive."

"Where's little Alfie then?" questioned Dan, suddenly realising that he'd not seen nor heard him. "Is he sleeping?"

Mrs Atkins couldn't keep up her brave facade for a second longer, and seemed to crumble pitifully into Dan's arms.

"Oh Dan, such a *dreadful* thing has happened....that poor little lad."

Dan was becoming impatient; he needed to know exactly what *had* happened, and the quicker he made a pot of tea, the quicker he would get any sense out of this flustered old woman. Literally carrying Mrs Atkins in his arms through to her chair in the back parlour, he swiftly had the water on to boil.

"Its Dan isn't it?" asked Mrs Greenbank as she stood at the foot of the stairs with the small swathed bundle resting in the crook of her arm.

"Mrs Atkins has told me all about you; I'm Mrs Greenbank from around the corner in Russell Street and this is little Hope, who arrived into the world yesterday."

Dan glanced at the tiny pink face, which was only just visible amongst the layers of the white cotton shawl.

I've been staying here with Mrs Atkins since that

awful beast snatched the little lad."

Dan froze in shock, "Are you talking about Alfie, Mrs Greenbank? Please, *tell* me what's been going on."

Mrs Atkins proceeded to fill Dan in with the previous day's events while Mrs Greenbank brewed a large pot of tea. Hope, who wasn't hungry, after all, had fallen back to sleep and was now temporarily resting upon the soft couch cushion.

"It was that awful brother in law of hers; he showed up here, pushing his weight around, and then, he stole poor little Alfie away, thinking that Rose would be chasing after him, so that he'd be able to get his wicked claws on her. The shock of it brought about her labour, and what a difficult labour it turned out to be too, leaving her in such a state of weakness. It was touch and go at one point; Doctor Chapman said that we was to count our blessings that they both survived." Mrs Atkins sniffed, trying hard to hold back her tears, which seemed to be continuously on the brink of over flowing these days.

"Poor, poor Rose," declared Dan, clearly disturbed by what he'd been told.

" Why don't you go up and see her?" suggested Mrs Atkins.

Mrs Greenbank, who had undoubtedly been listening into the conversation, came hurrying in from the scullery,

"Do you think that would be appropriate under the circumstances, Mrs Atkins?"

"What circumstances, Mrs Greenbank?"

"Well, with her being a married woman who's just given birth, of course, and Dan being a single man!"

"Oh don't be so stiff collard!" averred Mrs Atkins, "We both know full well that Rose is a widow; those two are more like brother and sister in any case, and besides, Rose *needs* a bit of cheering up. Where have you been hiding yerself, Dan, we haven't seen you for weeks; we was beginning to think you'd forgotten about us."

Although Primrose knew that there *were* more to Dan's feelings than mere brotherly love, she wasn't going to let Mrs Greenbank's prudish ways ruin the day, especially knowing how much his visit would mean to Rose.

"My Pa was sick for a couple of weeks, it left him weak, so I've had too much work to take care of on the farm and wasn't able to get away; I've missed you all, you know, and as soon as I've seen Rose, I'm going after Alfie. That damn brother in law had no right to take Alfie."

Angered at the sheer nerve of Sebastian Harper, Dan was ready and eager to go to battle with him.

"Oh, you don't wanna get on the wrong side of that savage, he's a ruthless brute from what I've seen of him," warned Mrs Atkins, nervously,

remembering how terrified she'd been.
"There's more than one way of fighting a battle, Mrs Atkins."

Rose was just on the verge of drifting back to sleep, as Dan knocked on her door. Thinking it was the doctor, Rose was pleasantly surprised to see Dan standing shyly in the doorway, with a tray of tea and bread and butter in his hands.
"Dan! Come in."
Instantly shocked to see how pale and fragile Rose looked and sounded, Dan had never been more certain of anything in his life, that the love and adoration he felt for this beautiful woman were genuine; he decided then and there that he could never love another as he loved Rose Harper. If only she was his wife, he thought, yearning to take her into his protective arms and assure her that he would make everything better. She looked so fragile; it made his heart ache. Rushing to her bedside he quickly placed the tray onto the floor, and took her hand in his, "Oh Rose, if only I'd had known, I would have been here like a shot... Congratulations, baby Hope is beautiful, just like her ma."
For the first time since the birth, a touch of colour returned to Rose's cheeks as she blushed, demurely.
"Did Mrs Atkins tell you what happened? Did she tell you that my loathsome brother in law

has kidnapped my darling Alfie?" Rose sniffed, reaching under her pillow for her handkerchief.

"Don't fret Rose," Dan comforted, "I'll soon be on his trail, I promise."

Their privacy only lasted for a brief few minutes, before Mrs Greenbank arrived with baby Hope in her arms.

"I think little Hope is hungry again," she declared, even though there wasn't a sound coming from the contented infant.

Rose stretched out her arms, gesturing Mrs Greenbank to deposit the small bundle into them.

"Here, Dan, why don't you take hold of her for a minute," suggested Rose as she quickly placed Hope into his hands, giving him little choice in the matter. Being far from happy with Dan's presence upstairs, Mrs Greenbank busied herself tidying Rose's bedroom, reminding her that the doctor would be arriving very shortly. Dan kissed the baby on her forehead, wishing he could do the same to Rose, but with Mrs Greenbank reminding him of a beady eyed hawk, he certainly didn't want to ruffle her feathers.

"Right then, I'm going after little Alfie," declared Dan, standing proud.

"Don't you think you ought to leave that to the peelers?" stated Mrs Greenbank pursing her lips. "He's an unsavoury character to say the least, and twice as big and with twice as much muscle as you."

Sensing Dan's embarrassment by Mrs Greenbank's insensitive comments, Rose insisted that Dan was just as well-built as Seb.

"Bushel Farm can't be *that* far away from my family's place, though strangely enough, I've never heard mention of it," mused Dan, "but not to worry, I'm sure it won't be that hard to locate."

"Take care of yourself, Dan, I'll pray for your safe return with Alfie...Oh my poor little boy...." breaking down into a flood of tears, Mrs Greenbank was quick to comfort her, as she offered a stern warning look towards Dan.

Downstairs, the local constable had arrived and was jotting down some notes in his small book, as Mrs Atkins retold the events of the day when Alfie was abducted; not that he really wanted to hear all the details again, he just needed to know the name and location of Sebastian Harper's farm.

"Are you saying that nobody has even gone in search of Alfie yet?"

The constable eyed Dan cautiously,

"And you Sir, are?" he questioned.

"He's a very dear and close friend of mine and I've known his family for generations." Mrs Atkins declared, proudly as she lifted her head high.

"I'm Dan Heyford." Spoke up Dan, clearly. The constable nodded as he jotted down his name, licking the end of his pencil first as though it was a most important part of the process.

"Due to the fact that the man in question resides in Northamptonshire, and has most likely returned to his farm to wait for the arrival of Mrs Harper, I'm afraid the case is now out of Oxford constabulary's hands and is now a case for the local Northamptonshire police force, but, be assured that we will keep Mrs Harper informed of their progress." The constable casually replaced the notebook into his jacket.

" Excuse me if I'm speaking out of line, constable, but it looks to me as though this case is not being treated with the urgency that it warrants; Sebastian Harper, by all accounts is an exceptionally dangerous man, and Alfie Harper is in grave danger."

Giving Dan yet another cold glare, he dragged his tongue slowly over his thick lips before replying,

" Do you actually know this man, Mr Heyford? I trust you're aware that he *is* the child's uncle and that they share the same family name. I doubt that any harm will come to the child; Mr Harper is merely using him as bait. He is of course in trouble, and what he has done cannot be condoned, but there are far more pressing cases to be dealt with which require our immediate attention."

"No constable, thankfully I can't say that I do know Mr Harper, but from what I *have* heard about him, I wouldn't trust him with one of my sheep let alone a helpless toddler, unable to fend for himself." Filled with frustration and anger, Dan had already taken an instant dislike to this pretentious constable, who was clearly oblivious to the seriousness of the situation.

"A few words of advice, Mr Harper, don't get involved in family matters which are of no concern to you." The constable's smug grin teased Dan to the point where he was finding it difficult to restrain from swinging for him.

"Upstairs, sits a very poorly young woman, who has been through one hell of a birth, and is living every second of her life worried sick for the safety of her first born, and physically unable to do anything about it; she has put all her faith and trust in the police force to find her son and you are doing absolutely *nothing!*"

"Calm down Dan," implored Mrs Atkins who was becoming quite anxious having to sit and listen to the heated conversation.

"Very well said, Mrs Atkins; this whole case is getting quite out of hand; now I must be on my way, I've wasted enough time already this morning." Placing his helmet back onto his head, he made his way towards the shop door, only to be met by Doctor Chapman as he stepped over the threshold.

Dan left Mrs Atkins' home, downcast and annoyed to the point that he felt like striking out with his fists; there had been few times in his life where he had harboured such strong violent emotions. He *would* rescue Alfie, he told himself, and bring him home to his ma.

CHAPTER TWENTY-THREE

The Bushel Farm farmhouse no longer resembled any similarity to a home. In his hot headed, fowl temper Sebastian Harper had damaged everything and anything he could lay his hands on. Why hadn't Rose come to fetch her son? He continued to ask himself, coming to the conclusion that the new man in her life had taken priority over Alfie, and that she just couldn't bear to leave him. Seb was riddled with jealousy, an emotion that he'd become well acquainted with where Rose was concerned. She was *his*, he persisted in telling himself and she belonged at Bushel Farm with him.

Spending hour upon hour pacing back and forth through the farmhouse, cussing loudly and every now and again grabbing the nearest object to hand, sending it hurtling through the air to its destruction, Seb had succeeded in working himself up into such a crazed state that he had lost all sense of reasoning, and had practically forgotten about Alfie who was still out in the barn. When it did suddenly occur to him that he had abandoned the infant to the outside, he took out a dish of water to the child, almost as if he imagined that he was keeping some kind of animal out there. Alfie would scream out on viewing his uncle, but it was nothing but a cry of fear, from the sinister monster that had stole him away from his loving mamma and all that was dear and familiar to him in his world. Seb would cover his ears and look at the child in disgust. Alfie had become lethargic, heavily soiled and half starved.

When Seb wasn't throwing a tantrum, he was sleeping, and as soon as the village ale house was open, he would be the first customer, his presence keeping many of the local men away, deterred by his overpowering stench, and his foul mouth, and not wanting to be involved in a fight with such a desperate man.

The only remaining livestock now left on the farm was a handful of scrawny looking hens, they too feared for their safety since Seb had long since bothered to shut them up in the hen house at the end of the day. They had however discovered a small gap in the side of the barn, a few feet off the ground, and were able to fly up one at a time and find security inside the barn for the night, safe from the countryside's hungry foxes. An unusual kind of friendship was formed between the hens and Alfie. He welcomed their arrival at dusk, every evening, becoming excited on viewing the first one as she popped her head through the hole. Most of the hens would allow Alfie to touch and stroke them and one had even taken to roosting alongside Alfie every night, allowing him to snuggle up to her and keep warm as the temperature dropped. The hens would also return to the barn

during the day to claim a bale of hay on which to
lay their eggs on; leaving Alfie to climb his way
up the hay mountain to claim his prize. He soon
acquired a taste for the raw eggs which to begin
with, would accidentally crack in his heavy
handed possession, leaving him to lick his messy
fingers clean. These precious eggs had become
his one and only sustenance over the days.

Seb sat scowling in his usual corner seat in the
ale house; he'd had enough of waiting and had
arrived at the conclusion that it was either Rose's
new fancy man or that interfering old biddy who
were preventing her from coming after her son;
they probably realised that once Rose was back
home where she rightfully belonged, they would
never set eyes upon her again. Seb had decided
that come the morning he would journey back to
Oxford and bring her home himself.

Leaving the ale house three hours later, even in
the pitch darkness of the moonless night,
Blossom was able to bring her master home with
no assistance from him. Twice, Seb had fallen
out of the saddle after nodding off and losing
what little body control he had, and twice he had
clambered back into the saddle in the most
undignified manner. The poor mare was left to
carry the uncomfortable leather load on her back
all night as her drunken master stumbled over
the threshold, giving no thought to her, and
leaving her to roam the yard. The farmhouse

was as black as a coalmine and just as dangerous with the amount of debris littering the floor. Seb tripped up over every obstacle in his path, swearing loudly in his struggle to reach the window where he last recollected seeing a candle. With immense difficulty he lit the candle which stood in a cracked tea cup on the window ledge and in the dim light, he viewed the appalling state of his surrounds, sobering up a little as the hard facts that this was not a place where any woman would wish to call her home suddenly struck him. He would wake up early, he thought, and put all his efforts into returning the hovel into its former cosy and inviting home, before venturing to Oxford. Thinking that he'd heard a sound from outside, Seb peered through the filthy window, seeing nothing but his own reflection in the black abyss; he was startled by such a grotesque looking villain staring back at him. Disgusted at what he saw, he savagely yanked the curtains together, before climbing up the stairs, on all fours, and falling into the bed. Seb's deep sleep was near to unconsciousness filling every corner of the ramshackle farmhouse with the ruckus from his long throaty snores. He fought in vain to wake up from his horrifying nightmare; he could just make out an image of Rose through the thick smoke, as he sniffed the air, breathing in the aroma of burning roast lamb. It wasn't like Rose to burn his diner, she was always such an expert in the kitchen, she was an expert at everything she did; the best and prettiest wife any man could wish for. Fighting to lift his heavy weight off the bed, Seb suddenly caught sight of Johnnie standing over him, he was livid and Seb could see nothing but his own repulsive reflection in his eyes as Johnnie's hands wrapped themselves around his neck, squeezing tightly. Seb gasped for air, only to choke on the thick black smoke, as he struggled to speak.

'Rose don't belong to you no more Johnnie Harper, so bugger off!' Johnnie was laughing out loudly and triumphantly as Mad Master Monty appeared behind him, a childish grin on his vacant looking face.

The blazing fire which had quickly kindled when the naked candle flame caught the curtains, now raged aggressively throughout the farmhouse, destroying everything in its path. The augmented crackle of its destructive flames intensified with every passing minute, as its vivid orange tentacles seemed to dance for joy in every direction, becoming loftier as they multiplied. The farmhouse had become like a small pocket from hell, and as the rafters came crashing down, the dense smoke had filled Seb's lungs, choking him to death.

Percival and Jayne Bird from the neighbouring farm were the first to arrive on the scene. After being woken by the sound of a distressed horse outside in the yard. When Jayne pulled back the curtain, she couldn't believe her eyes. The bright orange glow in the distance, across the fields, illuminated the dark night like a beacon.

"Percy, wake up, Bushel Farm is on fire!" she exclaimed, shaking her husband, who always managed to sleep more soundly than her.

"Go back to sleep Jayne, it's the middle of the night," he mumbled sleepily.

"Percival Bird!" she yelled in his ear, " We've gotta go an' help our neighbours; their place is ablaze." Jayne had already pulled on her brown serge skirt and was hurriedly buttoning up her blouse.

"His horse is down in the yard!" added Jayne. Percival had left his bed and was standing by the window,

"That looks like one hell of a fire, I hope to God that Harper has got everyone out to safety, and isn't pissed out of his thick head as usual."

"*Percy!* There's no call for that vulgar talk."

"Its only the truth love, he practically clears the *Fox and Fiddle* every evening with his presence; don't reckon the man's been sober nor had a wash for months, not since he buried his brother."

"Well let's hope we don't end up having to bury anyone else later today. I hope to God that his brother's wife, Rose, and child aren't trapped inside." Jayne declared with a renewed urgency.

214

The farmhouse was nothing but a ruin by the
time anyone arrived on the scene; a smouldering
shell of a home, now completely gutted. The
locals looked on in disbelief, many of the elders
having known Seb's parents and been frequent
callers at the farm in their youthful days.
"There's nothing to be done now, it's too late,"
announced one onlooker gloomily, "nobody
could have survived inside that inferno."
As neighbours mingled together, all having their
say and expressing their opinion on the tragedy,
most of them pointed the blame at Sebastian
Harper's drunken state, claiming that he was no
better than a cold blooded murderer by causing
the death of Johnnie Harper's poor widow and
child, nobody having realised that Rose had
abandoned Bushel Farm four months ago.
Jayne remembered the occasional chats she'd
had with Rose to pass the time of day when
they'd met in the village store. She was struck by
her beauty, a little jealous, if truth be told, but it
was also Rose's love of life and her effervescent
nature and kind heart that made her such a
lovely girl, who doted on her husband and son.
Jayne had held little Alfie in her arms soon after
he was born, when she'd taken Rose some calves
foot jelly and a knitted layette for her new born,
one of many which she had in her drawer.
Percival was always saying to her that when she
did find herself with child that she had better
pray she'd deliver triplets, since she'd knitted

enough garments for a whole tribe. Jayne lived in hope and prayed constantly for such a blessing, but after ten years of marriage it was looking more and more certain that it was not to be.

For a minute or two she imagined she was hearing things, but she *could* hear an infant's crying. She looked around for Percival, who was stood with the group of men folk who'd also left their beds. She was the only woman on the scene, the only able woman who didn't have to remain indoors to tend to her little ones. Not wanting to sound like a hysterical woman nagging her husband, knowing how embarrassed Percival would become in front of his fellow men, Jayne left him to his conversing for the time being. The distinct crying sound continued and this time it was accompanied by the distressed squawks of hens. She *wasn't* hearing things; she wasn't going insane from lack of sleep and the shock of the night's terrible events. Marching across the farm yard she untied the piece of knotted rope which held the barn doors shut. It was a miracle; young Alfie Harper was locked in the barn. But why, she asked herself. He was alive and that was all that mattered. The hens flapped and squawked noisily as they desperately fled through the open barn doors. Alfie stood in a bedraggled state, his wide eyes staring up at Jayne,

"Mamma," he suddenly declared, before falling

onto the ground. Jayne noted how poorly and filthy the small boy appeared, and hurried to rescue him. He was wet and soiled and quite unrecognizable as Rose's well kept son.

Something didn't add up here, thought Jayne, as she quickly peeled off Alfie's outer garments and wrapped him in her cardigan, taking him outside towards the group of men who had now thinned out, most having returned to their homes.

"I was just wondering...."Percival stopped in mid sentence, straining his eyes in the darkness.

"Look, look who I found in the barn!" exclaimed Jayne, full of excitement.

"Surely that's Johnnie Harper's boy isn't it?"

"Of course it is, who else do you think would be in the barn of the Harper's farm!"

The remaining men folk now all focussed on little Alfie. He became upset and clung tightly to Jayne's neck, hiding his face.

"Where did you find him Mrs Bird?" They questioned in unison.

Percival answered their question, and a fresh debate began on why and how the little lad had been in the barn in the middle of the night, and not with his ma. Not at all interested in what they had to say on the matter, Jayne could only think about getting Alfie back to her home where she could wash, feed and comfort the poor bewildered infant. It seemed to her that the locals were secretly reveling in the drama of the night, and forgetting that lives had perished, and a young child had become an orphan.

CHAPTER TWENTY-FOUR

"Would you care for a cup of tea and a slice of Mrs Greenbank's fruit cake, Doctor Chapman?" Invited Mrs Atkins, as the doctor returned back downstairs after Rose's daily check.

"Thank you Mrs Atkins, but I can't stop for your delicious refreshments today; I have a long list of patients to visit this morning before my afternoon surgery."

"You work too hard, Doctor!" declared Mrs Greenbank.

Doctor Chapman smiled,

"Well ladies, thanks to your commendable nursing, Mrs Harper is making excellent progress. I've told her that she can get out of bed for a short while this afternoon, if she feels up to it."

Mrs Atkins and Mrs Greenbank sat proudly at the small table.

"Oh Thank The Good Lord!" praised Mrs Atkins.

"And won't it just be the icing on the cake if young Dan brings Alfie home to her later today," added Mrs Greenbank.

"That would indeed be the best medicine for Mrs Harper," Doctor Chapman agreed.

Dan was slumped in his motionless horse cart beneath the shade of an ancient Horse Chestnut tree, a few miles away from Bushel Farm. He felt numb; how could he return to Rose and be the bearer of such devastating news, he asked himself, how could he face her and watch the sun disappear from her soul; but if it wasn't him who broke the news to her, it would most likely be that pompous, heartless peeler, who he'd taken such an instant dislike to. Dan felt like a coward, and he despised cowards; his eyes were wet. Poor little Alfie; why hadn't he arrived earlier, he scolded himself; he was no better than that bloody peeler; condemning him for not taking Alfie's abduction serious, when he had been just a neglectful by waiting until the morning to journey to Bushel Farm. Picking up the reins and giving them a firm flick, Pepper ceased his grazing and was soon trotting towards Oxford.

It was, however, Doctor Chapman who had the misfortune of delivering the gruesome news to Rose. Bumping into the pair of constables whilst on his morning rounds, it was decided that since Rose was in such weak health, and would probably require the doctor's medical attention, Doctor Chapman would be the better person to break it to her. It was an aspect of his profession which always left him feeling absolutely helpless.

Jayne Bird had spent the night with her arm lovingly wrapped around Alfie as he lay next to her in bed. After she'd bathed and fed him, he had given Jayne a little smile, and quickly fallen asleep; he had been exhausted. When morning arrived, it was a delight to both Percival and Jayne to find their normally quiet home filled with the sound of Alfie's young voice. He insisted on calling Jayne 'Mamma' which although pleased her, also broke her heart in the knowledge that poor Alfie had seemed to have suffered of late and was eager to adopt her as his ma. It remained a mystery as to why little Alfie had been found in such a state of neglect and abandoned in the Harper's barn.

Percival Bird knew the question which would soon come from his wife's tongue. His heart was saddened that they had not been blessed with children; Jayne was a natural and he was moved as he watched her strong maternal instincts shine through as she fussed over Alfie. He already had most of the Harper's livestock under his care after they had wandered onto his land through Harper's broken fence, and last night he hadn't just taken in the Harper's mangy looking chickens, but now he had little Alfie Harper under his roof too.

Jayne sat spooning little Alfie extra creamy porridge; he already looked much better and was on his second bowl, thoroughly enjoying every delicious mouthful. Jayne had cut down one of her blouses to size and Alfie was wearing it like a night shirt.

"You know, he's an orphan now, Percy, and I know for a fact that he no longer has any living relatives. If *we* don't take care of him, it will be the workhouse."

Percy looked solemnly, deep in thought, not feeling quite sure that he was ready to commit to anything just yet; it had been a long night.

"We'll talk about this later my love. I'm already running late this morning, and I must see to the beasts."

"I'll be out to do the milking shortly; I'm sure little Alfie would love to watch." Jayne desperately yearned to keep Alfie as her own son, and didn't want to let Percy think that he'd cause her to neglect her duties on the farm in any way.

"You stay in and take care of the little lad, I'll do the milking today, and if Molly turns up from the store, I'm sure she won't mind doing a bit of milking, besides, she knows that I always give her discount, and she does buy most of the milk anyway."

"Thank you my love." Percy delivered a quick kiss on Jayne's cheek, and ruffled little Alfie's fair curls before leaving the farmhouse.

Crossing the field to where he had a good view of the Harper's place, after he'd milked the cows and let them out to graze, he noted quite a lot of activities going on. A small crowd had gathered, together with a few policemen and what looked like the undertakers, with their ominous looking enclosed black wagon. Percy made his way to join them just in case he was needed as a witness. Everyone seemed to be talking simultaneously; Percy stood watching and listening. It seemed that they had only recovered one charred body from the wreckage, that of Sebastian Harper. The topic of conversation was that there was no sign of Rose Harper's body or that of her son's. Percy felt compelled to join in and inform the constables about Alfie, praying that they wouldn't drag the poor lad away to the workhouse. That boy had been through an ordeal already, and needed a good dose of kindness, love and stability, none of which would be found in the workhouse. Percy quickly added that he and his wife were quite willing to take care of the infant, maybe even adopt him, he had dared to say. Everything was scribbled down in the constables' note book, including Percy's address. A couple of the locals who had often ran into Seb in the *Fox and Fiddle* gave a detailed account of how Seb had continuously boasted that since his half brother had lost his life back on New year's day, Rose had declared her love for him and was now living as his wife. Nobody had believed his drunken statements, and knew it was merely wishful thinking, but this now caused speculation that perhaps Seb had done something terrible to Rose Harper; everyone knew what a devoted mother she was and how she would never abandon her son to the barn. Percy added that it was his wife's belief, judging by the state that she'd found him in, that he'd been locked in the barn for quite some time. It seemed like everyone had their own ideas and suggestions as to the whereabouts of Rose Harper, most of which appeared cruel and wicked, but it was the general speculation that she had somehow lost her life at the merciless hands of Sebastian Harper.

By mid day, Bushel Farm had once again become deserted leaving the bare shell of the burnt out farmhouse looking eerie as it cast disturbingly gruesome images through the minds of the locals as to what went on within its confines.

Jayne received a steady trickle of women folk calling upon her when they'd heard from their husbands about how she'd taken the Harper boy under her care. They brought their children's clothes which could no longer be passed down to any younger siblings, and other items which they considered would come in useful to their barren neighbour, along with an overwhelming amount of advice on the *do's* and *don'ts* of raising a child, as though Jayne were a simpleton. She took their gifts and advice gratefully, laughing out loud when they had left; they really were treating her like a foolish child who had never even laid eyes on a baby before, but she didn't mind, and her bouts of laughter proved to be contagious, causing Alfie to giggle uncontrollably for the first time, putting tears of joy in Jayne's eyes.

There was to be no more correspondence between the Northamptonshire Constabulary and that of Oxford, as far as the Northamptonshire police were concerned it was an open and shut case; all that was missing, was the body of Mrs Harper, and since the prime suspect had already met with his end, there seemed little point in pursuing the case further and wasting the time of an already thin and stretched police force, following a dead end case. A few days later, the case was virtually closed and filed under 'accidental '. The remains of Sebastian Harper were laid to rest in the family grave, a small family graveyard, later bought by the local parish and fenced off from Bushel Farm, which was to be sold at auction, the funds to be held in a trust until Alfie Harper reached the age of twenty one.

Johnnie had written to Lester and Nora to inform them that he was in Bicester and temporarily staying in Westmead Abbey as Sir Hugh Whitehead's house guest. Nora was curious as to why such a gentleman of high standing should form a relationship with Johnnie. Lester on the other hand gave it little thought, telling Nora that it probably wasn't quite as Johnnie had phrased it in his letter. Beth, saw it as an opportunity for Johnnie to perhaps find her the position that she longed for, to go into service, and begged her parents to ask Johnnie in their next correspondence if Westmead Abbey was in need of a kitchen hand or a parlour maid.

Life at Westmead Abbey continued with Johnnie trying his hardest to befriend Wilkins and to find a way in which to solve Sir Hugh's ongoing problem. After becoming more acquainted with his host, Johnnie had come to the conclusion that he was a weak and cowardly sort, probably attaining all his strength in the past from the capable and strong willed Lady Ophelia, and hiding behind her shadow. She had definitely been the head of the house, in body, if not in name and Wilkins had obviously grown to know his master well over the years and now preyed on his weaknesses. While Johnnie wracked his brains for ways in which to solve Sir Hugh's predicament, Sir Hugh was busy plotting a more final idea in his head and just needed Johnnie's support and advice before drawing up a successful plan.

CHAPTER TWENTY-FIVE

"I'm finding this heat a little too hot and sticky for my liking," complained Sir Hugh at breakfast. It was mid September, and unseasonably warm for the time of year.

"Well, since we're now in autumn, I can't see it lasting much longer, "replied Johnnie, as he spread the rich apricot conserve onto his toasted bread. "Which reminds me, that I really should be on my way, Sir Hugh. A humble farmer like myself could quite easily become accustomed to living in such luxury and I really need to continue searching for Rose; besides, I've been your guest for far longer than you intended, I'm sure."

"Nonsense man, nonsense. I thoroughly enjoy your companionship and you haven't yet allowed me to help you in your search, which I did promise on doing. Did I not?"

Sir Hugh had a worried look about him; one which Johnnie had come to realise was a sure sign that he was becoming anxious. Picking up the table napkin, Sir Hugh dabbed his forehead before taking out two large Cuban cigars from the inside of his linen jacket, offering Johnnie one. Not being partial to these pungent smokes, Johnnie declined the offer and continued with his breakfast. Hugh had the look of a worried child about him, as he feared that he might find himself left alone with Wilkins once again, who, since the arrival of Johnnie had stayed out of his way and behaved in an appropriate way in which a coachman should.

"Johnnie, there's a couple of pressing issues that I would appreciate your honest opinion on and I've also got a proposition to put to you. What say we take a leisurely stroll around the grounds?"

Being engulfed in a huge cloud of pungent cigar smoke, Johnnie could think of nothing better and agreed enthusiastically, taking a quick gulp of tea to wash down the toast.

It was a lot cooler outside with a gusty breeze blowing through the leafy trees, many of which had just begun to show signs of the impending autumn, turning to vibrant hues of yellow, burnt orange and maroon. They walked in silence across the lawn, heading towards the lake, both taking in the beauty of the changing season. Sir Hugh then suddenly spoke, his words shocking Johnnie, and causing him to come to an abrupt standstill,

" I'm planning to kill Wilkins, you know. I need your help Johnnie, but only as an alibi. I wouldn't dream of subjecting you to any risks. What do you say?"

It was an awkward moment. Sir Hugh must have been contemplating this for some time thought, Johnnie, still shocked by the casual way in which he had suggested such a final act.

"There must be another way, Sir Hugh, surely?"
pleaded Johnnie, not even trying to conceal his
shock from Sir Hugh. They continued walking.
"*No*, there *is* no other way, I cannot live my life
while I breath the same air as that no good
blackmailing bastard; he has to go. I don't even
think that he has any living family; Maisie tells
me that there is never any mail for him so I
suspect that even if I were to push him off the
edge of a cliff right now, nobody in the world
would miss him."
"Is that what you have in mind for him then, Sir
Hugh?"
"Good God, man, no, that would be pure folly;
no, I intend to send him on his way in the same
way that I ended the lives of my Lady Ophelia's
treasured beasts all those years ago."
They had reached the edge of the lake and
Johnnie requested that they rested for a while
using his sore leg as an excuse. He had to think
hard before agreeing to commit to Sir Hugh's
plans he warned himself, now wishing that he
had not been so indulgent of Sir Hugh's
generous hospitality and had left Westmead
Abbey weeks ago. He detested the idea of being
involved in such a cold blooded and risky
crime.
A lone eider duck made its way towards them as
they sat by the water's edge, probably hoping
that like Harriet and Maisie often did, they had
brought him some stale bread. Johnnie's

thoughts drifted back to the maimed bird which had, in a way been the start of his problem; if only Master Monty had just left that duck alone, or not even have caught sight of it, then he wouldn't be sitting here discussing how to murder a fellow human, he wouldn't be a cripple, and he wouldn't be separated from his darling wife and son.

"So what do you think, Harper?" Sir Hugh suddenly blurted out, bringing Johnnie back from his far thoughts.

" I'm sorry, Sir Hugh, I don't feel that I could become involved in a murder. Somewhere out there I have the responsibility of a wife and son; I just can't take such a risk, but I do have another idea that might just work."

Hugh sat up straight, excited to hear what Johnnie had in mind, a look of relief already loosening up the furrows in his brow.

Johnnie smiled, "I can't tell you just yet, I have to clear it with Harriet."

Sir Hugh looked confused, "Harriet? You mean my cook, Harriet?"

"Please Sir Hugh, not another word until I have approached Harriet on the matter, and she is in agreement."

"Dash it Harper, the suspense is already giving me indigestion, I beg of you to let me know what you have in mind."

"All in good time, Sir Hugh, all in good time," laughed Johnnie, seeing the transformation in Sir

Hugh's troubled face.

As they took a slow pace back to the house, Johnnie asked,

"What was the proposition that you mentioned, Sir Hugh?"

" Heavens above, what a half witted fool I am, damned good job you reminded me. Let's go to my study and all will be revealed over coffee. By the way, have you seen Wilkins this morning?"

"He was pestering Harriet in the kitchen earlier to give him a bag of apples for the horses," replied Johnnie.

"Well he has no right, there are plenty of laden apple trees on the estate; he's just downright lazy."

"Oh, I think it's more than that, Sir Hugh, I think he has taken quite a fancy to Harriet."

"No! you can't be serious," exclaimed a shocked Sir Hugh, "well I hope the woman has more sense than to get involved with such a devious man as Wilkins; it seems to me that he has a soft spot for any female who crosses his path; stupid fool of a man."

"Don't worry, Sir Hugh, according to young Maisie, her ma can't abide the man."

"Young Maisie I fear has taken rather a shine to you, Harper; tread carefully, she's not so young to know and follow her heart; I've witnessed the way she looks at you."

Shocked by this latest revelation, Johnnie felt inwardly pleased that such a pretty young woman harboured feelings for him; maybe his disability didn't make him a lesser man after all, he mused.

Maisie promptly brought the tray of coffee to Sir Hugh's study, and for the first time, Johnnie felt a little awkward in her presence.

"Thank you Maisie, can you make sure the door is firmly shut on your way out," requested Sir Hugh.

"Should I pour the coffee for you Sir?" she asked softly, giving a warm smile to Johnnie.

" No, that will be all thank you, Maisie."

"Take a look at these, young Harper and tell me what you think." Sir Hugh handed him a small pile of letters from various land agents in Oxfordshire and its neighbouring counties.

"What are they?" quizzed Johnnie, briefly flicking through them, but taking little notice." Sir Hugh stood up to pour the coffee, "It's to be my new project, and in honour of my Lady Ophelia. Do you remember me telling you how she so longed to run a horse farm, stocked with the very best breeds of horses? Well that's what I intend to do, but not here of course, no, here wouldn't be suitable, so I've got a few places to view, and I'd value your opinion bearing in mind that I would like you to manage the place for me." Sir Hugh passed a very thoughtful Johnnie a cup of coffee.

"What do you say then, Harper?"

Johnnie took the coffee in one hand while he
flicked through a few of the pages of farming
land; farms and large plots that were currently
on the market.

"It does sound like a good venture, Sir Hugh, but
I think that you are forgetting about my most
important mission in life at the moment, and
that is to find my family and my roots."

"You are completely mistaken my dear man, this
is for you and your family, and hopefully, by the
time I have found and purchased a suitable
place, and all the legalities have been finalized,
you will be reunited with your dear wife."

"I hope so," sighed Johnnie.

Sir Hugh took the letters from Johnnie's hand ,
excitedly pulling out odd ones from the pile,
"I thought we'd look at these two in Oxfordshire
first, there's a large plot of land on the outskirts
of Banbury, then there's this delightful sounding
Honeysuckle Farm in Oxford, though it's
probably not as appealing as its name, and
failing those two, we could stretch into
neighbouring Northamptonshire where
there's a Bushel Farm up for auction next month;
now that one might prove to be the best
investment, although it does state that the
dwelling needs extensive repairs."

Johnnie had the strangest of feelings all of a
sudden, there was definitely something familiar
in Sir Hugh's words, which sent a shiver through
his body.

"Bushel Farm?" he repeated, "I feel as if I know that farm."

"Well there's a good omen if ever I've heard one," declared Sir Hugh jovially, oblivious to Johnnie's change of mood.

The following few days found Johnnie going over and over in his mind, thoughts of Bushel Farm, becoming more and more convinced that it held an important link to his identity and his past. He could almost picture the farm and was sure that at some point in his life, he had lived there. Since Sir Hugh's plan was to visit the various estates in a few weeks time, Johnnie tried to push all thoughts about Bushel Farm to the back of his mind for the time being, and put all his efforts into the other problem of Wilkins. With some agreeable negotiations between him and Harriet, Johnnie prayed that his plan would work.

It was to be a few days later when Johnnie braced himself for a most critical performance; telling lies was a trait that he had never been accustomed to and he prayed that Wilkins wouldn't be able to see through his deception. The weather had taken a dramatic change, the sultry heat finally giving way to a night of deafening thunder storms and torrential rain. Wilkins had spent many hours out in the stables trying to console the anxious horses when every clap of thunder neared Westmead Estate, until it seemed to hang in the violent night directly above the stables. The huge pile of steaming horse dung and damp straw, adjacent to the row of stables, emitted an overpowering stench, which wafted into the cold damp air. Johnnie pulled up the collar on his oil skin jacket and covered his nose, as he tried to avoid the copious puddles across the yard. He could hear Wilkins' annoying whistle as he approached the tack room; it was always the same monotonous, irritating tune, which seemed to have a way of getting stuck inside of Johnnie's head, remaining with him for the rest of the day. He already felt angry, which was, he thought, an appropriate emotion to feel, as he was about to confront Wilkins, with a blast of abuse.

" Wilkins, you bloody, worthless scoundrel," yelled Johnnie, as he marched into the tack room, "you're a shame to the Westmead Estate." Immediately ceasing to rub the polish into the leather saddle in front of him, Wilkins stopped whistling and looked up, in shock at this rude intrusion, his jaw dropping. Before giving him a chance to reply, Johnnie continued,

" That poor woman, is sat bawling her eyes out in the kitchen, she is thoroughly shamed, and ruined, and it's all down to you, Wilkins."

" What the hell are you talking about Harper?"

"Oh don't play the innocent man now, *please* Wilkins. Everyone knew that you spent a good deal of time in Harriet's room back in the summer months."

"What's that conniving bitch been telling you, Harper?"

"Only the truth, Wilkins; only the sad truth."

"I haven't so much as touched a hair on her head. I'm innocent, and whatever it is that she's accusing me of is a downright lie." Wilkins had now stood up from his stool and was noisily tidying up his work bench, trying to ignore Johnnie's unwelcome presence.

" Well all I can say, Wilkins, is that I hope you will have the decency to marry the poor woman and be a father to your child. I dread to think of the scandal it would cause when Harriet is no longer able to hide her shameful secret."

"This is a bloody set up," yelled Wilkins angrily "I was mending the jammed windows in her room, doing her a favour. Do you honestly think that I'd be tempted by an old soiled cook, Harper?"

" Well from what I've heard since arriving here, you are rather taken in by the older and more experienced woman."

Wilkins marched angrily towards Johnnie, who was preparing to defend himself, coming to a halt close to Johnnie, his fists clenched and his face like an over ripe fruit about to burst open.

"I don't know what your bloody game is, Harper, or what your business is here at Westmead Abbey, or why Sir Hugh has developed such an attachment to you, but if you think I'm going to fall for your ridiculous games, well you must have more than just a crippled leg."

He had hit a nerve, and Johnnie had to remind himself why he was standing in front of this obnoxious man, and why it was imperative that he remained calm. Wilkins continued, angrily,

" Is it money that you and she are after? Is that it? Have you cooked this whole fiasco up together to make your fortune, thinking that you can take me for some kind of fool. You *do* know that blackmail is a crime, don't you?"

Finding it difficult to hold his tongue, Johnnie couldn't believe the audacity of this worthless man.

" Yes, of course, I know and it is one of the lowest crimes that a human could possibly stoop to and *no*, I can assure you that I don't want a penny of your money, I just wish to see justice done and see that poor woman's mind put at ease."

"Well there is no possible way in which that harlot of a woman is going to snare me and force me into a life sentence of raising her bastard child. It has nothing to do with me!"

"So you keep saying, Wilkins, so you keep saying; but Harriet is of a completely different opinion," spoke Johnnie, calmly.

Remaining cool as he enjoyed every minute watching a hot tempered and frustrated Wilkins crumble in front of him, Johnnie just prayed that

Wilkins wouldn't give Harriet a hard time; if he had any sense, he'd stay well away from her, thought Johnnie.

It was a few minutes to midnight, that same day, when Wilkins knocked on Sir Hugh Whitehead's study door, leaving his packed case outside.
" I'm sorry to trouble you Sir Hugh, but I have a small proposition to put your way." For the first time, Wilkins stood sheepishly, fiddling with his hands nervously as he spoke.
"Come and sit down, Wilkins," ordered Sir Hugh, looking up from his book.
Wilkins didn't move, but folded his arms in a bid to stop his uncontrollable hands from moving.
" I won't take up much of your time, and I think you'll be quite pleased to hear what I'm about to say."
Closing his book and placing it upon the table, Sir Hugh sat up straight, and alert, curious to hear his coachman's proposition.
"Go on," he commanded.
"I've finally decided to accept your cash offer, and move to pastures new. Once I've walked out of Westmead Abbey, I promise that you won't see or hear from me ever again."
Sir Hugh mulled Wilkins' words over in his head, he had no idea of what had gone on in the stables between Johnnie and Wilkins, but he did have an inclination that Johnnie Harper was somehow behind this sudden and unexpected

action by Wilkins.

"And what was my cash offer, Wilkins? Remind me."

"Seventy gold sovereigns, Sir," declared Wilkins, keeping eye contact with Sir Hugh, who was visibly shocked by the steep request, and couldn't recall offering such a price to be rid of this leech.

"And I trust that I will receive the letter which I wrote to you in return?"

Wilkins swallowed hard, a redness creeping over his cowardly looking face.

"*Well?*" demanded Sir Hugh, "I take it that you are still in receipt of my correspondence!"

There was no reply from Wilkins as he shifted nervously from one foot to another.

" You damned lying leech! You've been bluffing me all these years!" Yelled Sir Hugh, in a fit of rage. "Get out of my house and don't let me *ever* set eyes on you again."

An even angrier Wilkins marched forward, ready to grab Sir Hugh by his neck, with the intention to squeeze the life from him.

"Don't you dare touch him!" sounded Johnnie's voice, as he barged into the study, a pistol in his hand, "or you'll not live to see another sunrise."

"I might have known you'd have your crippled weasel on hand, you bloody coward, no wonder it was me that Lady Ophelia always secretly loved, she was wasted on you, Whitehead."

Sir Hugh suddenly fell back onto the couch, all colour having vanished from his face as he held his chest, gasping for air. Johnnie looked on in utter shock, as Wilkins made a swift exit from the study and from Westmead Abbey.

NEW BEGINNINGS

1879

CHAPTER TWENTY-SIX

"Ma, please come and tell Henry to be sensible, because otherwise I'm going to end up giving him the sack, he's not helping me one bit," declared Hope as she marched into the parlour from the shop, her head of brown wavy hair cascading over her shoulders.

Dan and Rose both tried to keep a straight face as they sat eating breakfast; they were quite used to Hope's rather bossy and demanding nature, and at only fourteen she had matured into a beautiful young woman, who was meticulous in all that she did, especially when it came to arranging the new stock and changing the window display.

"Please try and be patient with your brother, Hope, remember, he is five years younger than you, and you can't dismiss your own brother neither!"

"Well if he wasn't my brother, I'd have sacked him years ago, besides he's skinny enough to make an ideal chimney sweep."

"That will do Hope," spoke up Dan, as he got up from the table,

"Henry will be going to school in ten minutes, anyway."

Henry came running in from the shop,

"Ma, Hope is being bossy as usual; I've had enough of being ordered around by a silly girl.

Can't you give me another chore to do?"
"Still think that marrying me was the best thing you've ever done Daniel Heyford?" laughed Rose.
" Hmmm," teased Dan, "let's just pray that young Primrose grows up to be less argumentative."
Primrose looked up from her bowl of porridge, her huge brown eyes, melting her parents hearts, "I'm a good girl, aren't I Ma; I'm not *argmented,* am I?"
"No you're not my sweet darling, you're mama's little angel." announced Rose, as she stroked Primrose's full cheeks.
" But Henry and Hope are angels sometimes, aren't they?" She questioned, looking concerned.
"Yes my sweetheart, you are all my angels, now finish that porridge and let's clean up this house."
" But I'm the only one with angel's golden hair though aren't I Ma, like you?"
"No you're not!" protested Henry," our brother Alfie had angels hair too, didn't he Ma?"
"That's right my darling," agreed Rose sadly.
"Come on Henry, I'll walk with you to school." Dan intervened, not wanting Rose to become upset.
" Can we go and see our new home tomorrow Pa?" asked Henry eagerly.
" I wish we weren't going to live in the boring countryside," protested Hope, as she marched back into the parlour, "I'm a city girl; I will

simply loathe the country with all those smelly cows and sheep, and strange speaking people, I know I will."

After the terrible death of little Alfie, Rose took on the thoughts that her life was just destined for misery; first her parents taken from her before she'd even been given the chance to know and remember them, then her dear grandparents, followed by Johnnie and then her very own son, suffering so much in the last days of his young life. But, as she slipped into a deep dark place, she tried to console herself, that at least Seb had perished in the fire, and that she was blessed by having Johnnie's daughter. Those early days after Hope's traumatic birth always filled Rose with such a feeling of foreboding, as she remembered each long day being both a mental and physical struggle. Dan, Mrs Atkins and Mrs Greenbank had been like pure saints, and had stood by her like a guiding force until she'd managed to emerge from her depression. Dan had insisted on taking Mrs Atkins, Rose and Baby Hope out to spend a day on his family's farm, every Sunday, which proved to be an essential part of their recuperation, Mrs Atkins and Dan were as much in mourning for Alfie as Rose was. Dan had broken down and spilled his heart out to his ma shortly after that terrible day, also confessing the feelings he had for Rose. Mrs Heyford was able to sense the genuine love that her only son harboured, and it broke her heart to

see him so distressed and miserable. It was she
who had suggested the Sunday visits, taking to
Rose immediately, and feeling such empathy for
her, having suffered so many losses for one so
young. When the rest of Dan's family had
become aware of Rose's sad plight and the
involvement of their brother, they too welcomed
Rose and Baby Hope into their family,
encouraging Dan to propose marriage to her.
Still being unsure of Rose's feelings towards
him, it wasn't until Hope's second birthday that
he plucked up the courage and finally heard the
words that he'd dreamt of for years, when Rose
was overjoyed and accepted his marriage
proposal with no hesitation.

Prior to their wedding in October of 1867, Rose
had a special request to ask of Dan. It was just
after the harvest; Rose had seen very little of Dan
since he'd been busy assisting on the family
farm, while she kept the shop running and took
care of Mrs Atkins who was approaching her
ninety third year and had become very frail of
late. Hope had become a handful after turning
two proving to be a very strong willed child who
seemed curious about everything in sight; it was
a welcome break for all when she took her
afternoon nap.

" Dan, before we get wed, would you mind
taking me to Bushel Farm, only I want to say my
final goodbye to Johnnie, and tell him that I'm
going to marry such a lovely man who I

know will love and cherish me and his daughter
for as long as we live."
Feeling a little jealous, Dan wondered if Rose
would ever love him as she'd loved Johnnie, but
he couldn't deny her this one special request.
"Are you sure you won't find it too upsetting,
my darling?" asked Dan, struggling to speak as
an uncomfortable lump constricted his throat.
"I've never been back, I was always so terrified
of running into Seb, and then with one thing and
another....Well, I think I'm brave enough now to
face Bushel Farm, one final time to say my
goodbyes."
"Well, if you're sure.....You know that it will look
quite different now, I expect a completely newly
designed farmhouse has been constructed on the
land." Dan couldn't bring himself to say the
words 'burnt down' or 'fire', and wished in his
heart that Rose hadn't requested to partake in
such a daunting task.

It came as a huge shock to Rose on that last
Sunday in September, when they arrived in
Northamptonshire and to where Bushel Farm
had once stood. A high brick wall now
surrounded the perimeter of the plot, with a pair
of ostentatious wrought iron gates at the
entrance and two stone carved horse heads on
either side, sat imposingly on top of lofty pillars.
A large sign reading *LADY OPHELIA'S
STABLES* was suspended above the gates on

heavy metal chains and swung gently in the light breeze.

As they peered through the gates, into the far distance they saw a fine and very modern looking building, which was in complete contrast to the modest farmhouse where Rose had spent her first married years, and where Alfie had been born. There were no longer fences dividing the farm land, and in the far distance where her neighbours had once lived there was no sign of their home which had once stood on the horizon, but instead were what looked like row upon row of stables and a large paddock. A few unattended horses could be seen wondering in a nearby meadow. Dan had become nervous as he watched Rose spending such a long period gazing through the gates, "Come on Rose, before they set the hounds on us for snooping."

"It all looks so different, I can't believe that this is where my home used to be; it looks so grand and changed, and spotless. I wonder whatever happened to Mr and Mrs Bird too, their farmhouse has disappeared altogether, along with the bordering fence."

"Horsie, horsie," called out Hope suddenly, catching sight of the handsome thoroughbreds.

"Come on Rose, I can see the graveyard from here, it's been fenced off, look." Dan pointed to the nearby rectangle of partitioned land, which was unkempt and over grown with an abundance of bright red dancing poppies. Dan remained on the horse trap with Hope, while Rose walked slowly towards the entrance.

"Mamma," called out Hope, holding her arms outstretched.

" Mamma will be back in a minute," consoled Dan, as he watched Rose enter the small family graveyard. The cacophony of joyful birdsong on the bright sunny day did not match the sad and poignant occasion, and Dan sat quietly praying that Rose wouldn't return too upset and that they would soon be on their way again, away from what used to be Bushel Farm.

Rose placed the two small posies of flowers upon Johnnie and his ma's graves, speaking to Johnnie as though he could hear her every word, as she knelt by his grave.

" Oh my darling Johnnie, I always imagined you and me to be living here at Bushel Farm 'till we became old and grey haired. I thought we'd be surrounded by our grandchildren, enjoying every day of our lives together...I guess life doesn't ever go to plan...I have missed you so, my darling...you have our dear little Alfie with you now, and I have our beautiful daughter, Hope. She has your hair, Johnnie. I'm going to wed again....he's such a good man, but no-one will ever take your place in my heart my beloved." With tears streaming down her face, Rose had said her piece, and left the graveyard to the comfort of Dan's arms.

"Everything is so different here," Rose had stressed, "I feel as though I'm in a completely different place from what used to be my home, which I suppose is a good thing in a way. If anything, it will make moving on a lot easier." Rose kissed Dan's cheek as they rode back towards Oxford, "I love you Dan, and I can't wait to become Mrs Heyford, next month."

CHAPTER TWENTY-SEVEN

Shortly after Wilkins had scurried out of
Westmead Abbey, Sir Hugh Whitehead had
made a full recovery from his minor heart attack,
making him even more determined to put his
plan into action, now realising how precious life
was, and knowing how easy it was for death to
suddenly strike, with little or no warning. He
was interested in viewing the plot of land in
Northamptonshire even more so since the land
agent had informed him that the adjoining farm
was also up for sale. If he could put a decent
offer in for both, it would make a sizeable plot to
convert into a horse farm.

Johnnie, who had now temporarily taken over
Wilkins' duties in caring for the horses and
driving Sir Hugh around in his carriage, had not
been prepared for the shock that awaited him
when arriving at Bushel Farm. Soon after
reaching Northamptonshire, the roads became
more and more familiar, all the blurry clouds
which had concealed Johnnie's roots were
suddenly swept clear from his mind and he
knew exactly where he was and that he had
finally arrived home. Home, however, was
nothing like how he had left it, and the terrible
nightmare that had taken place at Bushel Farm
was soon told to him by the land agent who
recalled the tragedy with great enthusiasm,

unaware that the family he spoke of, who had all
perished in the great fire at Bushel Farm, were
Johnnie's kith and kin. Even Sir Hugh was
shocked as he watched Johnnie crumble in front
of his eyes, thinking that his young friend had
allowed this tragic story to get the better of his
emotions as he embarrassingly told him to pull
himself together. All thoughts and business
discussions we're put on hold when Sir Hugh
and the land agent came to know of the reasons
behind Johnnie's emotional breakdown. The
land agent now realising that Johnnie Harper
was most likely to be the rightful owner of the
land, though suspicious of him since he'd
already read his name on the gravestone in the
Harper family graveyard. It didn't take long for
Johnnie to put two and two together and realise
how his half brother had betrayed him in such a
despicable way. Johnnie knew that it was Master
Monty who had been buried under his name,
but the realisation that Rose had obviously
believed she was a widow for all those months
before the fire, and that now it was too late, was
too heavy a burden for Johnnie to comprehend.
He was devastated, and Sir Hugh, knowing all
too well the pain and stress of bereavement, took
it upon himself to gently care for his dear friend.
He also took it on board to buy Bushel Farm; not
having the patience to wait for such legalities to
be sorted out to prove that Johnnie Harper was
the rightful owner and was who he said he was,

regardless of his name being on a headstone in the family graveyard. It was a mere drop in Sir Hugh's financial ocean, and he also decided to keep silent about the fact that he'd made the purchase and happily handed the deeds over to Johnnie, congratulating him on gaining his home once again.

It was a few months later when Sir Hugh made an announcement to Johnnie, who had just finished his now daily activity of teaching Maisie how to play chess,

" You do realise Harper that it's not learning the movements of pawns and knights that young Maisie is interested in?" he teased. "How many times have I told you, the girl's madly in love with you, man, and you could do a lot worse you know...pretty little thing."

Johnnie sat setting up the chess board, still not convinced that what Sir Hugh insisted on had any truth in it,

"It's rather too soon for me to be thinking about romance, I've only recently discovered that I've lost my wife and son."

"All the more reason to put it behind you and start afresh. Now, Harper; changing the subject, I've got a bit of news to tell you, *and* another proposition. Perhaps some coffee might not go amiss, there's a lot to discuss."

Sir Hugh grabbed hold of the bell cord, leaving Johnnie silently praying that Sir Hugh hadn't found himself in any more sticky situations.

"Right now," Sir Hugh said commandingly as he watched while Maisie poured the coffee, "I have purchased a small dwelling on a pretty decent large plot of farm land."

Maisie left the room, allowing Sir Hugh to speak freely.

"Coincidentally, it's the farm next to your very own *Bushel Farm*."

Johnnie looked surprised, and a little shocked, "Surely you can't mean the *Bird's* place?"

"That's the one," confirmed Sir Hugh, smiling triumphantly.

"Well, I never in my wildest dreams expected them to sell up and leave," stated Johnnie.

"Apparently, Harper, they recently became parents for the first time, and have plans for their son to gain all the benefits of an education in Oxford, and they wanted something on a smaller scale; the agent informed me that they've found an ideal small holding in Kidlington."

"Percy and Jayne Bird will make excellent parents, they've waited so long. I think most of the local folk, had given them up to be forever childless. That's wonderful news."

Sir Hugh quickly continued in order to prevent Johnnie's mind from wandering back into the past.

"Now Harper, please don't think me presumptuous, but with your finances being somewhat on the dry side, I would like to invest in your land and my new acquired property, to transform the whole place into my former idea of a horse farm. That burnt out shell needs to be demolished, and I've taken the liberty of having the plans drawn up for a state of the art home to be constructed in its place, for you and your future wife and family. Now, where the former Bird's farmhouse and outbuildings stand, well, they will be demolished too and in its place, row upon row of the finest stables will be constructed, to eventually house the finest countries horses. There will of course have to be a few small but modern cottages built, to accommodate your employees and their families." An extremely excited Sir Hugh stopped briefly to take a gulp of his coffee, " You certainly *have* been making plans, whilst I've been moping around," declared Johnnie, still trying to imagine the finished project.

"Good Heavens, man, you've had a terrible shock and have been in mourning, I won't hear another harsh word said about you. Now hear me out, Harper, it's time to talk business. You of course will own fifty percent of the establishment, and live and manage the place, hopefully with that pretty Maisie on your arm. While I'm alive, all profits will be split fifty, fifty, but of course you will take an extra cut from my fifty percent to pay the staff and to subsidize your own salary. Don't worry yourself too much about these figures, Harper, the finances will sort themselves out once we're up and running. What do you think then, Harper?"

Johnnie stalled for a while, mulling over Sir Hugh's extensive plans and ideas, he seemed to have thought of almost everything,

" So, will you be staying here at Westmead Abbey?"

" Of course, this *is* after all my home, where I've resided for most of my life."

"Forgive me, Sir Hugh, that was a very silly question," said Johnnie, his embarrassment clearly visible.

"Ahh, what you really meant and were thinking, was if I am to live in this huge place, virtually on my own, and that only proves to me what a considerate and caring friend you have become Harper. But, my dear good man, worry not, because yours truly is to be married, and my dear wife to be will employ new and trustworthy staff for Westmead Abbey."

"*Married!*" voiced Johnnie, rather louder than he'd intended.

Sir Hugh broke into a hearty fit of laughter,

" If I were an artist, Harper, I'd capture that exasperated expression on your face and have your portrait hanging out there with the rest of the collection, it would certainly cheer me up on a gloomy day. I'm going to marry Harriet."

Johnnie's face expression failed to change,

"*Harriet!* What, you mean Maisie's ma?"

"The very same, we became quite close when

she cared for me after my heart attack you know... Dash it Harper, I beg of you to change your facial expression, I know she's twenty or so years my junior, but she's more than happy to marry me. Call me a silly old fool if you like, but my life is empty, I have no family, and even if her feelings for me are slightly less than mine are for her, I think that I deserve a little happiness and joy before this old ticker completely packs up; I've already had one scare."

"I'm sorry Sir Hugh, it's just that you *have* certainly succeeded in shocking me on this day, and given me a lot to think about. I'm sincerely happy for you *and* Harriet. I'm sure you'll both be very happy, marriage is indeed a blessed union." Telling himself to rid his face of the look of shock; however sweet and wholesome Harriet was, Johnnie couldn't help thinking that she had ulterior motives in marrying such a wealthy and much older man who already suffered from a frail heart, but who was he to protest.

"There are those who might call marriage a *'golden cage'*," joked Sir Hugh. "Now Harper, what's your opinion of my little venture?"

"Well, I'd hardly call it *little*, but I'm already extremely excited by it. Living on Bushel Farm's land will be a comfort to me and, in a way, keep me close in spirit to my beloved family."

CHAPTER TWENTY-EIGHT

"I knew I'd find you here, Alfie Bird, you were supposed to meet me ten minutes ago, you know,"

Alfie looked up from the leather bound book in his hands, quickly glancing at the wall clock, before giving all his attention to Hope Heyford. She was right, of course, it was now ten minutes past three, and her soulful brown eyes bore into him for an explanation and an apology.

"Oh, Hope, I'm really sorry, but you know how easy it is to lose track of time when you have a good book under your nose."

" Maybe I'm not that important to you then," replied Hope in a sulky tone.

" Don't be silly, you know how much I love you. Why, I spend every second of the day thinking about you; if we were both older, I'd whisk you away and marry you."

Blushing from Alfie's words, Hope took a random book from off the shelf, hiding behind its pages. It had been three days after Blackwell's book shop opened on New Year's Day of 1879 in Broad Street, when Alfie and Hope had met; Alfie had clumsily collided into Hope, causing her bag of roasted chestnuts to spill out across the pavement. That had been six months ago. He had been in a mad dash to make his first visit to the most talked about book shop in Oxford. As they both watched as the chestnuts rolled across the pavement where an old man was shovelling the fresh horse dung from off the busy thoroughfare, Alfie immediately put his hand into his pocket and paid for another bag.

" Please accept my apologies, I'm truly sorry." Hope thanked him and as their eyes met, a strong bond was instantly born, surprising them both.

"Alfie Bird, what in the world can you possibly find so interesting in looking at drawings of horses without their beautiful skins, they are positively horrifying."

"And to think that I've been stood, waiting like a lemon, and positively cooking beneath the afternoon sun."

Alfie's keen interest in anything equestrian kept him returning to study '*The anatomy of the horse*' by George Stubbs, from the shelves of the book shop; not being able to afford the purchase of a copy for himself, it was one of the items which was on his '*to buy list*' when he became twenty one and would receive his trust fund. His parents had casually told him about the healthy sum of money that he would receive on his coming of age, they were quite mysterious about the relative who had left it to him though, telling him that all would be explained when the time arrived.

"Come on; let's go to the tea room down by

the river, it will be cooler down there *and* there's less chance of us being seen together by anyone." Their clandestine liaisons had continued throughout the year, both of them knowing that if either set of parents should get wind of this blossoming young romance, they would surely put an end to it. The simple fact that Hope's beau was called Alfie would in itself cause her ma into a state of distress. There had been a few occasions where someone bearing that name had crossed the family's path, only to send her reminiscing about the day when Alfie was lost forever to her. Hope knew that it had been on the day she was born, and had always felt that her untimely arrival had contributed to the events which led up to her brother's death, leaving her wondering if subconsciously her ma blamed her in some way.

They sat at one of the outside tables beneath the dangling branches of a nearby weeping willow tree. A few brightly coloured dragonflies darted quickly, close to the river's surface, and a solitary swan graced the stretch of water as she glided effortlessly beneath the willow's dangling fringe. Alfie ordered two glasses of lemonade and a plate of mixed sandwiches from the waiter, all the while keeping his continuous gaze on Hope, thinking how stunning she looked today. She was always dressed so stylishly, everything matching in the softest shades. Her pale green dress with its pink lace trimmings reminded

Alfie of a summer meadow in full bloom; the wide darker green belt emphasized her tiny waist; she was blessed with a perfect figure. Becoming aware of Alfie's fixed stare, Hope suddenly felt a wave of shyness and could feel her cheeks blushing. Alfie offered her a sandwich, realising that he should divert his eyes.

" Oh Alfie, I wish I didn't have to move to the country; days like this will become impossible, you know."

"We'll find a way my sweet Hope, we might not see as much of each other, but a few miles isn't going to come between us. We shall make some kind of arrangement, maybe meeting on the first or last Sunday of every month, even if it's only for an hour."

" We can't even write to each other for risk of our parents finding out, and you'll be starting at St John's College soon, so you won't have a minute to waste on a foolish young girl like me." Hope sat pout lipped, sulking.

" I've just had a brilliant idea," exclaimed Alfie," We *could* correspond, we'll just give ourselves a couple of alias names, you could sign your letters as Harold, and I'll sign mine as Amy!" Everyone sitting at the surrounding tables focussed their attention to Alfie and Hope, as Hope burst out in to a fit of laughter.

"Come on; let's take a stroll along the river, before we're forced to leave for disturbing the peace."

It was a few weeks later that the Heyford family moved from the small corner shop, that held so many mixed memories for Rose. Dan waited outside with a solemn faced Hope and an over excited Henry and Primrose upon the large heavily loaded wagon, its two strong Shire horses waiting patiently to be on their way. Inside the small dwelling, Rose went from room to room, soaking up the nostalgia that every nook and cranny of the place brought about. Primrose Atkins' spirit seemed to be talking to her from every corner; she had become like a mother to Rose and a grandma to her children, all except for her namesake, who hadn't been born until two years after Primrose had peacefully passed away in her sleep at the age of ninety nine. She closed her tear filled eyes as she stood in the empty house, the clear image in her mind of little Alfie running around, his golden curls like springs bouncing as his Nanna chased him; he had been such a happy child, and Rose would carry his memory with her until she drew her last breath.

"Hope, go inside and fetch your Ma, and give this to her." Dan had pulled a large cotton handkerchief from his pocket, and Hope felt a sudden gush of sadness, knowing what her dear ma must be going through. She scolded herself for behaving so selfishly; her poor ma had suffered a lot, and lost so many of her family members, while she was selfishly making such a fuss and behaving childishly, just because she couldn't bear the thought of being so far away from her Alfie.

She found her ma as expected, her face red, flustered and soaked from her streaming tears. Hope put her arms around her and they held each other tightly, both now sobbing, but at the same time strengthening their close bond. It was at that moment when Hope decided that once they were settled in their new home, and her ma was away from the constant reminders of the son she had lost, it would be time to confess about her feelings for *her* Alfie. How she wished that he didn't carry the same name as her late brother.

The new Heyford home was a modest small holding, close to Dan's family farm, and just inside the borders of Northamptonshire. Mr and Mrs Heyford were approaching their mid sixties and since their two daughters had both married and now lived far away, one in the Highlands of Scotland, and the other in India where her husband was stationed with his regiment, they weren't happy with Dan and his family living away in Oxford and desperate to see more of their grandchildren too. Dan couldn't wait to be back working on the land again, with Rose also welcoming the prospect of returning to the countryside, even though, over the years, she had adapted well to living and working in the city. It was Hope who troubled her most. Rose knew how unfamiliar the countryside was to her, and how much she detested its remoteness; she was a city girl, who barely managed a week away at her grandparent's farm during the harvest season, always elated when the time to leave approached. Henry couldn't conceal his excitement and spent most of the long journey talking about how he was going to be in charge of the ducks and chickens on the farm, and how he couldn't wait to help his pa tending to the livestock; Primrose caught her brothers infectious excitement and was soon joining in announcing how Ma was going to teach her how to milk the cows and allow her help make cheese and butter in the dairy. Hope found herself wanting to leap out of the loaded wagon and run back to Oxford, she'd already had enough of mile upon mile of green fields, trees and livestock and missed the beauty which she loved so much in Oxford's familiar architecture. She missed Alfie, and wondered when they might see each other again, he had told her that his parents often travelled to Northamptonshire to visit friends, and that he would accompany them on their next visit, but even that prospect couldn't change Hope's mood on this day, she wanted her old life back.

"I'd almost forgotten how peaceful the

countryside is," announced Rose, "nothing but the melodious sound of bird song!"

"I prefer the screeching of the steam engines arriving at Oxford Railway station, and the constant buzz of city folk's chatter; it's far too quiet here," moaned Hope from the back of the wagon. "What's the point in dressing up when there's nobody to take any notice of you; I think I will spend every day in my nightgown, and not even bother to put the brush through my hair."

Primrose began to giggle,

"You're so funny, Hope, you *have* to get dressed in the morning, else people might think that you are sick! Won't they Ma?"

"Ooh, Dan, can we pull up here for a minute," requested Rose suddenly as they neared a small lonely cottage. Everyone, including Hope was intrigued as to why Rose wanted to stop by this sad, run down looking dwelling.

" Do you remember me telling you about old Evie Bancroft?"

Dan nodded his head slowly, a vague look on his face,

"From what I recall, she wasn't one of your favourite acquaintances."

"I know, but that was fourteen years ago when I was young and naive, anyway, she might not even be here."

Dan pulled up reluctantly, wishing that his wife would leave the past alone, and dreading the fact, that nothing but sad memories would be dug up by this visit. He prayed that there was nobody living there anymore, the place did look extremely neglected.

"Can I come too Ma?" shouted Primrose from the wagon.

" Me too, Ma!" added Henry.

"*No!*" ordered Dan crossly, "just stay where you are, your ma will be back soon."

"Awe," they complained in unison.

Rose stood at the cottage door, waiting. She knocked again, harder, just in case Mrs Bancroft had become deaf over the years. The neat garden was overrun with weeds, and the defined borders no longer existed. Rose remembered how this once pretty garden had impressed her all those years ago. There was no sign of anyone as she peered through the tiny window next to the door, so she decided to leave.

As she turned around to head back down the overgrown garden path, she was suddenly aware of a squeaking sound as Evie Bancroft slowly opened the door.

"Is that you, Rose?"

Shocked that Mrs Bancroft had remembered her after all the years, Rose hurried back up the garden path.

"Mrs Bancroft, how are you?"

"Much the same as when you last saw me, just a bit closer to the grave."

"You look well, Mrs Bancroft," Rose lied. Evie Bancroft was half the woman she used to be, thin and bedraggled, and sounding frail.

"I always knew you'd come back to visit me one day. I prayed for this day Rose. I did you a great injustice in not believing you."

"Oh, Mrs Bancroft, that's all water under the bridge now."

Squinting her eyes as she stared towards the huge wagon load on the road, Evie Bancroft, beckoned to Dan and the children to join her and Rose.

"Bring your family in Rose, I'd love to meet them, and have a proper look at young Alfie."

" Mrs Bancroft, Alfie was lost to us fourteen years since."

The look of shock that Rose was expecting to see on Evie Bancroft's face was more of a confused expression, as she just stared into Rose's eyes, shaking her head gently from side to side.

CHAPTER TWENTY-NINE

Dan hadn't wanted to take time out and stop at Evie Bancroft's place, he was eager to reach their new home and try and administer as much order there before the end of what he knew would be an exhausting day, but as usual, he could never refuse Rose anything, his love for her, like her beauty, only grew stronger with every passing year; at thirty four, her innocent girlish traits had long disappeared, leaving a strong and independent woman who's circumstances and life lessons had moulded her; she had become like a warrior, never giving up, and making the best of whatever life threw at her.

After introducing Mrs Bancroft to her family, Rose insisted that she should make the tea, while Mrs Bancroft sat and chatted to Dan. The state of the kitchen reflected on poor Evie Bancroft's health and deteriorating years, and Rose decided that she would make riding out to see this woman at least once a week, her priority.

"Dan, how far away is our farm from Mrs Bancroft's home?" She casually asked as she carried the laden tray into the overcrowded parlour.

"About half an hour's ride away I'd say," replied Dan, already reading his wife's thoughts.

"There, you see Mrs Bancroft, we are practically neighbours, and I can visit you often."

Evie's gummy smile, spoke for itself,
"Do you get any visitors, Mrs Bancroft?" pried
Rose, as she poured the tea.
" The vicar and his snooty wife call in every
Sunday after church, they bring me a few
donated groceries, and check that I haven't
passed away in the seven days since they last
checked."
Rose was reminded of when she had first
arrived in Oxford and how, as Mrs Atkins had
put it, that she was just waiting for The Good
Lord to take her. Mrs Atkins had lived another
eight years and they had become full and mostly
happy ones.
Rose poured the tea for the grownups; there was
nothing for the children and barely enough milk
for the three cups of tea. Hope was indignant
that she was being treated like her nine and four
years old siblings; when *were* her
parents going to view her as a woman, she
wondered, crossly.
There was little conversation, and Rose had to
issue warning glares to both Henry and
Primrose as they sat giggling at the way in
which Mrs Bancroft slurped her tea noisily, with
some of it trickling down her bare forearms and
dripping on to her skirt.
Dan as always could read Rose's thoughts, and
came to her rescue,
"Why don't we leave your ma and Mrs Bancroft
to catch up on their news for a while; we could

do a spot of gardening for Mrs Bancroft."

"Can we Pa?" exclaimed Primrose excitedly, already bored from having to remain still and quiet in the squashed parlour. Hope didn't share her brother and sister's enthusiasm, and announced that she couldn't possibly risk ruining her favourite dress, whereupon Dan instructed her to fetch some water from Mrs Bancroft's well for the thirsty horses.

"Your eldest don't look none too happy about moving; there must be a loved one who she's left behind."

"No, Mrs Bancroft, she far too young to be romantically involved, she simply prefers the city to the countryside."

Mrs Bancroft looked dubious.

" You know, Rose, I told that brother in law of yours that you'd fled to Oxford, hoping to throw him off your trail, and you obviously did the same to me by telling me you was heading to London. I realised after you left that he was a bad un, and then, one day, I was sat down soaking up the summer sun, when I heard the screaming of a little un, long before I caught sight of him. It made me shudder when that terrible man rode past like the devil, with young Alfie in his clutches. I recognized them both, I did."

"I always had the feeling that you didn't believe my story, Mrs Bancroft. I was terrified of Sebastian Harper, he was an evil being."

"Yes, I realised that when he called back, after you'd left."

"I hope he didn't hurt you, Mrs Bancroft," stressed Rose, full of concern.

"No, I've always been able to take care of me self, but he did put the wind up me."

"Well, Thank God, he is no longer around to trouble anybody anymore." Rose wiped her tears, it was impossible for her to mention Seb, without remembering Alfie, and filling her with gloom, as she thought of how his last living days were spent. She was instantly overcome with guilt, that she'd let him down as his mother, even though it was completely out of her hands.

"I've often seen that young lad of yours; going past with that kind couple...relatives of yours are they?"

"I think that must have been somebody else, Mrs Bancroft, like I said, my Alfie lost his life at the same time as Seb."

"Your Alfie ain't dead, I've seen him, and his hair is the colour of golden corn, just the same as yours."

Rose couldn't take anymore, Mrs Bancroft's memory was obviously playing tricks with her, and to carry on listening to her insisting that Alfie was still alive, was tearing at Rose's heart; she began to wish that she'd never asked Dan to stop. Leaving Mrs Bancroft with the promise that she would return just as soon as she had settled in her new home, she gave her a hamper of food supplies from off the wagon and bid her farewell.

Dan, Henry and Primrose had done an efficient job in clearing the pathway from its heavy over growth. Linking her arm through Dan's, Rose reached up to kiss his cheek, she knew how he wanted to get unpacked before dusk and that he was planning a quick visit to his parents before nightfall, but he didn't show any resentment towards her for delaying them, he was truly a treasure.

"I love you Dan and I can't wait to start our new adventure."

Dan couldn't resist Rose's soft lips, and returned the kiss, a surge of love forcing his heart to ache. The half hour ride to reach the Heyford's new home was spent with everyone suggesting a name for the place, and after a multitude of suggestions some of which had them all laughing out loud, especially Primrose's suggestions, they came to a unanimous decision of *'Golden Meadows Farm.'*

As exhausted as she felt after such a long and eventful day, as Rose lay in the strange new bedroom listening to Dan's light snores, sleep was far away from her. As she went over and over in her mind what Mrs Bancroft had said, about her sightings of Alfie, she found herself in a bubble of optimism, wondering if they were just the words of a perhaps slightly senile old woman who had let her imagination take over reality or there was, in fact a thread of truth in what she had told her. The fact that there had never been any findings of little Alfie's remains, seemed to suddenly rekindle her hope. She hadn't told Dan about Mrs Bancroft's revelation, not wanting to spoil the memory of the day they moved into their farm by dragging up the heart breaking past.

She would wait a week or two, if her patience would allow, and take a ride out to Mrs Bancroft's place.

Silently leaving the bed, Rose decided she'd make a start on cleaning and arranging the kitchen in the hope that she might divert her mind's thoughts and find sleep after a little more exertion. Lighting the oil lamp, she cautiously made her way down the unfamiliar steep stairs. The kitchen reminded her of Bushel Farm's kitchen, and was a far cry from the squashed scullery in Oxford. Rose couldn't wait to transform it into a warm and inviting room that would become the hub of her family, where tasty meals would be shared around the large kitchen table, and social times would leave lasting memories with her children, once they'd grown up. Thinking of her children suddenly reminded her that she'd not seen her monthly for a while; a new home and a new baby, how perfect, she thought as she placed her hand upon her flat belly.

Nora and Beth Baker, along with Maisie stood surrounding a distraught Harriet Whitehead, supporting her, as she struggled to compose herself by the open grave. The mourners gathered like a black storm cloud on this gloomy day in Bicester, where the sun remained in hiding as Sir Hugh Whitehead made his final journey. He had suffered a massive heart attack which had quickly snatched away his soul. Harriet had been at his side, on this day; a day that she knew *would* eventually happen. Her ten years of marriage had been blissfully happy ones, and she was confident that her beloved Hugh, who she'd found herself loving more than she could ever have expected, had lived his last decade in married contentment.

Johnnie Harper had been devastated when he'd received news from Nora telling him that Lester had not survived a bout of winter influenza; that was two years ago now and when Nora had to give up the lease on the farm, she welcomed Johnnie's intervention in finding her and Beth a position at Westmead Abbey; her as cook, and Beth partaking in a bit of everything. Sir Hugh had thrown all protocol to the wind shortly after marrying Harriet. They lived in a far more relaxed and informal way, taking each day as it came, and doing what pleased them, not what society dictated. Susie Baker had married a local farmer's son the year before her father's death, and they now ran their own farm; she had given birth to a boy, recently, naming him Lester, after her late pa. Beth was still searching for one of the characters in the copious books that she continued to plough through, not taking any notice of her mother's warnings over the years and when the trail of suitors had given up on her, at the age of twenty six, Nora declared that she was now a certified spinster and that she only had herself to blame. Beth, however had different ideas and was convinced that one day in the not too distant future, her dashing true love would cross her path.

Johnnie, surreptitiously wiped away a tear, as he remembered the good times that he'd spent in Sir Hugh's company, and that first ever day that they'd met; he had a lot to thank Sir Hugh for, and he would never forget his kindness for as long as he lived. He always laughed to himself when he remembered Sir Hugh's tireless efforts to unite him and Maisie in marriage. Although Johnnie had found it flattering that Maisie had fallen for him, he knew that it wouldn't be long lasting, and sure enough, Maisie *had* met a young man, closer to her age, and they went on to marry, and now lived in Oxford.

Westmead Abbey had a strange feeling about it with the absence of Sir Hugh, there were very few guests attending the wake, but as Johnnie's gaze passed over the handful of mourners he realised that they were all true and genuine people, reflecting on the careful way that Sir Hugh and Harriet had spent their short married life. After all the trouble with Wilkins, they had both been overly cautious as to who they entertained, and who they employed. Apart from old Mr Brown, who took care of the only two horses now at Westmead Abbey and drove the carriage, it was just Harriet, Nora and Beth who lived at Westmead Abbey and over the years Harriet and Nora had become very close; there was nothing visible in their friendship that resembled their status of Mistress of the house and employee. After all, Harriet would often say, Nora had just taken her old post, when she had been fortunate in becoming the wife to the master of the house. They had lived more like one happy family.

"How are you Johnnie?" Nora asked, "Such a sad occasion to meet up again."

"Yes, life does have a habit of dispensing doses of sorrow to make us all remember the frailty of the human existence," replied Johnnie somberly.

"That's quite true; you too have suffered your share of misery"

"And you also, dear Nora."

They were soon joined by Harriet, she looked every bit the grieving widow in her finely cut black silk taffeta gown; Sir Hugh would have been proud of her, she had always been a far too elegant cook, but during her marriage to Sir Hugh, she had transformed into a woman, fit to be called the Lady of Westmead Abbey, even though she had strongly discouraged having any title being attached to her.

"Such a sad day, Johnnie," she said with the strain of the occasion clear in her voice, " Dear Hugh was so fond of you, and always stressed how it was you that had dug him out of the deep hole he was in."

"Ah, well, dear Harriet, it was a joint effort I think, don't you?"

"What will you do now," concerned Johnnie, "you *could* all move in to Lady Ophelia's Stables, there's plenty of room there."

"You are, as always, kindness itself, Johnnie, but hasn't Nora told you of our plans?"

"I thought it was your place to tell Johnnie," Nora intervened.

"Oh there's no difference between you and I, Nora. How many times have I told you that you are more like a sister to me?"

Nora blushed, as she took a small backward step, to allow Harriet to disclose the brilliant idea that she'd come up with in the small hours of the morning.

"Well Johnnie, I know it's not really the appropriate occasion to discuss my future plans, but you and I both know that dear Hugh would have been all for it. I'm going to have the west side of Westmead Abbey turned into a hotel and continue to live in the east side. What do you think?"

Surprised at Harriet's plans, Johnnie wondered if perhaps, she was experiencing financial difficulties.

"It sounds like a splendid idea, Harriet, but if you are in financial trouble....."

Harriet was quick to interrupt,

"No, no my dear Johnnie, not at all, Sir Hugh left me very well off, God Bless him; no, I just don't want to spend the rest of my days, becoming lazy and gaining weight. I still have a lot of energy left, and with Nora here, as my right hand woman, not to mention dear Beth, I think we can make a great success of managing a hotel between us and I will obviously employ staff, which is where you could help Johnnie; I *do* trust your judgment, so if you know of any suitable candidates, I'd really appreciate it if you would send them towards the direction of Bicester."

"Well, I am impressed, and I can tell that you've thought this through very carefully."

Harriet and Nora exchanged a slight smile, pleased at how their impetuous idea sounded so well planned and convincing.

"*Wilkins*, get your backside off that crate and make yourself useful! How many times do I have to tell you, you're not indispensible you know and if you want to continue sleeping out the back, you've gotta prove yourself worthy and stop being so bloody lazy? The place is looking a mess; you ain't doing yer job." Gilbert Forester plunged the hot metal into the trough of murky water, the sizzling sound even after thirty five years of being a blacksmith never failed to thrill him. Wilkins leaned heavily against the wall, feeling like a school boy being scolded by his teacher. Life since leaving Westmead Abbey had slowly taken a downwards path and he was left with little choice other than to be at the mercy of the bullying ways of Gilbert Forester, who was a well respected pillar of the small town. Without a reference, nobody from Northamptonshire to London would employ Wilkins and by the time that he'd finished his fruitless search for employment, he was left in crippling circumstances. With no money and with his health deteriorating, he eventually returned to Bicester where Gilbert took full advantage of him, offering him a bed, which was no more than a couple of hay bales, in the back of his yard, in return for being what was tantamount to a slave at his beck and call all day. Wilkins took the brush to the floor and hung up the tools which Gilbert had been hand crafting all day, ready to be sold. The forge was a blessing in the winter months, but in the heat of the summer, Wilkins felt as though his very skin was melting. The only consolation for Wilkins was that he was only a stone's throw away from his beloved Westmead Abbey to which his heart and his beautiful memories of Lady Ophelia belonged. There had been many occasions when he had strolled up to the Abbey and sneaked in through one of the few gaps in its perimeter which only he knew of, having spent so many years roaming the extensive grounds. His intentions were to hunt out Johnnie Harper, who had proved to be the bane in his life from the very first time that he'd set foot over the threshold to the Abbey and become Sir Hugh's sly and devious companion. It didn't taken Wilkins long to realise that they had all contrived to get rid of him, and he wouldn't be surprised if Sir Hugh had even faked the heart attack that had made him flee from Westmead Abbey in such a hurry. After hearing the local gossip that Sir Hugh was to marry his cook, he felt it only right to honour Lady Ophelia's good name and work on a plan to disrupt the newlyweds, and somehow get rid of that bloody cripple, Johnnie Harper. Lady Ophelia must be turning in her grave and *he* was the only person who could perhaps ensure that justice was done. He was the only man in the world who had truly loved and cared for her and shared the same passion for horses as she did. The fact that Sir Hugh had so cruelly slaughtered every single one of the beautiful creatures surely proved the complete disrespect he had for his late wife.

"I must have needed my bloody head examined the day I agreed to let you live under my roof, and now I suppose I'm stuck with you 'till your last day, you're a downright lazy specimen, Wilkins!" Gilbert threw down his chisel sending it crashing onto the anvil and marched off to the ale house, leaving Wilkins behind, choking on a cloud of coal dust. The shock of seeing the crimson blood fly out from his mouth, only confirmed that the consumption which he'd been diagnosed with three months ago had now developed into the final stages. He felt his legs weaken beneath him; this sign seemed so final; how long would he have left, he thought to himself, finding his hands shaking with the shock; was it months or days? Looking around the dingy forge, he couldn't believe that he would end his days in such a depressing place, after spending most of his days in the luxury of Westmead Abbey, where his own room had been nearly equal to that of Sir Hugh's own private quarters and where he had the free run of the extensive grounds and of course the well stocked stables. In his early days he would often walk the grounds, pretending that he was Lord of the manor and that Lady Ophelia was his doting wife. He *would* return to Westmead Abbey, he assured himself, if only to get even with that bloody menacing cripple Johnnie Harper. He also decided that he would make Westmead Abbey his dying place, even if it had to be out on the grounds in freezing weather, should his life last for another season. Ignoring the surrounding mess, Wilkins abandoned his broom and went out to the back to rest his weary body.

CHAPTER THIRTY

With the arrival of autumn, Golden Meadows Farm had finally been put in order and had almost become a working farm. Primrose was elated with the pair of ducks that had been put in her care, and who were now in great danger of being overfed. Henry was now quite the young man, assisting his Pa, when he wasn't at school, and proud to be doing proper *'man's work'* as he phrased it, and not being ordered about by his older sister behind the shop's counter. With Hope's help, Rose had worked from the downstairs up, to arrange every room to her liking; there were four bedrooms upstairs, albeit three rather small ones, but it suited the family well. The second largest bedroom was shared by Hope and Primrose. Primrose wouldn't even entertain the prospect of having a bedroom all to herself; she was a child with such an imagination, and needed the security of having someone else near to her during the shadowy nights.

Dan had laboured tirelessly since the day they had moved in. The farm had been neglected over the years and most of the outbuildings and the barn required some extensive repairs before Dan could securely house the livestock which he was yet to purchase. He was also busy dividing the land into smaller and more manageable fields, with two of them allocated for growing their own crops. His excited enthusiasm kept him occupied during every daylight hour, making Rose feel a little guilty that she'd kept him cooped up in Oxford as a shopkeeper for so many years, and wishing that they'd made this move immediately after the passing away of Mrs Atkins; farming was in Dan's blood, and it might have been a lot easier on Hope too, if they'd left the city before she'd become so attached to that way of living. Rose was now sure that she was with child again and whilst unpacking one of the last crates she came upon a silver rattle which had belonged to Mrs Atkins and been used by her son and much later by Henry and Primrose when they were babies. She wrapped the rattle in a handkerchief and secured it with a ribbon, all the while a contented smile on her face. Everything would be just perfect, she thought, if only Hope showed some signs of accepting their new life. Rose knew how she was pining for Oxford, even the recent local harvest dance , which would have been an ideal opportunity for her to meet girls her own age, had not enticed her to put on her best gown and attend, instead she insisted that she fancied spending the evening at home, baking. The only occasion that a spark of genuine happiness dawned upon her was when she'd received a letter in the post from her friend in Oxford, and even though Rose had never heard mention of this girl, Amy, until very

283

recently, its effect on Hope seemed to change the atmosphere at home to the better, leaving Rose slightly reluctant to pry, for risk of sending Hope into one of her unpleasant moods again. The letter was read so many times, that Hope almost knew every word by heart; in Alfie's brief and carefully compiled communication, after the initial sentiments, typical of those written between two close girl friends, Alfie went on to inform Hope that his parents would be travelling to Northamptonshire on the Sunday after next, to visit old friends, and that he would be delighted if she could meet him at the first cross roads on the Oxford to Northamptonshire border. Alfie knew that this was close enough for Hope to reach by foot in twenty minutes or so, and far enough away from her new home, to hopefully not be recognized by anyone from both families.

Two weeks had passed until Rose, made the half hour journey to visit Evie Bancroft again. Having bought the unsold stock from Oxford with her, she took a small basket of groceries as a gift, greatly pleasing Evie, who declared that the only time she had seen tins of biscuits was at Christmas time.

Evie's house was in need of a thorough clean, and Rose was surprised when Mrs Bancroft said to her,

" you need to take it easy, young Rose, in your condition."

There was no denying the fact, as Rose looked shocked at Mrs Bancroft.

" How on earth can you tell? Why, I'm not even showing yet. I haven't even told a soul, not even Dan!"

"You have a certain look about you, Rose, and remember, I've been around a long time on God's Blessed earth to detect a fruitful woman when I see one, especially one that I know and love."

Rose was touched, but still insisted that Evie indulged in the last of the autumn sun while she quickly took a bucket of water and a mop to the small, dusty cottage, before they sat down for a chat, with Rose determined to pick Mrs Bancroft's brain as to what had compelled her to say what she had about Alfie.

Forty minutes later, and just as the black clouds came rolling across the horizon, they were back inside the spotless cottage,

"That was a very kind and neighbourly gesture, young Rose, but I hope it hasn't tired you too much. I thank you from the bottom of me heart,"

"It was nothing, Mrs Bancroft, the least I could do," replied Rose as she poured the tea and placed a warm buttered scone on a plate for a satisfied looking Evie.

"How's your eldest girl? Has she settled down now?" asked Evie, with the scone poised to her lips.

"Hope is yearning for Oxford and her old life,

Mrs Bancroft; she wears such a miserable face, day in and day out, and it's affecting the whole family."

"More like she's left her heart behind, with some young man," insisted Evie, "anything in life is easy to adjust to when you are a young lass, except for affairs of the heart."

"Well if that's the case," said Rose annoyingly, "she'll just have to get over it; she's *far* too young."

"Were you too young when your heart melted for that first love...Johnnie, wasn't that his name?"

"It was different back then, and besides I had no parents."

"Don't make no difference, whatever the circumstances; when the heart is infected with love, there ain't no cure for it."

Rose took a bite into her scone, angry that the whole conversation so far had been centred on Hope, who in her opinion was behaving like a spoilt child. No words were spoken for a while as they ate scones and drank tea.

" These are tasty scones, Rose, did *you* bake them?"

"I did," confirmed Rose, proudly.

"Nice an' buttery."

"Did you happen to see that young lad, who you said looks like my little Alfie, recently?" Rose casually asked.

"Can't say that I have, must be a good few

months since he's passed by, but mark my words, Rose, the next time I catches so much as a glimpse of him, I'm gonna flag him down and send him to visit you, then you'll see that I'm not the stupid old biddy that you take me for. You needs to get things sorted out girl, cos as sure as I am, that me name is Evie Bancroft, I know that your Alfie is alive and well."

The more Rose heard Mrs Bancroft talk, the more she began to believe her; she felt nervous all of a sudden, as she wondered what it would be like coming face to face with her first born after all these years. Would he have any recollection of his mother, she questioned; he had been so very young. Would she even recognize him? Would he bear any resemblance to Johnnie? There were just so many questions spinning around in her head, that she began to feel quite giddy, and swooned; later, to find herself coming round to the powerful reek of Mrs Bancroft's potent smelling salts which were being waved beneath her nostrils.

"Oh my goodness, what's the time? I have to get home....I don't know what came over me."

"Just calm down now, you simply fainted, that's all, quite normal in your condition. You needs to sup some cool water and take a rest before you even think about your journey home, my girl."

When Sunday arrived, Rose was relieved to see Hope in a somewhat jubilant mood, she had

woken early, prepared the breakfast, and was being extremely patient to Primrose's bombardment of questions. As the family all sat around the large table, Rose decided to take advantage of the morning's relaxed atmosphere and handed the small wrapped gift to Dan.
"It's not my birthday is it?" he asked jokingly.
"Why has Pa got a present?" cried Primrose, "It's not fair; have you got one for me too?"
"Be quiet, Primrose, let Pa open it,"
"You be quiet Henry, and stop telling me what to do!"
Primrose suddenly let out an exaggerated scream as Henry kicked her under the table.
"Ma! Henry just kicked me!"
Rose was beginning to wish that she'd chosen a more private moment to announce her happy news,
"Children, that will do, now let's have two minutes quiet from both of you, and Henry, there will be no apple pie for you later; how many times do I have to tell you about hurting your sister?"
Primrose smiled wickedly.
"Look what your ma has given me!" exclaimed Dan, laughing as he held up the silver rattle.
"She must think that I'm a baby."
His expression changed dramatically, as the hidden message in the gift suddenly dawned on him, and within seconds he and Rose had left their seats and were locked in an embrace, with

Primrose and Henry watching in confusion.

"Ma is going to have another baby!" announced Hope, confidently.

With everyone so excited by the news, Hope took advantage of the situation and announced that she was going to celebrate by going out for a country walk wearing her best dress. Her words were echoed by Primrose, pleading dramatically to accompany her,

"Ma, she can't tag along with me, I'm going to walk until my legs tire, and I won't possibly be able to carry Primrose all the way home."

"I can walk until I tire, too," declared Primrose. Sensing Hope's desire to be by herself, Rose was quick to intervene and persuaded Primrose that she could assist her with the pie baking.

There were barely enough minutes in the hour, before Alfie had to hurry back to join his parents. The weather had been kind to them and they both wanted nothing more than to walk hand in hand through the vibrant autumnal fields, Alfie excitedly describing his first weeks at St John's college, and telling Hope how Oxford was not the same since she had left, and Hope just content to be next to her beloved Alfie, listening to his every word. They spent their last precious minutes sat upon an old fallen log, both feeling pain that their assignation was drawing to its end, and not knowing when their next one would be.

"Oh Alfie, I'm going insane living out here, I want nothing more than to walk the pavements of Oxford again and meet with you in our special places."

Alfie wrapped his arms around her,

"We have to be patient, Hope; one day we will be able to spend every minute of our lives together, and nothing or nobody will separate us."

The parting was a wrench of agony; Alfie couldn't bear to see Hope in tears, which streamed down her flushed cheeks. They left each other in the same place where they had met, each heading along a different, lonely path and each feeling the pangs of sorrow.

Alfie couldn't face the prospect of having to make polite and friendly conversation with his parent's friends, and decided to make his way back to the cross roads and wait for their return. With his mind deep in thought and miles away, if it hadn't had been for the fact that his name was clearly being called out, he probably would have walked straight past the cottage where an old woman was leaning on her garden gate.

CHAPTER THIRTY-ONE

"Your name *is* Alfie then?"
Alfie looked puzzled at this old wizened woman
who appeared too old to still be breathing, let
alone raising her voice.
"Do I know you Mrs..?"
"I'm Mrs Bancroft, and I first met you young
man when the only sound that sprung from
your mouth was a baby's cry."
"You must be acquainted with my parents then?"
"I know your ma...Rose."
Alfie's brow suddenly developed deep furrows
as he stared confusingly at the eccentric creature
who still had her elbows leaning heavily on the
gate
" Oh, you are definitely mistaken then Mrs
Bancroft, because my ma is most certainly not
called Rose."
"Then that can only mean that she ain't your
bona fide mother then, can't it?"
" No, it means that you have made a big mistake;
I think I know who my ma is, and I definitely
know when I'm being made to look like a fool.
Who put you up to this immature prank?"
Evie struggled to suppress the laughter which
was itching to escape from her.
"Young man, do I look the sort to entertain
school girl dares?"
Alfie's patience was wearing thin; he even began

to fear that he had come upon some country witch and now just wanted to be as far away from this area as possible.

" I don't have to stand here and listen to this," he announced angrily, "I have to meet my parents." As Alfie began pacing along the road Evie Bancroft called out one last time to him, "Ask your parents who Rose is then; she has golden hair, just the exact shade as yours."

Alfie sat in the back of his parent's wagon, still disturbed by his meeting with Mrs Bancroft. After enquiring whether Alfie had enjoyed his time spent with his friend, Jayne and Percy Bird, were deep in conversation as they travelled back to Kidlington, near Oxford. The words of Mrs Bancroft refused to leave Alfie's thoughts; he couldn't find a reason as to why this old woman would say such lies; what were her motives, he wondered. He stared hard at his loving parents, and for the first time ever in his life viewed them in a different way. They both had mousey brown hair, and the more Alfie studied them, the more he came to realise that there were no similarities in any of his features compared to theirs. Why had he never noticed this before, he asked himself; were they his natural parents? And if they weren't, why hadn't he been told. The sun was just setting as they arrived back at their farm. Alfie helped his pa to unhitch the horse and stable him for the night, while Jayne headed off to the kitchen to prepare supper."Are you alright, son?" enquired Percy, "You've been very quiet this afternoon."

"I'm fine Pa," Alfie lied.

"If you say so, son, but it looks to me, like there's something bothering you, and in my opinion, it's always best to talk it out rather than bottle it up inside, but I'll leave that decision up to you, now let's go and see if your ma's got the supper on the table."

Alfie adored his parents, and he was in no doubt that they felt the same way about him too; he couldn't even remember a time when they'd raised a hand to him, or punished him, during his childhood. He had heard so often of how his fellow school friends had received a beating, or were made to do extra chores for various, mostly trivial, mistakes that they'd committed, but through all of his life, if he had behaved wrongly, his parents would talk it through with him, showing how disappointed they were. That in itself was enough of a punishment, which would motivate him to go out of his way to make up for his mistakes and to gain his parents forgiveness. How could he possibly upset them, by asking the question which lingered on the tip of his tongue, he asked himself.

Jayne as usual piled the food onto Alfie's plate, insisting that he was looking thin these days and needed to consume more.

Percy and Alfie would always exchange a playful glance to each other on these occasions, "Looks like your pa's going to get the scraps again," joked Percy.

"He'll be away to Oxford come the morning for another week, and I know they don't feed him properly in that college, and we don't want him coming down with a fever now do we, Percival Bird?"

"Give Pa some more chicken, Ma. I really can't eat all of this."

"Ah, don't worry son, there's plenty more food in the pantry if I'm still hungry."

Jayne lit another oil lamp and placed it on the table, the daylight was rapidly vanishing. It had been a long day, she mused, but a thoroughly enjoyable one, even though Alfie didn't make it to their good old friends, the Osbornes.

"Did you meet up with your friend this afternoon Alfie? Is he a young man from St John's by any chance?"

Alfie's deep hazel eyes held his ma's attention, "It was actually a female friend who I spent my afternoon with, Ma,"

Jayne's jaw ceased to chew the chicken leg, as her brain tried hard to take in this surprise announcement.

"Oh," was the only sound that escaped her mouth. Percy knew when his wife had been shocked into silence, and took up the conversation.

"So son, who is this secret young maid? Anyone your ma and I know? Is she from Northamptonshire? Have you been walking out with her for long?"

"He didn't say that he was walking out with her, Percy!" Jayne objected. "The boy's *far* too young to be thinking about walking out, and besides, he's got his studies to think of."

Alfie felt his parent's eyes on him as they waited for some answers; he felt annoyed and angered that they showed no respect for his emotions, like he was some silly ten year old afflicted by a childish infatuation. He decided to change the subject, and get what was bothering him more than anything off his chest,

"Who is Rose by the way? Only I was told today that she is my real mother."

Jayne's sharp intake of breath and the clatter as Percy's knife spontaneously fell from his grasp onto his plate, only proved to Alfie that there *was* truth in Mrs Bancroft's words.

"Who's been filling your head with such daft notions, Alfie?" asked Jayne, in her most convincing voice.

Percy was quiet as he focussed on his wife, who seemed to be digging a deep hole for herself. He had always known that the truth would eventually slip out, and had, on countless occasions pleaded with Jayne to disclose the truth to Alfie, especially in more recent years as he grew older and was becoming independent.

He knew that truth always had a habit of rising to the surface, and besides, he thought; nothing would affect their love and strong bond for each other. Alfie was a sensible lad, just as his natural parents had been, and as his adoptive parents were.

"*Jayne!* Alfie is a clever lad, and nothing in this world could change how much he loves his Ma; he deserves to know the truth, and besides, in five years time when he receives his inheritance, there will be no hiding the truth then."

Jayne looked daggers at her husband, wishing more than anything in the world that it had been her who had born her beloved Alfie. She doubted that even Percy realised how strong her love and maternal tie was for her son.

" Well, Percival Bird, looks as though we don't have any choice now, does it; as usual, discretion being your strong point." Jayne's hysterical voice, along with her watery eyes, made Alfie regret having opened this subject; his ma looked broken hearted, and it was all his doing.

Percy continued to tell Alfie the story of his late parents and how Jayne had discovered him in the barn on the night of the fire, and how from the moment they had rescued him they took the decision to adopt him, seeing it as a blessing and an answer to their constant prayers for a child of their own.

Jayne described how beautiful his ma had been, and how devoted she was to her son, which only mystified everyone as to how Alfie had been discovered in such a terrible state. Percy went on to explain how Alfie's pa had fallen in to the river and drowned when Alfie was just a few months old, and because Sebastian Harper had been such a ruthless scoundrel, it was the opinion of the local constabulary that Rose Harper had died in suspicious circumstances at his merciless hands.

Alfie listened intently, trying to remember every detail about this shocking revelation.

"So where did I live then? And where are the graves of my real parents?"

Those words hurt Jayne, *real parents*; she knew that Alfie would never again look at her and imagine that he'd once grown in her belly, and that it wasn't her who had suffered the pains of childbirth to bring him into the world. Percy might think that she was just being ridiculous, but it mattered to her.

"Well, son, the Harper's had owned Bushel Farm for three generations, they'd always been our neighbours, as far back as my grandparents day, but it was never the same after the fire destroyed the house, and we had such sad memories of the place, so it was a blessing really when that wealthy Sir Hugh Whitehead bought both ours and the Harper's land; *you know the place son;* Lady Ophelia's Stables, that is there now, right smart looking place too. The funds from the sale of what was Bushel Farm will be yours when you are twenty one.

The small family graveyard adjacent to the land is where your late pa rests, but they never found your ma's remains...very sad and tragic ordeal, I must say."

Jayne left the table in order to make the bedtime cocoa, hiding her tearful eyes.

It was getting late and they had spoken well into the early hours of the morning. Alfie doubted that he'd get any sleep with so much to think about, and with Mrs Bancroft's words still echoing in his head. She had not spoken of Rose in the past tense, but he couldn't bring himself to mention this to his ma, seeing how strained her face was looking. *Was* his mother still alive? *Was* that even remotely possible? But he decided that he'd have to make his own investigations and a secret pilgrimage to visit his family graveyard.

" You never did tell us who your young lady friend is, did you, Alfie?" asked Jayne as she placed the mugs of hot cocoa onto the table.

" She is called Hope, Hope Heyford."

CHAPTER THIRTY-TWO

There was very little sleep in the Bird household that night. Jayne kept Percy awake until the thread of early morning daylight shone through the narrow gap where the curtains didn't quite meet. She was a troubled woman with a conscience which made her feel as though she had deceived her dear Alfie, over the years, by not telling him the truth when he had been old enough to understand. Was *he* too feeling such pain, she wondered; would he ever trust her again after this day; would he love her less? Would he still look upon her and Percy as his parents, or would it now make breaking away from them an easy option, especially in a few years time, when he would be in receipt of his trust fund. The questions multiplied and filled Jayne's head until it ached so much, forcing her to forsake her bed to seek comfort in a mug of hot milk with a drop of medicinal brandy in it. The stove had burnt its last log, leaving the kitchen cold. Wrapping her woollen shawl tightly around her, Jayne stepped outside to retrieve fresh fire wood. The birds had already began to fill the new day with their cheery songs, each bird seeming to compete in tweeting the loudest; it was a sound which made Jayne feel comforted, as she praised the Good Lord for this new day with its amazing fiery red sky and its musical complement. Placing a chair by the window, she sat watching the sun come up as she sipped her hot milk, deciding, that she was, as usual, over reacting to the situation. Surely last night's revelation couldn't possibly erase the fourteen years of family memories from Alfie's heart; all the growing up, the picnics, the family meals, the Christmas and birthday celebrations, the care and devotion that he had received whenever he had been poorly. By the time she reached the last drop of milk, she had come to the decision that she would dwell on the matter no more, and in a positive mood she made a start on the breakfast.

The lack of sleep reflected in their faces as they sat around the table, their appetites lost, but in order not to upset each other further, they continued as though nothing at all had occurred, and it was just another ordinary Monday morning.

"Did you have time to pack your case last night Alfie dear?" enquired Jayne, a question she repeated every Monday morning.

"I did, thanks ma,"

"And what do you have planned for this morning, Percy? Will you be returning home after taking Alfie into Oxford?"

Percy looked tired; his eyes were red from lack of sleep.

"I'll be coming straight back home again, unless of course there's anything you want me to purchase in town?"

"Not today thank you Percy,"

Alfie quickly swallowed his bread and gulped down his tea, in the awkward and strained atmosphere. His ma would normally object to such hurried consumption, insisting that it was an unhealthy and rude manner in which to eat, but this morning was different.

"Its fine Pa you don't have to take me in today, didn't I mention to you on Friday that Burlington was spending the weekend at his uncle's home and he very kindly offered me a ride with them this morning, in their fancy carriage, complete with suspension for a smooth journey!" Alfie faked a beaming smile as he told his lie, hoping that his parents wouldn't catch him out.

"I don't recall you telling me, son...must be becoming old and forgetful."

"You're not old Pa. Maybe I told you when your mind was busy on other matters."

"Maybe," admitted Percy, rubbing his brow.

"Well that does sound like an opportunity not to be missed...wouldn't mind a ride in one of those fancy carriages myself, would make a fair change from the bumpy ride in our old horse cart," declared Jayne.

"You never know Ma; I might even buy you one when I'm a wealthy graduate!"

Relieved to be out of the house and on his own,

Alfie set off in the opposite direction from Oxford, taking the road towards Northamptonshire, and praying that it wouldn't be long before he was able to cadge a lift from a passing traveller. Thankfully, apart from the gusty autumn wind, the day made for ideal walking weather, and by the look of the sky would remain dry for a while. Alfie had decided during the night, when he had tossed and turned, unable to sleep, that a single word from his lecturer would not penetrate his brain until he had got to the bottom of yesterday's revelations. Evie Bancroft's words had plagued him and with the added information which his parents had told him, he knew that his life wouldn't return to normal, until he had visited the graves of his family for himself and delved into his roots. He prayed that he might by chance run into Hope on his travels, maybe she would be on an errand or out walking her siblings to school. She was the only person in the world that he wanted to confide in, and today of all days, he longed for her support and love more than he'd ever done before.

Managing to hitch a ride most of the way on the back of a hay wagon, it wasn't long before Alfie was once again stood at the gate of Mrs Bancroft's cottage. A horse and cart was tethered to a tree trunk alongside the partially broken picket fence causing Alfie to feel reluctant to march up the garden path and knock on the door, since Mrs Bancroft obviously had company. He sat for a while on the opposite side of the track, where the grass bank dipped, giving him an ideal place where he had a clear view of the cottage with only his head being visible from the other side, and, he concluded, with Mrs Bancroft being so old, her eye sight was most likely poor and she probably wouldn't even spot him.

It was about half an hour later that the door to Mrs Bancroft's cottage slowly opened to reveal a stony faced gangly woman. She was dressed in the darkest grey from head to toe, her matching hair was pulled back tightly into a bun and she carried a small bag in one hand and a grey bonnet in the other. As she paused to put on the bonnet before closing the door behind her, Alfie emerged from his hiding place and made his way to meet her.

His face broke into the widest smile as he doffed his cap.

"Good morning," he proclaimed, in a friendly manner. There didn't appear to be the slightest change in the austere looking woman's facial expression. She stared coldly at Alfie, as though he was some kind of pest.

" Is Mrs Bancroft at home?" Alfie enquired nervously.

There was a pause of awkward silence before the woman's steely eyes shifted from Alfie and she gave her reply.

" Mrs Bancroft is in the chapel, she has finally left this miserable world."

"But I spoke with her only yesterday," announced Alfie in disbelief.

"Well you must have been her last visitor before the Angel of Death arrived, young man. My husband, the reverend, and I found her in the late hours of the afternoon."

Alfie was speechless.

"I won't ask if you are a relative," she continued, "because I know she has none, well none that are alive that is to say, so might I ask what your business is?"

"I just wanted to ask her a few questions, nothing more."

The reverend's wife raised her eye brows and continued to stare at Alfie as she closed the door.

"Well, young man, I'm afraid it's too late for that."

She left Alfie standing on the path as she walked briskly towards her horse and cart. Alfie ran after her.

"I don't suppose you know her friend, Rose, by any chance?"

"Rose who, young man?"

Alfie stalled, suddenly feeling that all the odds were against his mission to delve into his origins.

"I think it could be Harper," he replied, trying to sound vague.

"Rose Harper!" she declared, and for the first

time, her fixed expression changed to one of confusion.

" There used to be a Rose Harper who lived some miles from here at what used to be Bushel Farm, but that place has long been gone, along with all the Harper family; there was a house fire you see."

Alfie doffed his hat once more,

"Thank you very much, sorry to have held you up. Good day."

"Goodbye young man, sorry you've had a wasted journey."

Watching as the unfriendly, frosty reverend's wife rode off, Alfie couldn't help philosophising that maybe this was some kind of omen sent to warn him off from his intended investigations. Poor Mrs Bancroft, he thought; of all the times to die. Maybe God had just kept her alive so that she could relay her message to him; if he hadn't of met her yesterday he would be none the wiser about his parents. With his hands pushed deep into his pockets, Alfie made the decision that since he had come this far, and it was now too late to attend college, he *would* continue with what he had set out to do, and make his way towards Lady Ophelia's Stables, where his life had begun, when it was Bushel Farm.

Desperately unhappy that her time spent with Alfie had passed so quickly leaving her still yearning to spend more precious moments with him, Hope had cooked up a plan, and if luck was on her side, a possible way in which she would once again be able to see Alfie more often. On Sunday evening, she announced that her friend, Amy, from Oxford had asked her to spend the following day with her, to help out with decorating her house for her elder sister's forthcoming wedding breakfast. Hope excitedly explained to Dan and Rose, over their supper how her friend's parents had ordered hundreds of hot house blooms, which had to be properly arranged throughout the home. Rose, being happy just to see a spark of excitement in her daughter, agreed to let her go, even though it meant that Dan would have to take time out in order to ride her in to Oxford. It was Hope's intention that once arriving in her beloved city, she would look for work in service, or in a busy hotel, giving her the opportunity to spend her free time with Alfie. She could just picture his delighted face when she would announce to him that she was once again living in Oxford. When Hope had asked Dan to drop her off just by the railway station, telling him that she was going to take a stroll past their old shop before calling on Amy, Dan, who already doubted Hope's story, became even more suspicious of her. She'd seemed a little on edge throughout the journey and reluctant to chat. He sensed that she was up to something, but thought it better to keep quiet rather than cause a scene; his main worry was that she wouldn't do anything to upset Rose, whose heart was already breaking from watching how sad and distant Hope had become since their move.

As the grey clouds above, slowly darkened giving way to a sudden and heavy downpour, Dan was now convinced that spending a portion of his savings on a couple of young mares, would be a sound investment. At nearly seventeen years old, Pepper was unable to handle long journeys and refused to travel faster than a gentle trot. Wrapping the tarpaulin around his shoulders, Dan continued at the dawdling pace towards Northamptonshire.

CHAPTER THIRTY-THREE

There didn't appear to be any signs of an end to the continuous heavy rain; it looked set to remain for the rest of the day. Alfie had taken shelter beneath a roadside tree for what seemed like hours, as he waited for a break in the weather or for a passerby to offer him a ride, but neither had manifested. Already soaked to the skin, he decided to throw caution to the wind and continue on his journey along the deserted and dismal muddy track. He still couldn't quite believe that Mrs Bancroft had died so suddenly after he'd met her, although, when he pondered over his initial thoughts when he'd first set eyes on her, she *did* give the impression of being extremely close to the grave and he couldn't remember ever seeing someone who appeared so aged in his life. He shuddered, there had been far too much talk in the past twenty-four hours of deaths and tragedies; it was a gloomy side of life that he preferred to ignore.
"Where you heading, young man?" came a sudden call, bringing Alfie out of his reverie, and relieved that at last there was a sign of life. "I'm on my way to the horse stables." Having forgotten the name of the place, Alfie's delayed reply sounded vague,
"Do you mean Lady Ophelia's?" questioned Dan, his face dripping with rain water.

"Yes, I do believe that's the name of it."

"Climb up then, I'm not going as far as there, but I'll be able to take you a bit closer,"

"Thank you Sir, that's jolly decent of you," accepted Alfie, not knowing why his language had strangely decided to mimic the toffs from St John's, who he despised so much.

Dan looked at him in a peculiar manner as Alfie hurried to climb up on to the seat next to him.

" It's certainly not the sort of weather you want to be hanging around in is it? My name's Dan, by the way."

"I'm Alfie."

Hearing that name seemed to instantly transport Dan back into the past, he had loved that little boy so much, and, it always reminded him of those early, heady days when he'd first set eyes on his beautiful Rose and fallen in love on the journey to Banbury.

"Ah, that's a good strong name lad; you should go far in life with a name like that."

"How far from here are the stables?" asked Alfie.

"Normally, I'd say about an hour's ride away, but with poor old Pepper not as young as he used to be, and with this dreadful weather, it will probably take over an hour to reach my farm, and then another hour's walk from there. Are you hoping to buy a horse then?"

" No, I'm just making a few enquiries, and going to visit the nearby graveyard."

Dan was puzzled,

"There ain't no graveyard there."

"But I was told by a very reliable source that there's a small family graveyard near to the stables."

"Do you mean the *Harper* graveyard? That's the only family graveyard that I know of."

"Yes, that's the one I'm heading to." Dan took a second to take his eyes off the muddy track and have a better look at this young lad, who like him was drenched. He was intrigued as to why he should wish to visit this graveyard, which conjured up such terrible memories and an ominous feeling inside of him.

"How old are you Alfie?"

"I'm nearly sixteen."

"I can't say that I've seen you around these parts before; are you from Northamptonshire?"

"No, I'm from Kidlington, near Oxford, do you know it?"

"Yes, I know Oxfordshire very well; I lived there for a good few years."

The conversation abruptly ceased, as Pepper neighed loudly, shook his head, and came to a sudden standstill.

"Oh dear, poor old Pepper, I think he's making a protest, and I can't say I blame him."

Both Dan and Alfie alighted from the horse cart, and Dan steered the contraption through a gap in the dense forest where the rain was unable to penetrate through the thick layers of foliage which had yet to shed their leaves.

Alfie took off his wet jacket, then removed his jumper, and used it to wipe down the soaked horse. Dan looked on, impressed by his companion's actions. After hanging a nose bag of oats over Pepper's head, and covering him with the dry blanket which had been tucked away beneath the seat, Dan and Alfie waited for Pepper to take his well earned rest.

"It's my fault," confessed Dan, "I should have let the poor old thing rest in Oxford before my return."

"Ah, that's a long journey for an old horse to make without a break," agreed Alfie.

"You must come and refresh yourself at my place before you continue on your journey, you need to dry out, and that woolly of yours needs to be hung before the fire."

"Thanks, that very kind of you," replied Alfie gratefully. He was cold, soaked and starving, and it now seemed like hours since he'd sat eating breakfast with his parents. The thought of reading old headstones under a relentless sky seemed more than unappealing.

Alfie had not noticed the sign for Golden Meadows Farm as they took the turning off the main road, the heavy rain had drenched the overhanging bushes, weighing them down and causing most of the letters to be covered. It was not a day to take in the surrounding sights, but the cosy looking farm house *was* a sight for sore eyes, and Alfie was inwardly celebrating a break from the abysmal weather.

"Come with me to the stable while I unhitch Pepper, don't want to give my wife a fright." Alfie assisted with drying off Pepper, and then waited while Dan went to inform Rose that they had a guest.

"Right, Alfie, follow me; we'll soon get you warm and dry."

Alfie followed obediently, and was soon stepping over the threshold into the warm and inviting kitchen, where Primrose was sat at the table. Removing his drenched cap under Primrose's watchful eye, Alfie was made to feel a little awkward; he wasn't very good when it came to conversing with young children, so he just gave her a wave, to which he received no response.

"Where did your ma go?" asked Dan as he began peeling off his outer garments.

"Oh, she's just gone upstairs to become decent." Dan gave Alfie a feeble smile, embarrassed by Primrose's way with words.

"Take those wet togs off lad, you'll catch your death standing about in them," insisted Dan just seconds before Rose entered the kitchen,

"What a storm we are having," she exclaimed, glancing at the young lad who her husband had invited in. Primrose jumped down from her chair and ran to her ma.

"Ma!" she whispered urgently, "he's got golden

hair just like me!"

"Primrose, it's very rude to whisper, even more so in front of our guest, now bring the mugs from off the dresser, while I make a brew."

"Yes Ma,"

"Alfie, this is my wife, Rose; Rose this is Alfie." Rose had the most peculiar feeling in her stomach as her heart began to flutter inside of her as though a hundred butterflies were trying to escape. She was unable to welcome their guest as he stood staring back at Rose, wandering if this was just a coincidence, or if this beautiful women, who *did* have the same colour hair as him could be his real mother.

Dan coughed, realising that hearing that name had sent his wife back into the past.

"Would you like to take a seat, Alfie?" prompted Dan.

"How old are you Alfie?" There was a break in her voice and she seemed unable to move from the spot where she stood.

"*No!*" She suddenly shouted, "Let me guess, you'll be sixteen in February."

"And you used to be called Rose Harper?" choked Alfie.

Dan watched in astonishment as the tears began to stream down Rose's face, and Alfie hastened towards her. They were suddenly locked in an emotional embrace and Dan now realised that Alfie had never perished in the fire all those years ago.

"What's wrong with Ma?" squeaked Primrose, completely bewildered by the goings on.
"I think I can safely say that your brother has come home," announced Dan, his watery eyes unable to divert their attention from Rose and Alfie.
Now thinking that all the grownups had gone completely mad, Primrose took the opportunity to sneakily help herself to a piece of fruit cake from off the plate on the kitchen table.

As the heavy rain continued to beat down noisily, the Heyford's kitchen was alive with excited chatter, emotional turmoil and revelations; there was just so much to talk over and so much to catch up on. Rose kept Alfie close to her side as they sat around the table, every now and again stroking his head, and bursting in to tears again, not quite believing that this day was really taking place. She had mourned Alfie's death for so many years, and tormented herself over how he must have suffered at the hands of Sebastian Harper, and now with her handsome son sat at her side, she felt as though she was floating on a cloud, and that all this might just be a mere dream.
As Rose set about telling her life story from the time when she had escaped from Bushel Farm and from Seb, the shocking realisation that Alfie's beloved Hope, was in fact his very own sister soon came to light. He explained to Rose

and Dan how he and Hope had been clandestinely meeting over the past months, and how they had bonded with each other from their first encounter, leaving him stunned at the fact that if their circumstances hadn't come to light, they could have possibly gone on to marry, which didn't bear thinking about. It was however, thought Rose, a blessing that Hope was staying with her friend in Oxford for the night; she would have to be told soon, and hopefully would be so euphoric with the news that her brother was alive that she'd be able to adjust to the new situation and look to Alfie in the appropriate way. Both Rose and Dan knew that the coming days would prove difficult and without doubt, be exceedingly emotional. Rose still couldn't quite digest the fact that everyone had just presumed she was dead, even without there being any trace of a body; it seemed to her that the local constabulary had been very lax in their enquiries, and couldn't wait to close the case.

It was decided that Alfie would spend the night at Golden Meadows Farm; what with the appalling travelling conditions, and Pepper needing his rest, even though Dan could have used his working shire horses, he knew that it was too soon for Rose to be separated from Alfie just yet. Alfie assured them that it would cause no worry to Percy and Jayne Bird, since they believed that he was at college, though, he did have a feeling that Hope's over night stay in Oxford with her friend, was simply a ploy to try and meet up with him outside the college gates and he prayed that she wouldn't stir up any questions as to why he hadn't been in attendance. When Henry arrived home from the local school in his soaking clothes, he took the news with great joy and celebrated that at last he had a brother. It took no time at all before he was in full conversation with Alfie, as though they had never been apart.

CHAPTER THIRTY-FOUR

After spending the entire day traipsing the streets of Oxford in the pouring rain, Hope still hadn't managed to secure herself a place of work. She had tried the hotels in Cornmarket and George Street, and called on dozens of the grand homes which lined St Giles, hoping that one of them at least would be in need of a domestic servant. The hem line of her lilac damask dress was now soaked up to her knees, and heavily soiled; it wrapped around her legs as she walked, causing her whole body to shiver. Hope was wearing one of her ma's handmade straw boaters, which was now a darker shade of wheat, and dripping chilly rainwater on to her shoulders. 'I must look an absolute state; it's no wonder that nobody is offering me a position,' Hope told herself as she tried in vain to stop her teeth from chattering together.

Deciding to take a break, and hopefully dry off a little, Hope called in at the Carfax tea rooms in Queens Street. The two waitresses whispered to each other and giggled under their breath as they watched Hope in her dishevelled state pull out a chair and sit down.

"Are you ready to place your order, Miss?"

"I'd just like a pot of tea please," requested Hope, as she eyed the display of tasty looking cakes and sandwiches. Even though she was absolutely famished and hadn't eaten anything but an apple since breakfast, she knew she had to be extremely cautious with her limited funds.

"Can I get you anything to eat, Miss?"

"Goodness!" sighed Hope, " I fear I can barely breath, after the huge luncheon that I ate earlier; I couldn't possibly manage another crumb, although I must admit, they all *do* look positively divine."

On realising how young Hope must be, and that she was trying to impress being much older, the waitress couldn't help thinking that she was in some kind of trouble. She was unable to stop herself from prying when she returned with the order.

"Are you sure that everything is alright Miss?"

Hope decided to take this opportunity to ask the question that she'd tired from repeating all day, and felt a sudden surge of guilt as she imagined the shock on her parents faces if they could only see how she'd spent the day, masquerading like a pauper.

"Well actually, I've spent most of my day looking for work, and have walked miles in this horrid weather in doing so."

"I thought you looked a bit out of sorts; that's a shame Miss, what sort of work are you looking for?"

"I'm not particularly choosy; I've been to all the big houses and the hotels, but nobody seems to be able to help me."

"Oh my, you poor girl," comforted the waitress, "I'll ask my colleague, she usually has her ears open to any upcoming positions; we don't want you being taken to the workhouse."

Feeling more like an imposter with every passing minute, Hope couldn't wait to finish her tea and depart from the tea room, telling herself that she should perhaps spend her last money on a Hanson cab back to Golden Meadows and to where she belonged. The waitress returned with an envelope in her hand and proudly placed it down onto Hope's table, a gleaming smile pushing up her cheeks, causing her eyes to almost disappear,

"Here you are Miss, apparently, this new place is looking for staff; only trouble is, that it's in Bicester, but it's a right grand looking place, almost as grand as the Randolph!"

Hope read the address,.

Westmead Abbey Hotel, Bicester, Oxfordshire. Thank you, you've been so kind, I will make my way there now, before it gets dark." Gulping down the final mouthful of tea, Hope quickly paid her bill and was given a gift of a bag containing two tea cakes with her change,

"They're yesterday's, and a bit stale, but at least they'll fill your belly and give you strength for the road."

"Thank you again, you've been so kind," replied Hope, her mouth already watering at the thought of food.

"Ah, don't mention it, but the next time you're in Oxford, let us know how you got on; might even join you me self if there's jobs going, I could do with a bit of luxury in me life! Take care now, Miss!"

It was forty minutes later when Hope arrived in Bicester town. It had cost her all of her money, leaving her penniless; the grumpy Hanson cab driver had refused to go as far as Westmead Abbey, complaining that it was too far off the main road, and he had to return to Oxford urgently. With the hour becoming late in the afternoon, Hope's priority was to arrive at Westmead Abbey Hotel before the darkness of night totally engulfed her, and not having a clue as to which direction to travel in, she walked towards the town's blacksmiths where she could see an elderly man resting on an up turned wooden crate. Hope paused briefly to brush the dried dirt from off the hem of her skirt; the rain had finally stopped when she'd left the tea room in Oxford, and her dress had since dried leaving a deep dirty water mark. She adjusted her straw boater, and headed across the street.
Wilkins did not offer the welcoming smile which Hope was expecting, and which most men readily greeted her with. Instead he pulled his cap down over his eyes, and leaned back against the wall as though he'd suddenly fallen to sleep. What a rude and inhospitable man, thought

Hope; if he thinks that he can trick Hope Heyford, well, he can think again,

"Excuse me Sir," called out Hope, now noticing how scruffy and filthy this lazy man looked, "but could you be so kind as to direct me in the direction of Westmead Abbey Hotel."

No sooner had the words, 'Westmead Abbey' been spoken, then Wilkins grabbed hold of his cap, and immediately began choking. Hope watched helplessly as he spat out a mouth full of bloody sputum on to the ground; his face looked sallow and he had huge dark circles beneath his tired looking eyes.

" What business do you have at Westmead Abbey, and *who* are you?" bellowed Wilkins, puffing profusely.

Wishing that she'd gone into one of the few stores to get directions, Hope felt uncomfortable in the presence of this angry man, but with little choice, and being a stranger to these parts, and with it now looking impossible that she would be able to get home on this night, she had little choice other than to try to be as civil and obliging to this rough man.

"Are you quite alright, Sir? Shall I fetch you some water?" Hope asked, in a sympathetic tone, as her eyes searched for a jug in the unorganized looking blacksmiths.

"Answer my question, and stop treating me like a bloody simpleton; I've spent the best part of my worthless life at bloody Westmead Abbey, and look where it's got me. You'd be wise to take my advice, and go back to whence you came from." With his voice becoming louder and louder, and his face looking contorted with pain, Hope prayed that this sickly looking man wouldn't suddenly keel over and die before her eyes.

"I have to get there soon; it's where I'm meeting my pa, for the journey home."

"Then your pa should have more sense than allowing his pretty daughter to be out roaming the countryside on her own at this late hour."

"My pa has enough sense, thank you kindly sir, and you know nothing of our circumstances, so I'd appreciate it you would just tell me which way I should walk, before the last remnants of daylight are completely lost!" declared Hope, angrily.

Once again Wilkins began coughing and choking, but this time it was accompanied by his laughing, making him look and sound like a rabid animal.

"Take the left fork when you pass the post office," he finally advised, still choking and splattering, "it's a straight road from there, and should take you about ten minutes."

Relived to leave Wilkins behind her, Hope quickly thanked him and hurried on her way.

No sooner had she passed by the post office, when large drops of rain began to fall from the rapidly darkening sky. The road took on an eerie feel to it as she left the town behind her and was surrounded on each side by sinister looking trees which swayed and creaked, casting foreboding shadows across the gritty track. Hearing noises behind her as she increased her pace, Hope was too scared to look over her shoulder, and was convinced that the awful man from the town was following her. How she wished that she'd never set out on this foolhardy journey and that she was in the safety of her home with her dear ma and pa. Having no idea as to where she would spend the night as well, she prayed that the proprietor of the Hotel was a kindly, sympathetic sort who would perhaps take pity on her and give her a room for the night with her promise of a future bill settlement. If he turned out to be as unpleasant as the man in town, she'd find herself in an even bigger mess, she concluded. Her parents would be beside themselves if they could see what she was doing and what she had been up to all day, thought Hope, a wave of guilt washing over her. Shocked at the sheer grandeur and magnitude of Westmead Abbey Hotel, Hope's depression immediately lifted. The wide driveway was adorned with a row of welcoming lanterns on either side, which had an immediate effect on Hope, making her feel safe again. She headed towards the large entrance, and soon found herself in the luxurious vestibule of the Hotel. It was Harriet Whitehead who was sat behind the counter, engrossed in reading *Wuthering Heights*. The Hotel was quiet at this time of year, and with only a couple of business men staying, Harriet had allowed Nora and Beth to finish early for the evening while she waited for their return from Oxford. Harriet looked surprised to see such a pretty young girl all by herself, so late in the day,

"Good evening, Miss, can I help you?"

Hope who was still smiling from the sheer relief that she'd managed to find the Hotel, replied confidently,

"Yes, I'd like to see the owner please, or the manager," she quickly added, not really knowing who she should ask to see.

"Goodness!" exclaimed Harriet, "that *does* sound as though you are on urgent business, perhaps you might inform me as to the nature of it?"

Hope was under the impression that the receptionist was ridiculing her, but when she caught sight of herself in the reflection of the large ornate mirror her confidence dramatically decreased on seeing what a ruffled and grubby state she had become. Suddenly feeling out of place in the grand surroundings, Hope answered Harriet in a lower and more humble tone,

"I'm actually looking for work; anything really, I'm not fussy, and I'm able to do all domestic work, and I'm extremely hard working, *and* I usually present a far smarter appearance, it's just that I've spent my entire day walking the streets of Oxford in the most awful weather conditions, in search of work, and I'm now without a farthing to my name, and too far from home, with nowhere to sleep tonight." Hope took a gasp of air, as she tried with all her might to stop her tears from shedding. "Oh dear, I've said too much, pardon me. Is your manager a kindly man? Do you think he might consider giving me a trial at least?"

"Hey, steady on young lady; first of all, *I am* the owner of Westmead Abbey Hotel; I'm Mrs Whitehead."

The large glass door of the Hotel suddenly swung open and the foyer was filled with the chatter and laughter of the two high spirited business men returning from Oxford, who by the sound of them, had spent the evening over indulging.

"Good evening, Mr Barnett and Mr Green, I trust you had an enjoyable evening? "

The gentlemen were polite in their reply and quickly took their room keys, in a hurry to retire for the night, leaving Harriet to return her attention to Hope, once more.

"Now, tell me young lady, how old are you, and where exactly *is* your home? And presuming that you have kin, are they aware of your whereabouts, or have you ran away?"

Hope swallowed hard, blinking rapidly to stem

the impending flood of tears.

"Come and sit down lass, and tell me your story over a hot cup of tea; you look as though you could do with one. I have a daughter of my own, and I know that I'd be out of my mind with worry if she were roaming the countryside by herself after dark."

Since Harriet had only employed two cooks since opening as a Hotel, she did need an extra pair of hands to help Beth out about the place, and, she concluded it would leave her dearest friend and companion, Nora, with more leisure time to herself. It was agreed that Hope would start work in the morning, and live in at the Hotel, but it came with the condition that she and Harriet would take a walk into town in the morning and send a telegram to Hope's parents, the cost of which would be taken out of Hope's wages.

CHAPTER THIRTY-FIVE

In all their constant and excited chatter, Alfie
had completely forgotten to mention to Rose, the
sad news that poor old Mrs Bancroft had passed
away, until the following morning. It seemed to
Rose, that whenever happiness showed its face
in her life, it was always accompanied by a
helping of bitterness. She had been hoping to
make a difference in the life of poor Evie
Bancroft, thinking that perhaps she could do the
same for her as she'd done for Primrose Atkins,
who had become like a beloved Ma to her. Rose
sometimes thought that she was spending her
life looking for a mother or grandmother
replacement, to fill an empty void in her life. The
news saddened Rose, but as Dan assured her,
Evie *was* finding life a struggle and being such a
kind hearted woman, she was probably in a far
better place now with all the children she had
adored and so sadly already buried. They were
all unanimous on the decision to attend her
funeral and say their final goodbyes to the dear
woman who had been the catalyst in reuniting
Rose with her darling Alfie.

The early morning yawning was contagious.
After such a miraculous day, sleep had no place
amongst the adults at Golden Meadows farm;
Primrose and Henry tried to prepare the

breakfast together, under Henry's supervision, but like always, it ended in tears, and with Primrose insisting that since she was the girl, Henry should listen to her when it came to domestic matters; Henry had already taken a solemn vow never to be bossed around by a female again, unless of course it was his ma or granny Heyford. Breakfast, of a sort, was eventually served, and once Henry had left for school, Rose and Alfie took the horse and trap to embark on their private pilgrimage to the Harper graveyard, leaving Dan at home with Primrose. Dan had mentioned that he'd like to pay a visit to the nearby Lady Ophelia's Stables, to purchase a new steed, but knew that on this day, emotions would be running high, and it would be a poignant moment just for Rose and Alfie, and besides, Dan still couldn't avert his jealousy when Rose shed tears by Johnnie Harper's grave, even after all the years which had passed.

With the heavy rain finally having subsided, there was a distinct autumnal chill in the air, and no sign of the sun yet, pushing her way through the dove grey sky. Alfie let Rose take hold of the reins, proud of the way she handled the horse. Although he knew the name of every single bone and muscles of a horse, living in the city had given him little experience of handling them; his pa would never hear of Alfie toiling on their small farm, and Alfie seldom used the horse and cart. Both Percy and Jayne insisted that Alfie would grow up to use his brains, and the only tool that he'd need would be a pen. Alfie, however had slightly different ideas, and aimed to one day qualify as a vet, and dedicate his life to caring for the beautiful beasts which he adored.

Now in his mid forties, Johnnie Harper seldom left the perimeters of his land; he was a successful horse farmer and breeder, and now employed a handful of workers to take care of the majority of the organization of the stables. He would often spend long periods locked away behind the closed doors of his farmhouse. He had wealth and success, but his life seemed to be without meaning or purpose. His occasional trips to Westmead Abbey were the highlight of his life; seeing Harriet, Nora and Beth, always took him down a nostalgic road, and reminded him of how precious life was, when he remembered the days he'd spent with Sir Hugh and Lester Baker. The women would never cease to nag him about finding himself a young wife, but Johnnie had never quite recovered from discovering the tragedy of how his precious Rose and son were lost to him and within his heart a candle still burned for the sweetest love that he had ever known.

"Are you sure that you're up to this, Alfie?"

Asked Rose softly, noticing how pale and silent Alfie had suddenly become as they neared the graveyard. "We could quite easily return another day, perhaps when we've both got over the shock of all what's happened. She held his hand, blinking profusely to hold back her tears." We've missed so many years together Alfie, can you ever forgive me?"

"There is nothing to forgive, Ma." It was the first time since he was a baby that she had heard the word '*ma*' spoken from his mouth, and she knew that her dear Alfie meant what he said.

" It wasn't your fault that I had such a wicked uncle and it wasn't your fault that my sister Hope's arrival into the world coincided with my abduction and it certainly wasn't your fault that the police miss informed you. Please, Ma, don't ever feel guilty for something that was completely out of your control; besides, it could have been worse, I could have been thrown into the workhouse, and never met you again. My other ma and pa have raised me well and I have wanted for nothing."

"Do you know Alfie?" interrupted Rose, tears now uncontrollably dripping from her face, " Jayne Bird came to visit me just after you were born, she held you in her arms, and I remember feeling her pain and how her heart was breaking, knowing how much she longed for her own children; I'd wished then that there was something I could do for her; isn't that ironic?"

"Come on Ma, we'll support each other, and say our goodbyes to my dear pa and my grandparents, but there will be no prayers said for my uncle Sebastian, that's for sure."

"No, Alfie, we must pray for all of them, and try not to bear any grudges; forgiveness is a rewarding act; haven't we seen enough misery afflict the Harper family already."

Alfie wasn't so sure that he could be as forgiving as his ma, but he made no verbal objections as they climbed down from the horse cart and made their way slowly and peacefully towards the graves, holding each other's hands in support.

Johnnie had been gazing out from his bedroom window. He had watched the horse and cart pass by, and thought little of it until a few minutes later when all he could see was the tail end of the stationary horse cart. He stood wondering if there was a problem with the passengers or their horse; he knew of no other reason for anyone to stop where they had. He opened the window, calling out to one of his workers, Joe, a young lad who had recently married and brought his pretty young wife to live in one of the small cottages that Sir Hugh, in his wisdom, had thought to have built,

"Joe!" he hollered, gaining the lad's attention, "Looks like there's a stranded wagon out on the road; go and see if they are in need of, help, please."

Joe waved in acknowledgment, and immediately headed towards the imposing iron gates. Johnnie left his bedroom and went down to the kitchen to heat up yesterday's pot of coffee.

As he stood outside the back door, mug in hand, he breathed in the cool morning air, as he waited for Joe to arrive and report on his findings,

" There's no problem out there Mr Harper, seems they've just come to pay their respects at the graveyard."

Johnnie was instantly puzzled,

"Thanks Joe, you can return to your work now....how's married life treating you?"

"It suits me just great Mr Harper," replied Joe, smiling proudly.

"That's good; give my regards to your wife."

"Thank you Mr Harper."

Johnnie strolled around to the front of the house, where he was able to get a good view of the gates, hoping that the mysterious visitors would pass by when they had finished and he'd get a glimpse of them. He couldn't recollect any other living relatives from the Harper family, and the longer he stood waiting the more curious he became, until he abandoned his mug of coffee onto the window ledge, grabbed his walking stick, and headed towards the gates.

A tearful Rose and Alfie were oblivious of the man who stood at the gates, as Pepper gently trotted passed on the return journey. Johnnie felt a sudden surge of activity within his chest, as his heart beat so rapidly, he could do nothing but slide to the ground. Had he imagined it, he asked himself; how could that possibly be his Rose? They had assured him of her death. He quickly pulled himself up, and sped out onto the road, only to watch the wagon disappear from his view. There was nobody who could compare to her beauty; this was too much of a coincidence, he continued to tell himself.

"Are you alright sir?" asked Joe, who had been observing Johnnie's strange actions, "do you need the doctor?"

"No, Joe, I don't need a doctor; is there a horse saddled up and ready to go?" puffed Johnnie, still very shaken by what he'd seen.

"There is, sir," confirmed Joe.

" I want you to catch up with those people who were visiting the graveyard; they've only just left, and their horse seemed old and slow so they shouldn't have got very far; I'd go myself, Joe, but you're a lot younger and faster than me, *and* you have two legs, I'm glad to say. Find out who they are if you can and where they live, please don't lose them Joe, and don't mention my name to them either."

Noticing the urgency in Johnnie's voice and his strained face, Joe was soon galloping out through the gates on a sturdy young mare, in search of the mysterious couple who had managed to disturb Johnnie Harper's customary tranquil disposition.

Joe soon caught up with them, but finding himself not quite sure how to follow behind them without causing suspicion, he overtook them at a fast speed, and stopped further up along the road. Dismounting from his horse and examining her front hoof, he hoped what he thought to be, a clever little plan, would render successful.

Alfie jumped down from the cart,

" She was going at a fair old speed back there; what's happened to her?" voiced Alfie, fearing that the horse's rider had over worked the beautiful golden brown mare.

"Reckon she got a stone caught under her shoe, but I think I've been able to free it now."

Alfie looked dubiously at the sweating horse, as he stroked her mane.

"Hey, didn't I just see you up by Lady Ophelia's stables?" enquired Joe, "that's where I work, *and* live."

"Really! Well, you live at the place where I was born," stated Alfie, excitedly, "but I'm sure it's all very different from when I was a baby."

"Most likely, it used to be a farm 'till it was destroyed in a fire; it's a real fancy horse farm now, one of the best in miles."

"It certainly looks grand enough!" replied Alfie, concealing his sadness.

"Well, if you're sure you don't need any help, I'd best be on my way, I left my ma waiting and

there's a nasty chill in the air today," replied
Alfie politely, in a hurry to rejoin Rose.
"Thanks for stopping by, er..."
"Alfie,"
"Thanks again Alfie, and I'm Joe."
"Bye Joe, nice to have met you." The two young
men shook hands and parted. Joe mounted the
horse and followed cautiously behind Alfie and
his ma at a gentle trot, hoping that they would
lead him to their home and that it wasn't too far
away.

Both emotionally charged, after their sad
morning, Rose and Alfie found Dan in a state of
stress as he paced back and forth in the kitchen
clenching a screwed up piece of paper in his
tightly tensed fist. Rose immediately knew by
the look on his face that there had been some
kind of bad news. She felt her heart plummet, as
she warned herself that it was quite normal in
her life for bad news to follow any joy that she
should have.

"What's wrong Dan? What's happened?" Rose
rushed to his side, taking the paper from his
hand. It was a telegram. With shaking hands,
she feared the worst,

"Hope!" She cried out, "Oh God, please don't tell
me something dreadful has happened to her!"
Alfie had now risen from his chair and was at
Rose's side, his face full of worry. Rose couldn't
bring herself to read the telegram but instead
threw it onto the table as though it was a

burning coal in her hand.

"Oh, Rose, I'm sorry," exclaimed Dan, "calm yourself my love; Hope is well, nothing has happened to her except that she has left us and taken up employment at a hotel in Bicester."

Rose sank down onto the chair with a sigh of relief. The news that she'd left her family seeming quite trivial now after Rose had anticipated much worse. Alfie, too, breathed a sigh of relief, and knew that the only reason Hope had made such a move was to enable them to be closer to each other. Poor Hope, he thought, she was going to be in for such a shock to discover that they were siblings.

Dan had insisted that Rose took to her bed for a rest, she looked pale and tired, and he knew how draining the early weeks of pregnancy could be. Rose had encountered so many shocks lately, and he didn't want to put her or their baby at any risk. Alfie and Primrose served their ma in bed with a cup of hot sweet tea and a warm buttered tea cake, both echoing Dan and insisting that she should take a nap.

Dan was finding it difficult to contain his anger; Hope had lied to them, and taken advantage of their trust; she hadn't once mentioned that she was looking to leave home and find work outside; Dan just couldn't understand why and felt utterly betrayed by her flighty inconsiderate behaviour.

CHAPTER THIRTY-SIX

"No Dan, please don't go rushing over to Bicester now, you'll only make Hope more determined to abandon us, and Alfie believes that she's only done this so that she'll be near to him in Oxford. Give her time, at least we know where she is, and that she's safe and God knows, she is in for a massive shock when we tell her about Alfie."

"You're right as always, Rose; where would I be without you?"

"And where indeed would I be without you my darling?"

As they walked hand in hand across their land, it felt good to be away from the listening ears within the house for a while and to have some privacy. Alfie had returned to Kidlington to who Rose now referred to as his *other ma and pa;* he wanted to sit down with them and explain everything that had come to light; it was planned that if all went well, the two families would meet up on the following Sunday. Rose had decided that they should also bring Hope back home for the weekend too so that they could break the news to her.

"How's our little chap doing then?" asked Dan, as he lightly brushed Rose's belly.

"Oh he is definitely feeling neglected," joked Rose," In all the commotion, I almost forgot that he was even in there, and it's too early for me to feel him wriggle yet."

Dan stopped walking and pulled Rose into his arms, kissing the fullness of her pink lips.

" Rose my darling, you are the most beautiful wife and mother to walk this earth, and if I don't tell you often enough how much I love you, then please forgive me; I've got a feeling that our life from now on will only get better."

Dan's attempt to kiss his lovely wife once more was suddenly interrupted by the distressed shouts from Henry and Primrose, as Henry came chasing her across the grass, Primrose's screams putting an end to all peace and tranquility.

" I might have known that our private moment couldn't last long," sighed Dan.

"Ma! Pa! Henry put a spider in my bonnet."

"Come here you brave girl," coaxed Dan, "I'll put a toad in your brother's cap!"

"He won't care Pa, Henry loves frogs and toads!"

Rose and Dan exchanged a loving glance and Dan announced that he had decided to see if he could purchase a new horse for a reasonable price from Lady Ophelia's Stables and put poor Pepper out to pasture.

Having not been able to settle for one minute since hearing Joe's account about the young man by the name of Alfie, when Johnnie caught sight of exactly the same horse and cart for the second time in the same day, he began to think that perhaps he *was* losing his sanity. This time it was a lone man who steered the cart in through the open gates and followed the path towards the large block of stables which stood where Percy Bird's farmhouse had once been. He watched as Joe came out to attend to the visitor, but nothing could hold Johnnie back. He had to take this opportunity and endeavour to find out as much information as he could and put his troubled mind at ease.

He grabbed his walking stick, which he was now forced to rely on since suffering from troublesome leg ulcers on his stump; walking too far had become a painful exercise, and he no longer prided himself on being able to pass as an able bodied man. It was approaching mid day, and most of the workers had gone in for a bite to eat; it was only Joe who had not yet returned to his cottage; he was a good honest worker, who relished in impressing his boss, and ,thought Johnnie, was slightly taken for granted by his colleagues.

By the time Johnnie reached them, they were already in what appeared to be a serious conversation.

"Good afternoon," announced Johnnie, as he studied Dan, trying to make out if he recognized him from anywhere. "Are you being looked after, sir?"

"Yes, thank you," replied Dan, feeling certain that there was something strangely familiar about this man.

"Joe, go and take your break, I'll see to this gentleman," insisted Johnnie.

Joe sensed that there was something untoward going on; he had noticed the anguish in his employer's face when he'd given him his report earlier, and he had also recognized that this was the same aging horse and cart returning to the stables.

"I feel as though I know you," announced Dan, as he stood racking his brain as to where he'd seen him before, "you looked very familiar."

"Ah, I think I must have one of those familiar types of common faces!" Joked Johnnie, not wanting to disclose his name just yet until he'd found out more about this man, and the two people who had been travelling on the same horse and cart earlier.

"So how can I help you, Mr...?"

"Heywood, Dan Heywood," spoke up Dan, " I'm looking for a good strong horse, at a reasonable price; poor Pepper here has served me well, and is now deserving of an easier life."

"Well I'm sure we can sort you out with a suitable replacement, Mr Heyford; follow me." Leaving Pepper behind, Dan walked beside Johnnie towards the impressive stables.

"My wife tells me that her previous neighbours once lived here, when it was a farm." Dan had no way of knowing that his small talk would soon unravel a huge revelation which would cause an avalanche of events.

"Your wife lived very locally then?" questioned Johnnie, rather dubiously.

Dan was proud in his reply,

"She used to live in this very spot, but that was before I'd met her *and* before the fire."

Johnnie didn't answer; he could feel his whole self tingling with hidden emotions. Warning himself to remain calm, they entered into the stable yard in silence and were met by numerous magnificent horses in various striking shades, most of which were hanging their heads over the row of stable doors.

"What an amazing sight," declared Dan, impressed with what befell his eyes, "most definitely one of God's superior creatures."

Johnnie barely heard Dan's words, his mind was in a state of turmoil and as much as he wanted to know more about Dan's wife, there was part of him that feared the consequences of hearing what Dan would reveal, should he continue to question him.

"I think this beautiful mare would be an ideal horse for you, Mr Heyford." Johnnie strolled towards a palomino that was gently shaking her mane as she lifted her head, "She's extremely placid but as strong as an ox."

"She is a grand looking mare," agreed Dan, as he patted her neck admiringly, "I expect she comes at a price that is completely out of my range though."

Johnnie held Dan's eyes with a fixed stare, and knew that he *had* to know the truth. The moment was awkward; Dan was still trying to think of where he'd seen this man before,

" What price is too great for such a beauty as Rose," said Johnnie flatly.

"Is she actually named Rose?" questioned Dan in astonishment, "it must be a sign that she's the right choice; my wife *will* be impressed."

"*No!* Rose is no name for a mare," snapped Johnnie.

As tears spilled over from Johnnie's eyes, trickling down his face, Dan was instantly reminded of Hope; she had the very same look about her whenever she became upset. Feeling the hairs on the back of his neck standing up, Dan was suddenly overcome with the darkest of feelings.

"Rose is the name for the most beautiful woman, Rose is my wife *and* Alfie is my son."

Feeling as though he was in the middle of a nightmare, the truth almost wiped the breath from out of Dan's lungs, as he grabbed hold of the stable door to steady himself; what a disastrous mess this was, and what would be the solution, he thought, still not quite able to acknowledge what he'd just heard.

"And Hope is your daughter then," spoke Dan, his voice breaking, like his heart.

Johnnie looked up in surprise.

"I have a daughter?"

"Yes, Johnnie Harper, you have a fine beautiful girl who is the image of yourself."

Unable to take a second more of the torture, Dan hung his head in despair and walked away from Johnnie. He needed no more words with this man, who's shadow he had lived in for the past fourteen years, he needed time alone, time to think over where he now stood; was he even Rose's legal husband, he wondered, and would she run headlong in to his arms the minute she heard that Johnnie was still alive; how could this colossal mistake have been made? How cruel life could be, he mused, with tears blurring his vision.

As Johnnie suddenly realised that Dan was no longer at his side and was heading off his land he spontaneously jumped onto the nearest saddled horse, and raced after him. He needed to know more, and knew that life would remain stagnant until he was enlightened about the missing fourteen years since he had been presumed dead. Rose was *his*, were the thoughts running through his head, and he *had* to meet with her, and with his daughter who until minutes ago he'd been oblivious to her very existence.

Dan's thoughts were trying to justify who had more right over Rose; he had been her husband for more than a decade and they had two children and one to be born in the spring. Panic set in, as he feared that such another shock might cause Rose to lose their baby, but his one deep seated worry was that the moment Rose set eyes on Johnnie Harper again, all love for him would fly away like the dust behind a horse wagon. That was a thought that Dan couldn't bear; if he lost his precious Rose, he knew that he would crumble inside, and die.

The sound of Johnnie's galloping steed soon brought him out if his reverie. He glanced over his shoulder, half sensing already that it would be him.

"Mr Heyford, please, we have to talk," called out Johnnie as he pulled hard on the reins, stopping alongside Dan.

"Rose is with child!" declared Dan, "our third child, and I fear that another shock would be too much for her."

"Another shock?" quizzed Johnnie.

"It's a long and complicated story," replied Dan. "Please Mr Heyford, won't you come back to my home; there is much to discuss, and many unanswered questions. I'm a reasonable man, and I already know how much you love my Rose."

Those words, *my Rose*, seemed to grate on Dan's very soul, leaving him feeling raw and in the most excruciating emotional agony, but, he also knew that this terrible situation had to be resolved in one way or another, and he also reminded himself that Rose was a woman of such strength of character, that the end solution to this, would be in her hands, and ultimately her decision. He accepted Johnnie's invitation, and returned with him to Lady Ophelia's Stables.

CHAPTER THIRTY-SEVEN

There had never been a more heartbreaking two hours for Dan than those spent in the company of Johnnie Harper. With them both having so much to lose and with emotions so painfully raw, the only conclusion that they arrived at, was that with love came pain, and it was the price one had to pay for such an experience. Dan was adamant that Johnnie should stay away from Rose until he had broken the news to her as gently as was possible. Johnnie on the other hand seemed to be under the impression that he could just waltz back in to Rose's life and take up where he'd left off, all those years ago. He seemed undeterred by the fact that Rose had bore Dan's two children and was with child once more. He was in denial that Rose had lived a full new life with Dan, and spoke repeatedly of how he had been Rose's first love, which in his eyes meant that she couldn't possibly love another. Being eager to be united with his own children, Johnnie was shocked to hear that it had only been in the last few days that they had found out about the existence of Alfie, prompting Johnnie to swear and curse at his half brother, who had caused the ruin of every single member of the Harper family. Their lives had become like an unravelled garment, with loose ends hanging from every direction. Dan was not to know that

Johnnie was so well connected with Westmead Abbey Hotel, and as soon as he mentioned that Hope had clandestinely taken employment there and that she had no idea that her beau was in fact her brother, Alfie, Johnnie saw this as an opportunity to at least make himself known to the daughter he knew nothing about, but since Dan was so determined to shield the whole family from him, he had decided to keep it to himself, feeling sure that yet again Dan would insist that he pre-warned everyone beforehand, as though he was some kind of ogre, not their real pa who wanted nothing more than to make up for lost time and become acquainted with his children.

Dan and Johnnie parted with Johnnie agreeing to wait for a day or two before coming face to face with Rose, giving Dan enough time to break the news to her and for Rose to take on board the great burden which she was about to confront.

The sweet aroma of freshly baked apple pie filled the Heyford's warm and cosy kitchen. Dan felt mentally drained by the time he arrived home and Rose instinctively sensed that something was amiss. Never in a million years would she be able to guess the reason behind her pale faced and troubled husband, and could only imagine that the reasons were to do with finance, since Dan had arrived home without the new horse he'd intended to buy. Dan's urgent need to take Rose in his arms and hold her had never been greater; he feared for the future and wished that he could whisk his family away to the other end of the world and keep the news of Johnnie Harper to himself.

"What's ailing you my love?" asked Rose as she rested her head upon Dan's broad chest, "has something happened this afternoon?"

"Oh Rose, why does life have to be so bloody complicated?"

"Life is always full of obstacles Dan, but we've got each other, and we've always managed to get through them, haven't we? I'm sure we can wait a little while longer for a new horse...it's hardly the end of the world now is it? It's been an emotional few days, and we're both feeling the strain of it. Everything will sort itself out, have faith my love."

"Just remember my darling," uttered Dan, "that whatever happens in life, I love you with all my heart."

"Tell me what's bothering you Dan, *please.*" Rose broke away from his embrace, the grief etched on his face told her that there was a problem bigger than the lack of finances to purchase a horse and she became instantly concerned.

"Have you heard word from Alfie, or Hope?" She questioned in a worried tone.

"No my love, it's something else, but nothing for you to worry your beautiful head about."

Dan could not bring himself to open the subject which hung heavy on his heart, and quickly changed the subject, forcing an upbeat ring to his voice,

" How's the youngest Heyford baby doing, and where have Henry and Primrose got to...it's far too quiet in this house today!"

Rose felt her heart ache; she knew when Dan was concealing something from her and from the drawn look on his face, she sensed a huge problem.

"Henry and Primrose are out searching for wild flowers and anything, at this time of year, which will add some colour to the posy for Evie's grave; she's being laid to rest tomorrow morning, you know. It's such a shame that Alfie and Hope won't be able to attend." Dan's heart went out to his wife, she wore the saddest expression, and he couldn't bear the thought of seeing her suffer anymore.

"Joe, do you mind hitching up a horse and trap for me, please," requested Johnnie, as he passed him on his way to the stables.

"Shall I accompany you on your journey, Mr Harper?"

"No Joe; thanks all the same, I'm going over to Bicester, to the Westmead Abbey Hotel, should I be needed."

Joe repeated the name of the Hotel under his breath, and set to make ready the horse and trap.

Johnnie had sat in contemplation, since Dan's departure, unsure of what to do next, but finally reaching the decision to take a trip to Westmead Abbey where he would be able to see his daughter for the very first time, without arousing any suspicion; it had been a while since he'd paid Harriet and Nora a visit. He just couldn't sit around at home twiddling his thumbs, while his daughter lived a few miles away. If it hadn't had been for the fact that Rose was expecting, wild horses wouldn't have stopped him from descending upon her, no matter what Dan Heywood had said, but there had been far too much grief in all of their lives, and he didn't want the loss of her baby on his conscience, should the shock cause her emotions to spiral out of control.

With barely any light left and with the temperature rapidly dropping, it looked set to be an extremely chilly autumn evening. Johnnie pulled up the collar on his tweed jacket, and flicked the reins, encouraging the young horse to break into a faster trot.

Unable to make the return journey back to the blacksmiths in Bicester, Wilkins struggled to catch his breath as he concealed himself in the hay loft above the stables at Westmead Abbey. He had spent many a night there, safe in the knowledge that the work hand who had replaced him returned to his home and family every evening, but tonight, Wilkins was on a different mission, and had been plagued by troubled thoughts since his encounter with the young maiden who had asked directions to Westmead Abbey earlier that week. He hadn't believed the girl for one minute when she had told him that she was to meet her pa at Westmead Abbey for a ride home. Why had she made a bee line for him, and clearly gone out of her way to gain his attention, there was something not quite right, and then there was her uncanny resemblance to that bloody pain in the neck, Johnnie Harper. Wilkins smelt a rat, and even though he was probably in the final days of his life, he had a feeling that the young maiden would lead him to Harper, and if he could get even with him, he would go to his grave with a sense of victory like that of a martyr. In a lethargic state and gasping for every breath as his chest rattled noisily, Wilkins was suddenly aware of the sound of a horse and carriage approaching the Abbey. Using every ounce of energy, he dragged himself to where he was able to dislodge the loose wooden slat, and peer out. Even in the twilight, there was no mistaking Johnnie Harper, and as Wilkins watched him climb down off the wagon and enter over the threshold to Westmead Abbey with a distinct limp and with the aid of a walking stick, even through his agony, Wilkins was able to spontaneously produce a grin of delight, which was shortly followed by his now customary hacking cough with its bright crimson deposit.

' I'll get even with you tonight, you bloody cripple, Harper,' he announced triumphantly under his breath, ' If it's the last damn thing I manage; mark my words you bastard, *your* time is up too.' Pulling out the neat bulldog revolver from his inside pocket, his hands were shaking; a combination of his advanced illness and nervous excitement. He slid down the short wooden ladder from the loft and scurried out of the stables, keeping his body low as he made his way to the back entrance of Westmead Abbey. The rush of adrenaline shooting through his veins seemed to temporarily ease his pain, producing a spurt of energy.

As Johnnie entered through the large glass door to the reception area of the Hotel, he was warmly greeted by Nora who was sat behind the desk writing out a list of stock that was needed. Immediately leaving her position, Nora was soon stood at Johnnie's side, fussing over him and practically dancing for joy at his arrival.

"And about time too!" she declared, her voice an octave higher in her excitement, "we were only saying this very morning how you hadn't shown your face around here for a while; in actual fact, we were thinking of taking a trip out to visit you this coming Sunday! Ooh, wait 'till Harriet finds out that you're here. Now come and sit down and tell me all your news, while I've got you all to myself."

Nora led Johnnie to the brown leather Chesterfield sofa which was positioned near the desk where she'd been sat. Feeling a bit like a young boy returning from boarding school to his female aunts, Johnnie had always thought that Nora, Beth and Harriet would be the closest he'd ever have to any female relatives; they certainly treated him like one of their own kin, which always warmed Johnnie, giving him a sense of belonging. He suddenly became aware of a young girl who was quietly stood halfway up the wide staircase; she had her back to him as she lightly brushed the frames of the hanging oil paintings with a lengthy feather duster. Noticing, how Hope Heyford had captured Johnnie's attention, Nora made a quick announcement to him,

"That's our new girl, only fourteen...very young. Miss Heywood."

Johnnie's spontaneous paternal instincts took on the form of a feral animal, wanting nothing more than to rush towards Hope and declare to her who he was and to embrace his daughter after all the stolen years. Nora was becoming a little concerned as she noticed the interest that Johnnie was showing in Hope, even though she had made a point of declaring to him how very young she was. But thankfully the awkward moment was suddenly broken as Harriet arrived, a smile of delight on her face the second she saw Johnnie,

"Well, I never!" She declared loudly, "mention the sun, and it does shine! We were only talking about you this morning, weren't we Nora? *Johnnie Harper*, you are indeed a sight for sore eyes!"

The feather duster fell from Hope's grasp, its wooden handle clattering noisily down the stairs, as she spun around on hearing a name that had been mentioned to her so many times throughout her life. The two women looked up the stairs, both showing signs of annoyance over Hope's clumsy action. Johnnie had made his way to the foot of the staircase, and stood holding on tightly to the polished oak banister. There was no mistaking Hope was his flesh and blood, he could see it immediately, and Dan had been correct in saying how alike they were in appearance. As Hope froze, one flight up the stairs, she too felt the shiver of a ghost as the strangest feeling swept through her, causing her feet to feel as though they were nailed to the spot.

Harriet let out an over emphasised cough with the intention of regaining Johnnie's diverted attention, but even a thunderbolt couldn't have dislocated the bizarre interaction between Hope and Johnnie.

"Hope! Hope Harper! I am your father."

Before his spoken announcement, Hope already knew who he was, even though a small voice in her head kept repeatedly telling her that her pa was dead and buried. She seemingly floated down the stairs, tears of love and joy overflowing, and before anyone had a chance to notice the bedraggled looking stranger who had stepped in through the rear doors and into the reception area, Johnnie and Hope were locked in a tearful union, oblivious to anything or anyone else in the world.

It was Harriet's shrill and hysterical scream, which gained everyone's immediate attention, as she suddenly caught sight of the weapon in the hand of the stinking vagabond who had suddenly appeared from nowhere. The shocking events of the next few seconds happened too quickly for anyone to take any action to prevent them. Wilkins was unrecognizable; it was only Hope who remembered the sickly looking man from the blacksmiths in Bicester town. The sudden deafening sound as Wilkins pulled the trigger which sent both Johnnie and Hope falling to the floor caused Nora and Harriet to scream out in horror. Wilkins too had fallen to his knees, choking on his bloody spittle, and as the women's wide eyes stared in fear of him, he pulled the gun around until it was pointing directly at his head.

CHAPTER THIRTY-EIGHT

The message in the telegram received by Dan and Rose the following morning failed to explain exactly what had happened, but its urgent summons to report to Westmead Abbey Hotel, immediately threw them into a state of panic.

" It must be Hope!" cried Rose, "I had a strange premonition last night that she was calling out to me, she's ill, I know she is!"

"Rose, please calm yourself, think of the baby; you're gonna make yourself ill if you carry on like this," pleaded Dan. "Wake the children while I go and hitch up the horse and cart, the sooner we get over to Bicester the better."

Dan hadn't thought for one moment that Johnnie would have ventured over to Westmead Abbey, and he had no intention of adding to Rose's anxiety by telling her about Johnnie just yet, deciding to deal with one problem at a time. It *had* crossed his mind though that perhaps Alfie had not waited, as they'd agreed, and had sought Hope out to disclose exactly who he was to her. Maybe she had over reacted to the news and caused a scene at the Hotel.

Doctor Fitzgerald had not been anticipating such a busy night in the normally quiet town of Bicester. With one patient confirmed dead on his immediate arrival, and another not expected to

356

last more than a few hours, he was thankful that the young maiden had only suffered a surface gunshot wound in the fiasco which had taken place at Westmead Abbey Hotel. She was however in a state of shock and completely incoherent.

The local constabulary was already present on the scene and the undertaker had removed the lifeless body of Wilkins.

When Dan and Rose eventually arrived, along with Henry and Primrose, the forewarning that a major catastrophe had taken place was soon felt by the uncomfortable atmosphere which cloaked the impressive building. The doctor, who was in deep conversation with two constables in the foyer, soon broke away when Harriet discreetly whispered to him that she presumed the party who had just entered the Hotel was Hope's family, thus concluding that the beautiful woman was also the wife of Johnnie Harper. Nora, who was in a terrible distressed state, was trying to calm her nerves by busily arranging some refreshments. She couldn't take her eyes off the woman who she'd heard about so often over the years; she experienced a sudden flash back of the period when Johnnie had been fighting for his life, over fourteen years ago, and screaming out for *Rose* in his delirium. Now once again Johnnie was fighting for his life, only this time, the doctor had informed them that there was very little hope of him surviving. Nora broke down into tears, again, the cruelty that Rose had arrived back into Johnnie's life far too late, breaking her heart.

As Doctor Fitzgerald sympathetically informed Rose and Dan about the graveness of the situation, it was all too much for Rose. The doctor's words sent her into a distant and murky place, with Dan just managing to catch her in his arms as her legs suddenly buckled, giving way beneath her. Harriet immediately rushed to her aid with the bottle of smelling salts. After a brief rest and a quick and tongue tangled explanation from Dan, it was decided that while Dan sat at Hope's bedside, Rose should sit with Johnnie for a while. Beth Baker who was more than pleased to leave the gloomy premises took Henry and Primrose out for a walk around the grounds assuring them that their sister was going to be fine after plenty of bed rest.

In her bewildered state, Rose followed Harriet who led her up the sweeping staircase and through the wide landing until they reached the room where Johnnie would spend his final hours.

It was there that Rose was left alone. The semi dark room on any normal day would have intrigued Rose with its sheer grandeur and luxurious furnishings, but on this day all what filled her eyes was the sight of Johnnie upon the four poster bed. His face was ashen, his eyelids

closed but occasionally twitching and he looked
so much older than when Rose had last seen him
on the morning of New Year's Day all those
years ago. Still not believing that this was
actually happening it seemed more like a dream
as Rose gently kissed Johnnie's cheek before
sitting at his side. His breathing was laboured.
Rose soaked her handkerchief in a glass of
water, gently dabbing it on Johnnie's dried lips.
She took his hand in hers, and spoke softly to
him; unsure of whether he was able to hear her
voice.

"Oh Johnnie my love, how could this have
happened...I just don't understand? Where have
you been all these years? I never stopped loving
you Johnnie, I want you to know that, and I have
spent what feels like my whole life mourning
you, though I now know that our married life
was sabotaged and you were so cruelly stolen
from me."

Rose's burning tears fell freely, dripping onto the
back of Johnnie's hand as she held it tightly,
close to her face.

"Please....don't cry." His voice was frail, and his
eyelids barely opened as his heart swelled with
the sight of his beloved Rose's loveliness. "My
beautiful Rose, Rose..."

She stroked his forehead and rubbed more water
on to his lips, allowing drops to trickle down his
throat. She wanted to hear more from him. Her
heart was sending its heavy beats throughout

her entire body.

"Don't tire yourself my darling, my love."

"I have already seen our beautiful daughter, Rose, and you are here next to me...that is enough." As Johnnie's voice was becoming even weaker, Rose let go of his hand and lay alongside him on the bed. He knew she was there, and managed the ghost of a smile, feeling her softness next to him. His senses were sharp; he could smell her sweet skin which took his mind back to their first treasured days together. Johnnie's final words would stay with Rose forever,

" Be happy my precious Rose," he quietly whispered, as he slipped away on that final breath.

In the adjacent room, Hope had been greatly comforted by Dan's presence, and in the knowledge that she wasn't going to die from her gunshot wound which Doctor Fitzgerald had described as a lucky graze which would be sure to heal quickly and leave no lasting scar. Dan had broken the news that her father was not expected to live much longer. Everything had happened so quickly and Hope didn't appear to be too effected by the brief encounter which she'd had with Johnnie Harper,

" You are my only Pa," she had assured Dan, deciding to use the tender moment to confess to him about the other special man in her life. "Pa, I think you should know about someone who is very special to me, my true love, and my beau, Alfie."

Dan felt his heart plummet and knew that he had to break the news to Hope, even though it wasn't the ideal timing.

" Hope, there's something I *must* tell you. I want you to be especially brave, and think of your dear ma when you hear what I've got to tell you."

Hope at once believed that there was something wrong with her ma, thinking that perhaps she might have lost the new baby that she was carrying. Pulling herself up and wincing from the soreness of her arm, she focussed on her pa's troubled looking face.

"What's happened to Ma?"

"Your Ma is overjoyed that she has found someone that she believed was no long living and lost to her forever."

"I know all about Johnnie Harper, Pa," interrupted Hope, "he told me who he was."

"I'm not talking about *him*; I mean her son, and your brother, *Alfie!*"

Hope's face lit up, "Alfie's alive too?" she cried, in excitement, "that's a miracle, Ma must be so happy; where is he? Does he live nearby? When can I meet my long lost brother? This is like something you only read in books."

Dan had been hoping that by now Hope would have put two and two together and made the connection. His task now seemed even more daunting as he watched the flood of euphoria remove the previous trauma that Hope had so recently suffered.

" There is only *one* Alfie in this equation, Hope," said Dan, sternly, as he fixed his eyes on her. A few long and painful seconds passed before Hope understood what her pa had been trying to tell her; she crumbled like a withering bloom, sinking back down in the bed and covering her anguished face with the sheet. Dan tried to comfort her, but she pushed him away, angry that he had delivered such heartbreaking news. She didn't want Alfie as her brother, she loved him with all her heart; how could she possibly accept that one day he would marry another?

The miserable and soul destroying day came to its end with Evie Bancroft's funeral, where only Rose, Dan and the reverend's wife were in attendance. There was no shortage of tears, with Rose and Dan already in a state of grief at the end of what would always be remembered as one of their worst days. Rose held on to Dan's supportive arm, with the sudden realisation that if Johnnie had survived this day, she and Dan would no longer be together as man and wife; it was a harrowing thought, one that filled her with sorrow. They had come a long way since their very first encounter; Dan had never left her side in all the years, and was there for her like a solid dependable rock; she loved him dearly and in a way that she now knew she'd never loved Johnnie, even though he had been her first love. She tightened her grip on his arm as she looked up at his strong and handsome face, knowing in her heart that together, with a little time, they would be able to mend the hurt and frayed edges of their family and find happiness once again.

EPILOGUE

"Come on Hope, just one more push, you're almost there," cried Rose as she wiped her daughter's sweating brow.

" Your ma's right," encouraged the experienced mid wife, excitedly" your beautiful baby is almost with us."

Taking a huge breath and using what little strength she had left after nearly a full day and night of agony, Hope expelled the tiny, screaming infant, a baby boy. His sharp cries instantly reached the ears of Howard, who felt the same surge of relief as his wife upstairs, and could finally cease pacing back and forth in their modest Oxford town house.

"It's a healthy boy!" declared the mid wife as she tied the umbilical cord and wrapped him in the woollen shawl before placing him in his mother's arms.

"Oh, he's beautiful, Hope, and he has a fine pair of lungs; look at his head of dark hair, he definitely hasn't inherited his grandma's golden locks."

Hope was lost for words as she cradled her son in her arms, completely mesmerized by him, and not quite believing that she was now a mother.

A gentle knock on the bedroom door was followed by Howard's anxious voice, wanting to be assured that all was well with his wife and baby.

Turning red faced, the mid wife increased the speed at which she was trying to bring normality back to the area,

" You have a healthy son, Mr. Cinderford, and your wife is in a tired but good state of health; now, kindly return back downstairs until the appropriate time." The flustered mid wife's tight curls bounced as she shook her head and tutted annoyingly, "The birthing room is no place for a husband and if I had any say in the matter, all husbands would be made to leave the house completely, they're nothing but trouble."

Rose and Hope exchanged a wary glance, "Oh, dear, poor Howard," whispered Rose, as they heard his footsteps returning back downstairs.

Howard and Hope had met when he had been staying at Westmead Abbey Hotel. Hope had returned to Golden Meadows Farm only long enough to recuperate from the ordeal of the disastrous night of the shooting and of Johnnie Harper's death. She had been dreadfully unhappy, feeling as though she would never recover from finding out that Alfie was her brother. She had refused to meet him for nearly two years, until shortly after falling in love with Howard Cinderford, a handsome well bred business man, who, once a month stayed at the Hotel for a few days while conducting business in Oxford. Although his initial stay at the hotel was somewhat forced due to the Oxford city hotels all being full, in his pursuit of Hope, he continued to return to Westmead, even if it meant a longer journey into Oxford every day. Howard was welcomed into the Heyford's family, with everyone warming to him straight away, and Rose and Dan at last being able to breathe a sigh of relief, knowing that Hope had finally comes to terms with the fact that Alfie was her brother. They were married in the summer of 1885 on Hope's twentieth birthday. This day had been specifically chosen in the hope to shake off the dark cloud which always reminded Rose and Hope that it was the day that Alfie was stolen away from his mother. Now it would become the wedding anniversary of Rose's first daughter, and perhaps take away the sombre memory which always accompanied that day.

Rose had given birth to another beautiful daughter in the spring, following Johnnie's death; she was like a bright ray of sunshine in the Harper's lives during the dismal months where everyone was struggling in coming to terms with the unfolding secrets of the previous years. She was named Joy after the huge impact that her arrival brought to the family. Primrose was delighted that she was no longer the youngest, in the family, but Henry spent a few days sulking about the prospect of having three nagging sisters and that his only brother, who he saw very little of, didn't live under the same roof as him.

A new and strong relationship had formed between the Heyford and the Bird family and although Jayne found it difficult at first to accept that Alfie now had two mothers who he adored, she soon came to realise that there was nothing changed between her and Alfie's relationship, and since she already knew that Rose was such an adoring and kind woman, who had a heart of pure gold, and that she had suffered so much in her life, Jayne brushed all her feelings of jealousy away, deciding to make the best of the new situation. Over the following years, Rose and Jayne became as close as sisters to each other, often giving Alfie a difficult time, with their motherly demands.

Alfie continued to live with Jayne and Percy in between the weeks boarding at St John's College. He was now even more determined to fulfill his strong ambition to qualify as a vet. His graduation coincided with his coming of age in 1885 and with the long awaited inheritance of Lady Ophelia's Stables plus the unexpected lump sum which was a surprise to everyone, with nobody knowing that Sir Hugh had purchased the land as a gift for Johnnie, all those years ago. At twenty one years old Alfie was wealthy, educated and was one of the most eligible bachelors in the area. Henry, who was now fourteen had left school, but declined his brother's generous offer to pay for his higher education, and was more than happy to work alongside Alfie at the stables. Alfie had also insisted that Jayne and Percy sold their small holding in Kidlington and moved back to where their former farm had been. Although their former farmhouse had now been replaced by the stables they were quite happy to move into one of the new and modern cottages and after a life time of farming, they welcomed the opportunity of a more relaxed way of life, and were also now financially comfortable.

To the sheer joy of Nora Baker, Beth Baker had finally found her dream man, *and* to her delight he was a doctor; Doctor Fitzgerald who had attended Westmead Abbey had fallen in love with Beth on their first meeting during the tragic night of the shooting and although he was twelve years older than her and a widower, the bond between them was mutual. Nora, who would spend sleepless nights in the worry that her daughter would never live a full life and bring her own children in to the world, was euphoric when Doctor Fitzgerald asked for her permission to marry her daughter. A grand wedding reception, which was an extra wedding present from Harriet Whitehead, was held at Westmead Abbey in the early spring of 1881, and eleven months later, Beth gave birth to the first of three sons which she bore over the following consecutive years.

Life for Rose took on a more relaxed pace, with the foundation of her family being built on love, which had fuelled her and given her strength throughout her whole life, there were now no more loose ends to shock her and she and Dan were able to enjoy the coming years with their beloved children, and the first of many grandchildren to come.

Printed in Great Britain
by Amazon